God himself in his first stumbling efforts could not have created a more beautiful setting: cool and fresh and green; shaded by palms twisting up toward the sun, up to unbelievable heights; a few rays of sunlight slanting down through the tops of the trees; the air scented with the clean fresh fragrance of flowers; the sedate murmur of rushing water; the crashing of great waterfalls; water lilies and ferns; multicolored butterflies (some as large as a man's hand) floating about weightlessly; pineapples, bananas, coconuts, mangos, oranges. And all of it just waiting there.

But for five American GIs on an odyssey through an obscenity called the Vietnam War, this was a mirage. For reality was—

DEADLY GREEN

DEADLY GREEN

L. S. WHITELEY

To My Friend

Phill — "row" oops sorry
phillkrow

hove a Merry, "Deadly"

Christmas!!

your Friend,
Elliot

Ⓢ
A SIGNET BOOK

NEW AMERICAN LIBRARY

PUBLISHER'S NOTE

Grateful acknowledgment is made for permission to reprint selections from the following material:

"The storm has come" by Soshi, from *Haiku,* Volume 1 by R. H. Blyth. Reprinted by permission of The Hokuseido Press.

The Hills Beyond by Thomas Wolfe. Copyright © 1935, 1936, 1937, 1939, 1941 by Maxwell Perkins as executor. Reprinted by permission of Harper & Row Publishers, Inc.

"San Francisco (Be Sure to Wear Some Flowers in Your Hair)" by John Phillips. Copyright © 1967 by MCA Music Publishing, a division of MCA Inc., and Honest John Music, New York. Used by permission.

"Green, Green Grass of Home" by Curly Putnam. Copyright © 1965 Tree Publishing Company, Inc. International copyright secured. All rights reserved. Used by permission.

"Piece of My Heart" by Bert Berns and Gerry Ragovoy. Copyright © 1967 Webb IV Music. Reprinted by permission of Webb IV Music.

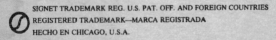
SIGNET, SIGNET CLASSIC, MENTOR, ONYX, PLUME, MERIDIAN and NAL BOOKS are published by NAL PENGUIN INC., 1633 Broadway, New York, New York 10019

First Printing, October, 1987

1 2 3 4 5 6 7 8 9

PRINTED IN THE UNITED STATES OF AMERICA

For my father

The storm has come:
The empty shell
Of a snail.

> —Soshi

Time passing as men pass who never will come back again . . . and leaving us, Great God, with only this . . . knowing that this earth, this time, this life, are stranger than a dream.

> —Thomas Wolfe,
> *The Hills Beyond*

1

At the time I couldn't speak. My mouth, my teeth, my tongue physically couldn't form the words. I was that weak. I had lost that much blood. And even afterward, for a long while, it was mostly—yes sir, no sir, I don't know sir. And once I finally got home (home: there's a joke that'll clear the bar) I still had a great deal of difficulty expressing myself. So now it's taken me these sixteen, seventeen, eighteen some odd years to at last reach the point at which I can actually take pen in hand and say: All right, page 1. And Jesus, even now, sitting here at my desk in this climate-controlled, color-coordinated room with the curtains drawn and only an occasional late-night motorist slipping by outside, it still haunts me. I can still smell the jungle rot and the *nuoc-mam* sauce and the foul stench of unwashed bodies. I can still feel the heat and the muggy closeness of the air and the eyes on the back of my neck. I can still hear the helicopters circling and the mangy dogs yapping at nothing and the cry of the babies and the shrieks of the monkeys and birds. And what's more, I can still see it—I can see it all; it's all right there, right there in front of me, just the way it was then: the red-clay soil, the rice paddies, those

7

goddamn silly-looking water buffaloes, the palm trees, the dense and foreboding jungle (the green, green, the soft and inviting and deadly green) and the clumps of bamboo, the looping vines, the flowers, the shacks of weathered wood, tin, and thatch, the ruined and blasted temples with the bits of colored tile still sparkling in the bright sunlight, the cooking fires and the kids in the dirt, and the young girls with their hair long and silky and their eyes slow and mysterious.

But I'm starting in the middle. In my ignorance and inexperience I have erred and misbegun. I should have started with: As the plane touched down, I looked out the window and felt my palms beginning to sweat, and I turned to the man seated next to me and said, "Shit," because that was all that I thought; it was all that I could have thought; it was all that anyone, no matter how articulate or well-schooled, could have thought that first time: sitting their tense, tired, watching the ground rushing up from underneath, the whirl and the swirl, the sense of urgency, purpose, the organized and methodical chaos. Then there we were in line, in the aisle, filing out the door; the stewardess in her crazy little hat standing by the door as calm and detached as a surgeon: "Good-bye. Good luck. Good-bye. Good-bye." And I was already out the door and halfway down the stairs before it hit me—the absurdity: bouncing off a 707 with a stewardess smiling and wishing me well. It was one hell of a strange way to go to a war. The famous twelve-month, teenage-tourist war catered for your comfort and convenience by the industries of America. Jesus, gimme a fucking break!

So we, like puppies in a pen, jostling and pushing, spilled out into the heat, into the sunlight, into Vietnam, tired yet excited, brave yet afraid, young yet soon to be old—some as old as they'd ever get. And in that initial thirty-second celluloidic exposure, I looked around in extended amazement and recorded it all forever: young girls with black hair, dressed in flowing white or rumpled army green, sly, beautiful, off to one side, behind a low concrete barrier, pointing and giggling; an old man in black, a wisp of white hair sprouting under his chin, squatting on his haunches in the shade with a pipe clenched between his teeth, looking at nothing yet seeing everything; helicopters, jets taking off and landing, loading and unloading; little jeeps racing about in minute self-importance; coffins, metal and waiting, stacked six high in the sunlight; and the miles and miles of asphalt and barbed wire and heat. And this time I didn't even say it ("shit"); this time I didn't even need to, because I was in it and I knew it.

But I'm still starting too soon. I must back up. There must be something first, some explanation, some reason or rationale presented, because one just doesn't say, think, or write: I arrived in Vietnam; because one didn't just arrive in Vietnam as one might have arrived in, say, England or Japan or Mexico, because one didn't go to Vietnam except for one reason—at least, for only one reason at the age of eighteen in the early autumn of 1969 wearing olive drab. We were there (we had been told) to help a people, a people oppressed and suffering, a people with a burning desire to be free from the threat of tyranny, a people who needed and wanted our help. It was our obligation, our sacred and inherited trust, to support the rights of these people, of people everywhere, to be free because we were the bastion of freedom and the kingpin of the Free World. Besides, we knew (and here again, we had been told, led to believe through books and boasts) that we were right and just and fair. We had God and Jesus and John Wayne and History on our side; we could do no wrong.

But if I were to say or write anything that would lead anyone to believe that I was there, there in the sunlight and heat, in the noble and mistaken belief that my small and insignificant presence could help stem the tide and save lives or forms of government or any other cancerous cause formed by and forwarded from that slack-jawed, disease-ridden, multiheaded hydra of self-interest and self-enrichment, then that would be a most sorely misconstrued conception. Because even if I were naive to the point of having absolutely no foreknowledge whatsoever of the grind and gore of battle and butchery, at least I was not disillusioned as to the motives or the goodness of my government, my country. Yes, my country: leaders shot down, college unrest, black riots, flags burned in the street, turn on, tune in, drop out; the very fabric and thread of our existence as a nation pulled taut to a fray. No, I was not there to help save the East or preserve the values of the West. I was there for a totally different and selfish reason: I was there because I no longer cared; I no longer cared for anything or anyone. In fact, I cared so little that I enlisted.

And now we're getting to it. Now we're getting to the crux and the crud of the matter: because I enlisted. And it is the reason for that enlistment that we now have a story before the story that must first and quickly be told before one can step out into the sunlight and heat and look around and say to oneself, "This is Vietnam. And I am here. Shit."

But this now please understand: it is not so much my story that I wish here to tell, because neither my story nor I myself am of any real importance. It is simply that I lived, ducked quick, dodged right and was lucky, whereas they died, were killed. So now I am the only one left to tell, forced to tell, forced by the faces, their faces in the night, forced to tell their story—but then, and yes, it is my story too; my story mixed and intertwined, wine and water, with theirs, so that to tell theirs I must also tell mine. My story. My confession, confession of . . . of crimes? You judge. I lived it. I am far too close to it to pronounce verdicts or plead for vindication. Survival in itself is senfence and satisfaction enough. So now, now that the deeds are long done, the words long spoken, and now cannot be undone or unspoken, now let us transfer and transport back, back to a summer, the end of summer, in the South, in Tennessee, in 1968, and there begin again.

The water was cool, the night was hot, and the laughter from the house drifted out into the dark like a cloud of dust across a desert highway. And as she lay there floating in the pool with her elbows anchored against the edge and her long legs kicked out straight, I looked up at the silver serving tray filled with stolen cocktails and asked, "Steph, want another?" She laughed and set her empty glass down beside the pool and said, "Another and I'll drown." Then she let go of the edge and pretended to drown and I pretended to save her and we came together laughing and kissing.

God, my God, she was beautiful: long blond hair, big blue eyes, nice small eager breasts, brown and almost boyish legs. And she was brave, too; brave in an erratic sort of way. She had that blank dare, that sudden and spirited challenge which allowed her total ease and comfort in the all-night black blues bars and safe passage at dawn between the knife fights and back-alley ambushes with an almost legislative immunity. She was a mad comet, a blazing winter star. She had a subtle type of segregation, a heightened separation, a serene dignity at the doorstep of danger; all, no doubt, inherited from that old and crazy, hot-blood and hot-spur cavalry officer of a great-great-grandfather shot down—some say (detractors all), back-shot—in a suicidal blind-chance charge with forty against four hundred. And the same chance and dare inherited and compounded again from the great-grandfather, the only son of that crazed and hell-bent colonel; the son who built and fortified a fortune in land and cotton and cattle and close-chested Tennessee politics in the carpetbaggered wake and ruin, and lived to recapture and reclaim the family land and increase its range and extent threefold. Then twice more (bing, bang) with her still inheriting, still compounding: the next two—the son and father, and the son and father again—who were able to hold on to that land and wealth through the bad times (the Depression: standing there on the front doorstep of the family-controlled bank—the family shifting now away from cotton and cattle and into banking and building—with the anguished crowd of bewildered and upturned faces gathered around clutching bank shares and bank books: "I'll buy outright, right here and now, any shares that any man here

12

wants to sell at twice its par value"—no takers; the bank stood and went on to serve as the springboard for future ventures) and the good (which in all fairness can actually be sometimes harder, more difficult, one tends to get careless and let things slip away—"What? Gone? Get the gun!"). Yes, she was truly brave and beautiful and royal and recklessly blooded.

"Austin," she said; she turned around. I undid the knot. She tossed the flimsy little top up and out of the pool and onto the brick walk. And I, ever the cautious one, the wary, looked up toward the house, the mansion, the mausoleum. It was bright and filled with the high rich laughter of kingmakers (little kings) and market manipulators, and the pool, our pool now, was dark and safe and we were alone. We glided down to the deep end with her wrapped arm and leg around and about me, and with me trying to swim or at least keep my head above water. Now clinging to the side: weightless, hovering, with her pressed between the wall and me; the slap of the bodies and the slap of the water; the old one-eyed German shepherd that she had reprieved from the dog pound and that she called Max, coming over to watch; the birds and the cicadas and the horses restless in the stable and the moon and the music from the house; and around all, around everything: the land, the family land, the passed promise and pledge stretching out into the night, out to the river, out to the road, out to the railroad tracks and beyond; and looking off to the south on a clear night: the lights of a city, that city, Memphis, glowing in the distance, radiating with the heat and energy of people and their lives, beckoning and yet, at the same time, repelling. And as we, corrupt and young, plunged and pistoned the night and the water into a churning chaos, I bent and kissed one of her breasts just below the waterline, and tasting the chlorine and the flesh, I knew that I was already hopelessly damned and already hopelessly in love.

Then it was fall again, and she was up there in that fancy and guarded fortress of a Connecticut boarding school for the daughters of diplomats and families with familiar last names that cost more in tuition for half a year than some people make in two. I was in school now also, in Atlanta, and constantly having to write letters home: yes, I'm still in school, send more money; and here, stretching the meaning of the word "still" into a whole new realm; spending most of my time down on Peachtree, listening to the music in the park and buying bags of marijuana for ten dollars off the street—"Grass? This?" "So what's wrong?" "Whose yard did you cut?"—and shouting and marching and jumping and dancing and grabbing girls—"Yeah. Yeah. Peace now! Hell no, we won't go! Let's go home to your place and get high. Oh yeah, sure, sure, peace, love, dope, and the Lord loves a cheerful giver. C'mon."

So there she was up there with all that smooth sophistication and all those bland young ladies with their clean, soft hair swept back away from their faces and their empty untroubled eyes (they knew that it was all only a matter of time, of waiting), writing me long and crazy letters about love and the stars and what Fitzgerald and D. H. Lawrence had said, written. And I was writing back my own minor masterpieces of poetry and prose. "Here!"

Then she would call me up and say, "What?"

And I, calm, cool, drawing on the side of the phone

booth in the dorm, writing her name and underlining it twice, would say, "Can't you read?"

And she, back again, with the same calm, the same coolness, would say, "Yes. Can't you spell?"

Then it was Thanksgiving—no turkey; tacos, with the folks away in France. And we—she and I—were back at the house and really thankful, lying in a too-large double bed with a fire roaring away in the bedroom fireplace and all the windows up because it was a warm November.

And she, calm and beautiful, propped up on one elbow, dipping a tortilla chip into the cheese dip and saying, "Austin, no good can come of it."

And I, rubbing her back, her back soft and smooth, asked aloud, asking myself as well as her, asking, "Can it be so wrong?"

And there in front of the fire was old one-eyed derelict dog, derelict Max, happily snoring and farting away.

I got up and opened the sliding glass door and said, "You should've left him."

And she, up now too, naked, calm, beautiful, patting him on top of his head and saying, "He can't help it. He's just old."

Then it started to rain; the rain light then hard, through the trees, onto the roof. She moved back to the bed and pulled the covers up around her. I opened another beer. And the room was still too hot.

Then she, calm, still, peaceful, watching the rain, said, "It's strange and sad."

And I, pausing, thinking, asked, "What? The rain?"

And she, calm, just sat there watching the rain.

Then back to school and back home again and Christmas and Sweet Baby Jesus. And there she was stand-

15

ing long and beautiful across a room filled with poinsettias and maybe forty or fifty friends of the family, talking to some congressman, who, so everybody said, if he didn't get caught or blow it, might one day have a shot at the "big job." I was just watching her, not really thinking about anything much, when suddenly she popped her head out around the congressman's shoulder—he got caught, he never made it—and gave me a wink, her tongue rolling out lazily along her upper lip. I laughed and damn near spilled my eggnog all over my new suit. And afterward, like we did every night and sometimes even during the day, sneaking off together, or in separate cars, to some motel somewhere and sitting in the parking lot ("Okay, your turn") and thinking up outrageously improbable names to register under, hoping that the clerks would challenge us. And once, in fact, one did pause for a moment too long and she turned her steely dare eyes on him and said, "Yes?" And he (the clerk), fumbling with the card still in his hand, stumbling back against the mail and key slots, said, "Oh, nothing. Nothing at all, Mrs. Fishhead. Room 211. Out the door, to your right, overlooking the pool." And we, trying like hell to hold the laughter in at least until we got out of the lobby, calling each other Mr. and Mrs. Fishhead or whatever, and ringing up room service and having drinks and food sent around and always leaving a big tip. "Thank you, sir!" "Don't mention it." And then falling back onto the bed again.

Then Easter and the birds and flowers, and I was sitting in the dining room alone, reading the afternoon paper and eating breakfast when she came downstairs and asked Lucy to please fix her a cup of coffee. I

16

could see that she was still wearing the little necklace that I had given her for her birthday that she had worn the night before—her birthday night—and had probably forgotten to take off. She always had a certain look about her in the mornings, a certain innocence that you just knew wasn't real, and it would only take a cup of coffee and a few minutes of sober reflection before that mirage of childishness and bewilderment would vanish. But there was still something in those first few minutes between the waking and the being awake, some shyness and vulnerability that made you just want to hold her and protect her, because in spite of all of her energy and her quick and sometimes cruel wit, there was still something of a very scared little person about her.

Finally Lucy brought in the coffee, patted her on top of the head, and smiled at her and said, "My, my, my, child," and then turned and walked back to the kitchen. And she looked over at me with the question (what?) unspoken and I looked back at her, and then we both looked away because that was just Lucy and there was never any explanation.

Then she took a sip of her coffee and said as calmly and as nonchalantly as she might have said anything, she said, "I'm pregnant."

I spilled my coffee over my eggs.

"What?" I demanded.

And then, while smiling and moving the index finger of one hand in and out of a small hole created with the thumb and index finger of her other hand, she said, "You know, pregnant. Knocked up."

And again: "What? What?"

And she: "Yes."

And I: "All right. Who?"

17

And she kicked me underneath the table. Hard.

"All right," I said, "but who will you tell them?"

And she smiled again and reached out her hand for mine and said, "The sweetest boy with the greenest eyes."

I gagged and said, "Abort."

She said, "Murder."

"All right," I said, "but I must think." And I got up and left. I jumped into my car and got almost to the end of the drive before I happened to glance down at the gas gauge: empty. I pulled back into the garage, stormed back inside and shouted, "Keys!" She looked up, smiled and pointed across the room. I snatched the keys off the sideboard, stalked back out again, started her car and made a wide looping half-circle through the front yard with Mother screaming at me out of a second-story window, "Austin! You, Austin! You stop that this very minute!" I hit the drive, then the highway flying. Two hours and fifteen minutes later, with two speeding tickets and a six-pack, I checked into a Nashville motel room where I quickly drank five of the beers and threw the sixth one through the television screen because the picture wouldn't stop rolling, then departed amid howls of protest from the night manager, and was back home again before midnight.

The next morning I woke up unusually early, stumbled up to the window, and looked out. Outside, in the front pasture, I saw her and her jumper, Shiloh, a wild bay that no one else could or would ride, going through the jumps. I raced downstairs and outside and up to where they were clearing the last jump with that singular majestic grace of frozen and suspended motion and violence.

"What the hell do you think you're doing?" I demanded.

And she, sitting high, her back straight, patting her horse's neck, her cheeks flushed slightly, smiled and said, "Good morning."

"I thought you said that you were—"

And she just leaned out of her saddle and kissed me and then rode off laughing.

Then two weeks later I received a postcard in the mail, and the picture on the card I still remember—a dogwood tree in full bloom. And the card read: "Austin"—no "Dear," no greeting, no salutation or warning of any type, no indentation, pause, or punctuation, just one line, straight out, like a summons or a telegram maybe—"Austin I have quit love always Steph." Nothing more. And still holding the postcard— the dogwood standing out alone, white against a background of thick green and soaring blue—I went downstairs (I was back at school now; my roommate, a fellow from Texas, had picked up my mail along with his own and delivered it, the card, to me in our room on the third floor) and placed a call through to Connecticut and had the fact confirmed by some anonymous, cheerful female voice on the other end of the line—"Yes, she never came back from the Easter holidays. We've already sent all of her things home. Hello? Hello?"

That next Friday I bailed myself out for a weekend and went home to check things out. I arrived at the house around ten o'clock that evening and was informed by Lucy that she was already asleep. "She goes off to bed right after supper now," Lucy told me, "and sometimes she don't even wait for supper neither." I went upstairs and tapped lightly on her door. There was no answer. I tried the doorknob. The door was locked.

The next day, Saturday, I woke up around nine and waited downstairs for her. It was a long wait. I was already on my third cup of coffee and beginning to think about beer when she finally appeared. She stood there in the doorway looking in at me as I looked back at her. I could hardly believe what I knew I was seeing: this girl, her eyes dull, her cheeks hollow; this girl, her hair, her long and lustrous hair, chopped off short and jagged, almost as if she had barbered it herself in some wild moment of self-defacement and despair; this girl, looking tired, distracted, wearing a long gray smock and carrying a large black book; this girl, not the one I had last seen only three weeks ago, not the one I had known, held, kissed, caressed, not the girl so vibrant and sparked with life and love; but this girl, now something empty (yes, *thing*, not *one*, some*thing*), something bloodless and removed from life. I was stunned, turned upside down. I tried to speak but the words like triple-barbed hooks stuck in my throat. Finally, she—seeing my difficulty, my inability—picked it up and broke the silence.

"You're home," she said, her voice cold and matter-of-fact.

"So are you," I managed to spit out.

"Yes," she agreed. She smiled slightly and then turned and passed down the hall into Father's study.

I sat there alone for a moment, unable to move, almost unable to breathe. What? What? my mind shouted, demanded. What? There was no answer. There was only the loud ticking of the clock from across the room. I pulled myself up out of my chair, went into the kitchen and got a beer. I drank half of it in one long gulp, then moved down the hall and entered Father's study. It was dark inside; the curtains were drawn against the sunlight. Under the dim light of a single floor lamp, curled up in a large leather chair, she sat. She looked so incredibly small and fragile. She seemed to be reading to herself from the large black book that I had noticed earlier—her lips were moving. I came up quietly beside her, and with my hand resting on the back of the chair, I stood there looking down at her. She didn't appear to be aware of my presence, or at least she made no move to acknowledge it. I just stood there—confused, hurt, worried— wanting to reach out to her, wanting to hold her again, but something held me back. Suddenly my eyes focused on the book in her lap, on the pages of the book. And I shuddered. The book was the Bible! I was distraught. I couldn't believe it. The Bible! The easy crutch. The ready answer to all the questions. Twist it, turn it, make it come out right. I grabbed her by the shoulders and shook her.

"What's this?" I demanded, pointing at the book.

She looked up, calm, consumed, like someone coming out of a trance.

Again I shook her. Again I demanded, "What? What's this?"

She turned the book up, showing me the cover.

And again: "Yes! But why? Why?"

And she, like a robot, like a computer voice accenting each word, each syllable in a slow, mechanical tone, said, "Because I have sinned and now I must find my salvation."

I was enraged.

"Sin?" I cried. "Salvation? Shit! What's wrong? What's the trouble? Tell me! This book isn't for you. Not these old wives' tales, these old myths and legends! Not for you! Never for you!"

And she, robot, computer: "Yes. For me. It has shown me the way. It has shown me the path. And I am at peace."

And I, fumbling on my knees beside her now, my hands covering the pages: "Peace? Peace? Jesus Christ, you look like you're dying! You look like you're dead! Do you hear me? Dead! Chuck it! We'll go for a ride, for a walk, but not this, not this blotting out, this obsession with old words and phrases. It's a death, don't you see? A death as final and complete as any grave. They're just words. Sunstroked Jews and Arabs wandering around in the desert, smoking hash. Visions? Oh hell yes, you'd be having visions too, wandering around lost and stoned in the fucking sun! But not prophets! Not saviors! Not saints! Men! Just men and myths! Campfire stories! Just a way of explaining! All right, granted, some of it's well written and poetic, but that was all later. This isn't the answer. This isn't the . . . the . . . the path! Words! Just words!"

And she, calm, dead, touched my head lightly and said, "It's all right. You don't understand. I forgive you. And you must forgive me too."

Then she turned back to the book and I went outside and walked off into the woods and sat down under a tree and listened with morose dissatisfaction to the sounds of spring and life bubbling up all around me.

And then that night and then the next morning and

that was it; it was over. I went out that evening drinking beer with a friend. We hit all the usual spots and told all the pretty girls all the usual lies. The bars closed at three and we left empty-handed. We stopped and got a bite to eat at some nearby slop joint, then I drove my friend home to his parents' house. We sat in my car in the driveway, smoking joints and talking for nearly an hour. Finally I said that I had to go, and I left.

The night was thick and hot. I could taste it and feel it on my skin. And as I sped down the road with the sky around me brightening slowly into the lazy hues of morning, I had a strange feeling, call it a premonition, a certain foreknowledge void of foundation or reason, that my life was about to be severely altered, cleaved in half if you will, and that there had never been a time in my brief and so far ill-spent existence in which there was less that I could have done to have swayed the swirling course of events. Then suddenly, like an electrical shock, a short circuit, I felt a clear and distinct surge of white-hot pain shooting through my brain and collecting and reverberating in my ear. I lost control of the car. It swerved violently to the right, just missed a telephone pole, ripped through a barbed-wire fence, and finally came to earth in a soybean field. Then as suddenly and as inexplicably as it had begun (the pain), it ended and there was nothing. No pain, nothing, only a slight light-headedness, a feeling of something passed and gone.

I just sat there in the car in the soybean field trying to collect myself. I don't know how long I sat there. It might have been only a few minutes or it might have been for over an hour. Finally a squad car, followed up quickly by an ambulance, raced by, shaking me back into the functional present. I started my car again, backed out of the field and back onto the road. Up ahead, vanishing into the distance, I could see the final sweeps of the flashing lights, red and blue. I proceeded down the road in the direction of the fleeing lights. I was nearing home. Soon I came within sight of the lights again. They appeared to be stationary now; still closer, they seemed to be coming from the entrance road to the family property. I sped up and slowed down simultaneously. I pulled in behind the last squad car—there were three of them now—and promptly slid off the shoulder and into a ditch. I sat there in my car at a decided slant for nearly a full minute, listening to my head and heart pounding, before I could force myself to open the door. Once out, I ran, then stopped, turned back, then stopped and turned again and ran on into the lights.

Next to a truck there stood a truck driver crying and shaking his head. He was trying to explain to anyone who would listen that he had not seen her, that she had come out of nowhere. "It were like she jumped outta them bushes there like she meant it. I been driving these here roads for nigh on twenty years now and I ain't never—" And I didn't even need to lift that bloody sheet covering that small and crumpled body because I already knew who was under it. "And you must forgive me too," she had said. But what was there to forgive? There was nothing. There was only what could have been. And as I turned away from the blinking bright lights and the staring white faces and walked back to my car—my legs rubberized, with my hands trembling so badly that I could barely get the key into the ignition, yet still shedding no tears (they would come later)—the truck driver's words echoed in my brain, and I wondered if I too had ever actually seen her or if she had not really just come from nowhere for a moment, like a flower or a moth that lives but a day and then is gone, leaving nothing but a passing memory and a little dust.

Then two days later, after the funeral and the afternoon rain, I was sitting with Max on the veranda, watching Shiloh grazing in the front pasture, when Father came out looking tired and defeated.

He pointed and said, "She loved that damn crazy horse. I remember the way she looked when I first brought him home that day for her sweet-sixteen. Her eyes all big and shiny. She wouldn't let anyone else touch him. Even slept out there with him that first night. Said he'd get lonely. Remember?"

"Yes," I said, looking at the horse, trying not to look at Father or let him know that I knew that he was crying. He was a very proud man.

"I can't have him here anymore. I can't even look at him," he said. "Nope. Gonna sell him tomorrow."

"Yes," I said, still trying not to look.

And then he walked out to the edge of the veranda and leaned up against a column, where all I could see was his back, and said, "Did you know that Ste . . . Ste . . . your sister was pregnant?"

And I knew the word and I already had it—the "no," the lie—working in my lungs, trying to form the audible release, when suddenly Father turned and walked quickly back into the house. And there, alone, I sat while the sun sank into an orange twilight and the night rose with its moon and stars; the stars, unchanged, no brighter, no dimmer, revolving on through the skies as if every day were yesterday and nothing were new or lost or different. Then, almost before I knew it, realized it, the sun was up again and the birds were singing, and I got up from the chair and stretched, and then I drove downtown and enlisted.

2

In-country: Vietnam; September 1969. Heat and sun-light. Two days of stand up and sit down while the gears of the green machine slowly began to click into place. On in gaping amazement to the Combat Center for one week of survival training and war stories. Then really in-country: Fire Base Fable.

So a little sleepy and still more than a little amazed, I found myself silently sitting on a stretch of tarmac, rifle and gear in hand, with six other replacements, waiting for a helicopter and watching the sun rising majestically out of the South China Sea. The breeze, thick with sea, felt good and cool. And three hours later—the sun full up and full fed and now no longer any breeze—we were still waiting and watching and starting to turn red. Finally the helicopter crew, joking and passing a joint, showed up, sneered at us, and then swept us away in a mad wash of rushing wind and violence. It was nothing short of magical (my first time in a chopper). Now: hurtling through space, exposed, open, vulnerable, small; the scenery diminishing, chang-ing, falling away; the lush green countryside, flat, sec-tioned, then rolling up into hills and peaks—green, gray, large and laughing; the rivers winding and twisting; the canals straight and steady; then a sampan; a boatman in a straw hat; a pagoda; a water buffalo; and all vanishing, vanishing away like a dream. Touch me. Asia? Even the word like a song.

Suddenly we dipped to the right and plunged at a near-impossible angle down a long steep valley; the land, green, rushing back in a blur on both sides; the wind and the noise. Seated next to me was a boy, a rather simple-looking fellow with a large red face and a fractured smile. He turned and grabbed my arm and screamed at me above the roar of the wind and the helicopter engine. "I'm from Kansas," he shouted. And I was a little taken aback; I really didn't know quite how to respond so I just held up a thumb and screamed back, "Wheat," and he smiled and nodded his head. Then up and over a rise and then, full view, I saw it: Fire Base Fable. A war in the midst of paradise. Fire Base Fable, like a painting that had been too beautiful and too green, so someone, an instructor, say, had taken a knife and had scraped away a small square of green from the middle of the prodigy's work and had said, "Too good," and had flung in a blotch of contrasting and contradicting brown. And that was it: Fire Base Fable: a brown, ugly scar on the beautiful green body of the earth.

Approaching now, lower, faster; the tension mounting, feeding on itself; the door gunners hunched over their machine guns; then a loud thump on the underside of the chopper, then two, three more; the gunners opening up, swinging, smiling, in love. And the gunners like some type of insane insect: the green fatigues and the flak jackets; the arms, powerful and tan; the bright orange flight helmets; the wires running up to and away from the helmets; the black visors covering the eyes; and the swinging and the smiling. The air laced sweetly with the acid scent of cordite; the spent shell casings raining backward, still hot; the wind; the fury; the love of the gunners for their guns; and the urgent heartbeat of the blades.

I looked over at the man next to me, the boy from Kansas, and he opened his mouth and started to bleed. And I just sat there watching the gunners swinging and firing, and the noise and the wind, and I felt nothing; I felt distant, removed. It could all just as easily have been a movie: an observation, not a partic-ipation. Oh sure, yes, an M-16 and clips and a helmet and boots and a flak jacket and all, but still only watching, watching with a detached, near-suicidal in-difference, and an indifference not so much to death as to life, to living, to the living.

Then touch down: Fire Base Fable. Although not really touching down, hovering some four, five feet off the ground. The gunners still firing and swinging, then one of them stopping and looking around—only the mouth close to being human, furious—screaming and pointing down and out.

So we jumped. Six out. One remaining, the body limp, slumped over, the head cocked, the mouth open, the eyes fixed in a blank stare of surprise and disbe-lief. So we jumped, jumping into a red swirling cloud of dust and wind and noise; jumping blind and scream-ing. I landed once, then I landed again. The second time: terra firma. And reaching and feeling in the biting blind red dust, I found a small arm, then a little leg, and the arm and the leg kicking and punching in unrestrained outrage. Then the helicopter and the noise and the wind lifted and the cloud with it, and I saw that I had landed on two little soldiers: ARVNs—our allies, South Vietnamese. They were wild, cursing and screaming. So I stood up, then they leaped up, shrieking and pointing up into the sky.

The helicopter overhead circling, gaining speed; a small body hanging from the skids; the helicopter rising and circling; the legs kicking; one of the gunners leaning out of the door now, whaling away with a stick or a bat; the body and the gunner and the helicopter lifting higher and higher, getting smaller and smaller; then the body letting go, turning slowly, falling silently.

The body landed some thirty meters from where I stood, nearly hitting a small cluster of ARVNs watching. A couple of the ARVNs screamed and pointed and jerked up their rifles, aiming at the chopper. Then from behind us there was a sharp metallic click. I turned around and saw an enormous shirtless fat man with rolls of skin working down from the neck, getting larger and more obscene in their progressive descent. The fat man shouted, "Down, asshole!" And asshole dropped. And looking back, I saw the fat man standing over a machine gun, patting it and smiling, and looking forward, I saw the ARVNs smiling and bowing and backing away.

3

Fire Base Fable: fifteen hundred men—roughly three-fourths Americans, one-fourth Vietnamese, some afraid, some apathetic, yet all tired, tired of bad food and little sleep and tired of being shot at, sniping in the morning, sapper probes at night, mortar fire whenever, sometimes seemingly forever—perched precariously on a shell-pocked, rat-infested pimple of bright red dirt, serenaded by near-continuous rock music (someone always seemed to have a radio nearby), and surrounded by endless coils of concertina wire, claymore mines, and trip flares, and an entire animated jungle brimming with exotic blooming plants and colorful strange-sounding animals; and within the jungle, nestled there in the trees, tunneled into the earth, squatting next to the animals, an unknown number of Vietcong, silent and invisible and constant. Within the compound itself, scattered about among the entranceways to the underground bunkers and the long airless sandbagged huts of corrugated iron and wood, lay large piles of rotting garbage, mounds of spent howitzer shell casings, and the twisted and forgotten skeletons of burned-out trucks and jeeps and helicopters. Machine gun posts and fortified foxholes were placed

along the embattled camp's outer perimeter at suppos-
edly strategic locations. In the center of the camp,
within an interlining of defenses, were the field hospital, the command and communication bunkers, the
howitzers and the mortar pits, and the flags of the
United States and the Republic of South Vietnam. On
the far side of the camp, in the Vietnamese sector,
were the ammunition dumps, the fuel-storage tanks,
the latrines, and the rows of shower stalls.

In short order I was assigned to a company, a platoon, and then a squad, and told to report to the
squad leader. After several inquiries and several sets
of misdirections, I finally located the area and then the
hole reputedly belonging to my squad leader. I stood
silently at the edge of the hole looking down. The hole
had not been dug but rather exploded out of the earth
by an artillery shell. The sides were baked by the sun
to a crusty consistency approaching that of concrete.
At the bottom of the hole, with his legs propped up
leisurely against one side and his back resting against
the opposite side, sunning himself, was an individual I
could only suppose had been misplaced and certainly
miscast and was surely a member of no army west of
Haight Ashbury. In his right hand he held a can of
beer; in his left burned a joint. His hair, long and
straight, once black, now streaked heavily with gray,
hung down to his shoulders. A white length of silk
inscribed with Oriental symbols and lettering, like the
headbands worn by Japanese kamikaze pilots, was
wrapped around his head. Aviator-style sunglasses
shielded his eyes; deep furrowed lines ran out from
these glasses and down from the corners of his mouth.
His tanned face was stubbled with several days of

growth, and caked with a thick coating of red dust. A neglected black mustache, with no betrayal of gray in it yet, drooped sadly across his upper lip, accenting a row of white teeth. Around his neck hung a thin silver chain anchored with a small gold Buddha amulet. And in spite of the gray hair and the lined face, by looking at the tanned and taut shoulders and chest, you could tell that he was young and strong.

"Sergeant Strider?" I asked after a few moments of silent observation.

The hand holding the joint pushed the sunglasses back on the head. The head turned slightly. The eyes opened. And the eyes were blue.

"Sergeant Strider?" I asked again.

"Asshole, don't ever call me 'sergeant.' I just plain don't like it," came the reply, low and slow.

"Yes, sir," I said, straightening up slightly.

"And never, and I mean absolutely never under any circumstances whatsoever, ever call me 'sir,' " he said, looking up at me.

"Yes, sir . . . uh . . . yeah, all right," I fumbled.

The day was hot. The jungle looked cool. And the sun blazing down upon my helmet made me feel a little faint.

"Just Strider will do for now," he said, letting his eyes run from top to bottom, from helmet to heel, measuring me with the weary patience of a pawnbroker only too used to dealing with goods of questionable value. "And as for you, I don't wanta know you at all—not your name or anything about you. Jesus, they come and go so fast! I don't wanta be your friend, your father, or your mother. Only a fool makes friends out here. I don't wanta know about your prob-

33

lems or your hopes or your dreams. I don't care if you're happy or you're sad. I don't give a damn if you have a girlfriend or a wife or a baby. I don't want nothing to do with you. I just want you to do your job when it needs to be done and stay the hell outta my way. All right?"

"All right," I said, shifting my weight to my other leg and looking out across the wire, out at the jungle.

"And now you'd better get your ass down into this hole. I'm surprised you ain't been wasted already. Ol' Charlie must be sleeping. You fucking new guys sometimes have the most unbelievable luck," he said, slipping his sunglasses back down over his eyes.

I slid quickly down into the hole next to him, whipped out a clip, and slapped it into place. I pulled my helmet down low over my eyes and lifted myself up onto one knee. I was ready.

After several minutes of being ready, Sergeant Strider lifted his sunglasses and gave me a doleful look.

"Might as well just relax, tiger," he said, placing the remaining half of a burned-out joint between his lips and relighting it. "Start working on your tan. We ain't gonna be doing nothing round here for a few days yet."

"Oh?" I asked.

"Yeah," he said, passing over the joint. "We're 'bout to have us a change of command."

"Oh, really," I said, accepting the joint. "Is the colonel going to be leaving us?"

"Yeah," he said. "He's gonna get a big promotion."

"General?" I asked.

"No," he said, smiling. "Specific."

*　　*　　*

The joint and the unaccustomed heat and humidity made me a little drowsy and I guess I fell asleep; one of those vague intermittent suspensions, not quite pure sleep and not quite consciousness either. I was aware that I was hovering pleasantly through half-dreams of dragons and lions dancing in the sun and helmets filling rapidly with sand, when suddenly a tremendous explosion shook me out into a last-light sundown wild with machine-gun fire.

I found my rifle and helmet after a quick search and pitched myself up onto the rim of the hole. The entire perimeter was erupting with a deafening violence. Flares hung in the air, drifting gently down and illuminating the fields of fire between the concertina wire and the black and ominous jungle into ghostly hues of transparent blue. Tracer bullets from the machine guns laced off beautifully into the jungle, disappearing. Off to the right, a siren wailed at an eerie pitch. And from behind me came the feeble, the all too humanly fragile voices of men running and stumbling in the fading light.

I looked back down into the hole. Still at the bottom, still resting with the same relaxed attitude of nonmovement and unconcern, was Sergeant Strider: his sunglasses still on, his feet kicked up and crossed, his arms still resting behind his head. I slid down next to him and shook him and shouted at him, unsure whether or not he was even awake; I shouted, "What? What?"

And he, still unmoving, still unconcerned, still in the same low voice void of all emotion, said, "The change."

Then suddenly there was a crash from above. I

looked up and a figure—the face contorted and smeared with green and black camouflage paint—leaped out of the darkness and into the hole. The figure, wild, out of control, pounced on Strider, laughing and beating him about the shoulders and the chest. (I almost shot the son of a bitch.) And Strider, unmoving, only covering up slightly, smiled. The figure: howling, laughing, screaming; the hair, long and blond and pulled back in a little ponytail at the nape of the neck; the eyes, burning red, insane; the teeth, white and wild with laughing. Excited, frenzied, frantic, the figure thrust himself into Strider's face, inches away, and screamed, "I got him! I got the motherfucker! Court-martial me? Shit on that noise! Blew his ass away! Whoo-whoo-whee!"

And Strider, still unmoving, calm, relaxed, smiled and said, "Good work, Billy."

Then the figure, the figure Billy, his eyes alive, dancing, jerked up Strider's M-16 and threw himself down on his back and began firing the rifle on full automatic straight up into the air, firing and laughing and screaming; screaming: "VC! VC! VC!"

4

The morning after the attack, after a thorough search for bodies around the outlying perimeter and along the jungle trails, the scorecard clearly reflected another shining American victory: one colonel, U.S. Army, and two parrots and six monkeys, all obviously VC, dead. Eight to one. A good kill ratio. One, I was assured, the colonel would have been proud of.

So with the command of the camp reluctantly assumed by a major who did not actually want the responsibility and may have been more than a little put off by the mutiny and murder in the air (he never left his bunker during his entire tenure of command), word soon came down that we'd hold fast for a couple of days and wait for the new C.O. The men, seeming to sense the logic and justness of this decision, adjourned themselves from their duties and retired to the tops of the bunkers to catch a few rays and drink a few beers and get stoned. To a casual observer it might have appeared as though the war had been called off. Indeed, it was rather strange: the silence, the silence amid so much potential violence. As one old-timer (all of twenty-four) put it: "Maybe the dinks declare a holiday if you blow up the C.O." Maybe. No one knew and no one seemed to care.

The day was hot, as (I soon learned) were almost all the days, but there was a slight breeze blowing in across the hill from out of the east, so it was not too unpleasant. Around noon a helicopter came in and picked up the colonel's body. Someone fired off a one gun salute; someone else said, "Fuck it." I was sitting against the rim of Strider's hole, working on my third warm beer and listening with vague disinterest to Billy explaining to Strider how he had trimmed the late colonel's wick.

"So I just knocked on the side of the motherfucker's hooch and he hollered out, 'Enter!' you know the way he always did, always trying to sound so bad, and I was just standing there in the dark, being real quiet, holding on to that damn grenade, still not really sure if I wanted to do it, thinking: All right, maybe I'll take my chances with the court-martial—when he hollered out again, 'Enter, goddammit! Enter!' I don't know, but it was just something 'bout the way the mother-fucker was always shouting and screaming, so I pulled the pin and stepped into the doorway and said, 'All right, fuck you, Colonel Motherfucker.' Then I pitched it at him, and right after I let go I knew that I'd fucked up, 'cause you see, I was excited and I'd forgotten to wait, so the sorry motherfucker still had a good three seconds or so and he could've shot for the door. He would've made it, no sweat, but he just looked at it, then he looked up at me, and then the stupid mother-fucker reached for it like he was gonna John Wayne it or something. I just hit the fucking deck laughing 'cause I knew damn well he'd never make it. And he didn't. So far as I'm concerned, the motherfucker fucked himself. He had a fair chance and he blew it."

Granted, there was something strange and more than a little disconcerting about listening to a man fingering an M-16 and calmly confessing to a cold-blooded murder, but then there was also something equally strange about sitting on top of a ripped-out little hill in the middle of a steaming jungle with a weird assortment of armed psychopaths for company, waiting calmly and assuredly for that blue-black pain that was going to punch your lights out and send you screaming to hell.

But none of that really mattered much to me at the moment. I took a sip of my beer and looked over at Billy.

He was a handsome-enough fellow, I guess. Probably about nineteen, with a wild shock of blond sun-streaked hair pouring over his ears and down his neck; not quite as long as Strider's but he was working on it. He had a smooth angelic face, almost feminine, with a slender nose and a shining set of white teeth. His eyes held a grayish tint and seemed a little too liquid in the harsh glare of the sun. He was clean-shaven and surprisingly well-scrubbed; even his fingernails were clean. He was of medium height and weight and had the graceful movements of a trim and trained athlete. His body was well-tanned and an endless source of amazement and admiration for him. He was constantly touching himself: massaging his shoulders, running his hands aimlessly up and down his chest, and forever combing his fingers through his hair. On the whole, he looked to be just another nice kid from any nice small American town. Maybe it was that outward appearance of sand-lot baseball and 4-H clubs and Saturday nights at the drive-in picture show that made his confession and his total lack of remorse seem so much more unreal.

"Yeah, the sucker was most definitely too gung-ho," said Strider, popping a banana from the stalk that he had harvested while on the morning jungle sweep.

"You 'member that combined-action operation down in Long Don?" asked Billy.

"Yeah," groaned Strider. "What a fucking mess!"

"You hear 'bout it?" asked Billy, turning toward me.

"No," I said.

"Well, we was going down into this little gook ville," began Billy with near-girlish enthusiasm. "It was 'bout five klicks out. We were suppose to be checking ID cards or something, but you just never know when you're out with the dinks. Like you might start off doing one thing half the morning, then by afternoon wind up doing something else entirely different. So anyway, we go on down into this little rat-shit ville—you know, damn kids running round naked, papasan and mamasan and all them sans of a bitches all smiling and squatting in the dirt—and we go in and start kicking a few asses and checking a few IDs. Well, hell, the damn cards are all fake anyway and we know it and they know we know it. They're all squatting and smiling and talking that dink shit, and the colonel, he's looking round and talking loud and putting on a big show. Then this ARVN captain comes up with a couple of real hard-case-looking twelve-year-olds that he's just real sure are VC, so we say great and start back. Now we're walking back down the same damn trail we just come up not more than two hours ago when right round a turn in the trail the fucking VC got a little ol'

L-shaped ambush all laid out. They got 'em an M-60 from somewhere set up at the turn and half a dozen AKs worked in back down along the trail. Well, so, the point and two or three other guys up front get wasted most immediately and everybody else just drops like shit where they're at. I was 'bout midway back down the column. I could hear but I couldn't see nothing. I was too far back, you see. So anyway, I was just laying there thinking: Well, now, this ain't too bad a spot to be—when Colonel Motherfucker comes hauling ass up the trail hollering, 'First Platoon! Up front! Move!' I turned over to this guy, Coconut—we called him Coconut 'cause his damn head was shaped just like a fucking coconut—and I said, 'More Colonel Motherfucker's motherfucking shit.' And Coconut, he just looked at me and started laughing. He was always laughing. And let me tell you one thing, them damn combined-action dinks weren't putting out no combined action neither. Them son of a bitches was just hugging and praying. So anyway, we get on up the trail and damned if we don't lose another couple of men to the AKs moving up. I tell you that damn Colonel Motherfucker was just too fucking gung-ho. Am I right, Strider?"

"Tell it," said Strider, unmoving, probably not even listening.

"I mean the man just didn't think right. Here he was, we could've called in artillery or at least out-flanked the AKs and circled in behind the M-60. We had us plenty of men, plenty of time. But not Colonel Motherfucker. No way, José. His plan was a frontal assault! On an M-60! Yeah! Can you believe it? A fucking frontal assault! So anyway, he sends out First

Platoon like some kinda glory charge. And he don't lead no fucking charge neither. He wasn't crazy, just insane. Sends out one of his new fucking lieutenants. So anyway, somehow, I don't know how, but somehow, part of First Platoon made it up to a little clump of bushes which weren't really nothing, 'bout fifteen or so meters away from the M-60, and this lieutenant that hadn't even been with us but a couple of weeks—Hey, Strider, what was that fucker's name?"

"Which fucker?" asked Strider, absorbed with another banana.

"The lieutenant. Goldman or Goldberg or—"

"Goldstein," said Strider.

"Yeah, I knew it was some Jew name. So anyway, this fucking Goldberg starts crawling up toward the M-60 with a couple of grenades. I tell you all them damn officers have just seen too fucking much John Wayne. I mean like if you can't chunk a damn grenade fifteen meters you might as well just quit. So anyway, Golden goes crawling up toward the M-60 and naturally he don't get but a couple of yards 'fore he gets his fucking head blown off. So there we are, pinned down in the middle of fucking nowhere with half the men either hit or fucking dead and this damn Colonel Motherfucker on the radio screaming, 'Charge! Charge!' Some great frontal assault, huh? So, anyway, after 'bout four or five minutes of some hard time hell this guy Johnson—he ain't with us no more, got it out on night ambush—this guy Johnson—a real nice guy, too—rears up and makes a beautiful toss and that was it. But, man, what a fucking waste! A real Colonel Motherfucker mess! Every damn time we'd go out with the motherfucker—and he loved to go out—we'd just know we was gonna get into the shit. Am I right, Strider? The motherfucker was the worst."

"The worst," said Strider, flipping a banana peel over his shoulder.

The sun was sliding down now behind a mass of hills a few kilometers away. The slow shadows reaching out from the jungle were almost to the perimeter wire. Rain clouds, heavy and low, were edging their way carefully through the sky. Soon it began to rain and continued thickly for nearly an hour, soaking everything and casting a hard chill into the air.

Billy persisted through the rain and then through the last bit of sunlight again with the telling of his war stories, which were now beginning to encompass not only mere hearsay and rumor but also out-and-out fiction. And since Strider was now obviously not listening—he seemed more asleep than awake—this left me in the untenable position of not only being an audience but also of being an actor as well, as Billy would stop from time to time and enter into a dialogue with me for the confirmation of an eluding detail concerning a person or place of whom or which I had absolutely no knowledge. I was, in fact, almost to the point of saying something extremely rude to break off the conversation when a jeep jerked up onto the scene and Billy was forced to surrender the stage.

A young lieutenant, his fatigues pressed to a knife-edge, his boots shined, leaped from the jeep and trotted toward us, waving his arms and shouting for Strider. He stopped in front of the hole, breathing rapidly.

"Strider! Strider!" shrilled the voice; the face red, the eyes glaring, filled with hate and disgust. "Good God, man, what in the name of all that's holy do you and your men imagine you're doing?" he asked, kicking a beer can out from under his feet. "This ain't no picnic!"

"Holy?" burped Strider, sliding down farther into the hole.

Billy lit a joint and smiled thoughtfully at the lieutenant.

"Trooper! Trooper!" piped the lieutenant, pointing at Billy. "What's your name? Strider, I want that man's name! He's on report! You're all on report!"

"Aw, cool out, Lieutenant," said Billy with a smirk, passing the joint over to Strider. "Ain't no big thang!"

The lieutenant, his hands on his hips, looked down at the joint and at Strider and Billy, and then began to shake.

"Strider, goddammit! Strider, goddammit!" shrieked the lieutenant, flapping his arms again. Turning with his arms still flapping, he took two exaggerated steps back toward the jeep and then stopped and turned again. His eyes were blinking fast. "Captain from Division Staff wants to see you, Strider," called out the lieutenant. "Now! Immediately!" He stood there for a moment longer, looking, watching, blinking, waiting for a reaction or something. But there was nothing. Strider didn't move. Finally, presumably disappointed, he jumped back into the jeep and cranked the engine. The engine sputtered, hesitated, then caught. "You hear me, Strider?" screamed out the lieutenant again as the jeep lurched away. "Immediately!"

"Fucking lieutenants!" Strider yawned, readjusting his sunglasses. "Give 'em a fucking bar and they think they own the fucking world."

"They just never learn, do they?" Billy smiled, massaging his M-16.

When Strider returned from his interview with the captain, he brought with him word that he, unbelievably, was suspected of complicity in the murder—yes, at least they knew that much now—of the colonel.

"Who? You?" Billy laughed.

"Yes, me," sighed Strider sarcastically.

"And what did you tell them?" asked Billy, his interest visibly picking up.

" 'What?' " replied Strider.

"What?" I asked.

"Yes, 'What?' " repeated Strider.

"Oh, 'What?' " I said.

"Yes, 'What?' Ignorance. Me no know nothing," said Strider as he popped open a beer and settled back down into the hole again.

Twilight and fading: the sun down, finished, yet the ground, the earth still retaining its heat; the voices low, secretive, conspiratorial; the feet moving slow, dragging; the birds calling; the monkeys shrieking, ripping along through the trees.

"Wake me if anything happens," I commanded, awash with a sense of false bravado.

And Strider looked over at me and smiled and said, "Something just might, new guy. Better sleep light."

"Yeah, sure," I said, and nodded off; the world floating away, leaving me wonderfully indifferent and unconcerned.

Little did I then realize that the marijuana of which I had been partaking so freely of late was so much stronger than anything to be found stateside, or that some of the men, such as Strider, were in the habit of multiplying the effect by lacing their joints with a little No. 4 heroin, and for an innocent, near-virginal youth like myself, this, combined with an ample application of sun and other assorted stimuli, was often more than my delicate system could stand. So I slept. I slept a lot those first few days. It was easy—sleeping.

How long I slept I don't know, but when I awoke again there was shouting and shooting and screaming and bright flashes of light and explosions everywhere. Above, swirling in circles, flares drifted slowly, slowly down. Machine guns raked away with a fascinating precision and beat. Incoming mortar fire exploded into sharp orange patterns. Outgoing mortar rounds from behind thumped like the dead beat of a bongo, then hung, then exploded with the muffled audibility of a ship's horn sounding its way through a fogbank. And from all sides, from out of the dark, came quickly, in jerking and jingling succession, the sharp cricket snaps of rifles popping off in rhythmic chorus.

A dream, I concluded to myself through my opiate daze, a most pleasant surrealistic dream. Wake me when the champagne is served.

Then I looked into the bottom of the hole. A boy laid out opposite me looked up and screamed, "Jesus Christ, I'm hit! I'm hit! Mother of God! Oh fuck, it hurts!"

I sobered and stared.

The face was young and blanched a pale dead white; the eyes were set in a permanent bulge of terror; the mouth, red, spilling blood down the chin, worked feebly; the shirt was ripped open; the gaping wound, raw, exposed, gurgled blood in and out, in and out.

Next to him, Strider was crouched, holding his hand and massaging his forehead. "Calm, partner, calm," Strider was saying, his voice slow and quiet as though he were trying to coax a shy young girl into bed. And then he stood, and in a voice louder than I would have thought humanly possible, he screamed, "Medic! Doc! God damn! Over here!"

A sweep of automatic weapon fire ripped the ground overhead from right to left. Following close behind the flying pattern of dirt and death, there came a man running, then leaping, and finally landing in the hole.

"He's hurt, Doc," said Strider, turning toward the man. "Bad. A sucking chest wound."

"I don't wanta die, Doc!" cried the wounded boy, lunging up and grabbing the medic's shoulders. "God, I really don't wanta die!"

The medic leaned close and wiped a smudge of dirt off the boy's cheek and said, "Be cool, ace. I'll have you fixed up and outta here and on your way home in no time." Then he popped something into the boy's mouth.

The boy released his grip, gagged once on his own blood, then slid back down to the ground, crying silently.

And the man called Doc under a flare in a hole in Vietnam: a small compact man—looking more like a boy really, nineteen or twenty at the most—with a quick and lean body that spoke of constant motion. Laboring over his patient, he assumed an air of fiery intensity void of everything except the frantic working: the hands, the instruments, the eyes, the tissue, the sweat, the bandages, the blood. He seemed totally enthralled, overwhelmed, like a scientist, an archaeologist on the verge of some great find. His head, seemingly too small even for that small frame, would snap back, appearing momentarily over his shoulder, growling, continuously calling for extra bandages or water or cursing Man and his follies. His black hair—considerably shorter than Strider's or Billy's but still a long way from what could even be remotely described as "military"—would whip loosely about his face and eyes, adding to the magical sense of fury and struggle. His face, broken only slightly by a thin rat-tail of black hair dangling off his upper lip, shone with a wistful intelligence. His eyes were brown and reassuring, like those of a faithful dog, and yet under close scrutiny they appeared profound and almost bottomless. He moved about the hole—jumping here and there; sometimes with his back or head appearing for long seconds above the rim—with a distinct disdain for danger or death. And for one observing (myself), it appeared as if he held no value at all for his own walking and breathing, and that all that mattered was the successful execution of the task to which he had been assigned and by which he was now utterly consumed.

"What d'ya think, Doc?" asked Strider after a moment.

And Doc just lifted his head, the eyes calm and incredulous, and looked at Strider. Then Strider turned and looked and saw and then quickly, without waiting for further communication or intelligence, he moved back toward the firing.

As Strider moved back to the rim, my mind registered once again on the sounds—the firing, the explosions, the screaming and the cursing—and then for no apparent reason, like a dormant container long on a shelf in some dark and forgotten corner that suddenly and mysteriously erupts into flames, I remembered a girl and a smile and a moment—a moment repeated a thousand times in dreams and nightmares with a thousand variations, so that the initial moment itself is obscured and no longer exact or definable, but twisted now by time and distance and metamorphosed into a crowded collection of emotions, most only half-understood yet all wholly painful. And as I sat there meditatively letting a fist full of sun-baked earth (dust to dust) play through my fingers, like sand in an hourglass, I thought: Well, it's all waste and want, sweat and squalor, hot nights, hell and heartache; so what's there to lose but the lingering? And with that resigned acceptance of fate dark and unalterable, I grabbed my rifle and threw myself down next to Billy.

An incoming round exploded close by, throwing off bits of bone and tissue and dirt. A soldier, apparently blinded by the blast, his arms groping through the smoke, stumbled a few yards, then collapsed. Billy flicked a little something that once might have been human off his arm and turned toward me with a look of sickened disgust. I rolled over on my back and watched Strider as he bobbed up, clipped off a couple of short bursts, and jerked back down.

And as I watched I tried to be objective, I tried to be clinical and nonchalant and maybe even brave, but I couldn't; it was all too immediate, all too terrifying. And with me, at that moment, it was not a fear of dying, of death, of blackness and nothingness that held the terror; the terror lay in the simple fear of fear, the fear of the unknown, the fear of pain and how I would react to it, the fear of being maimed or blinded, of spending the rest of my life in a half-existence in a wheelchair or with a cane pegging and plodding along at the mercy and pity of others. (I'm just not that strong; I know it.) And yes, what mercy? What pity? And this now you must understand: for I was far past the point of simple loss or losing; from here on out a sniper's bullet—the first shot clean and without warning—through the heart or the head was all sheer gain, a quitting of memory, a release from guilt. And here you might think or say: Well, all right then, just stand up. But no, that wasn't it; that I could have done myself without having had to travel the twelve thousand miles and without having had to eat all that diarrheic shit to reach the spot most suitable for my design. (Two suicides—she had tried [sweet angel] to make it look like an accident, but they knew; they never said anything, but they knew—in one family would have been too much for my parents.) What I wanted, needed, was for someone else to do it for me, to do it when I wasn't looking, hopefully, to have it appear to be the natural result of the risk and progress of war. And yes, I know that it was a complex and ambiguous and very possibly absurd position with which to hold, but that was my thinking; that was how I felt.

Another mortar round landed directly behind me. A scream went up for a medic. Off in the jungle, the night lit into a spectacular shower of flames and arching missile trails as a weapons cache or something went off.

Billy spun over on his back, flipped out an empty

clip, slapped in a new one, then turned and looked at me and screamed, "Fire, asshole! Fire! Just pull the fucking trigger, goddammit! It don't matter, you probably ain't gonna hit nothing anyway! But just fucking fire! Okay?"

So I coiled up tight, feeling every nerve and muscle twitch, counted to three, then counted to three again and lunged up over the rim, screaming and firing off a deadly burst of silence. I slid back down panting and sweating, clipped off the safety, and cursed myself. I rolled over again onto my back to watch Strider and Billy for courage and timing; then I coiled, counted, jerked and fired off a blind burst into the night. I collapsed back down below the rim, feeling drained and yet simultaneously exhilarated. And I don't know whether I was shaking from fear or excitement, but I do know that the adrenaline was pumping fast and I was infected with a kind of insanity, and it felt good. So up onto the rim I went, again and again and again, firing into the blind dark, firing longer and longer bursts each time, firing then falling back, laughing hysterically and shaking with utter amazement.

It was during one of my more uproarious breaks that I happened to look up from my laughing, and I noticed Doc and I stopped laughing. He was curled up into a tight little embryonic ball: his feet tucked up underneath; his knees drawn up to his chin; his arms wrapped about his legs. Next to Doc, sprawled out on the bloodstained slope of the hole, lay the wounded boy, now past all wounds or pain: one hand thrown back behind his rigid head in a kind of mock surrender; the other clutching the wound as if the hand could hold in the already vanished life; the eyes and mouth open; the mouth objecting; the eyes fixed on Doc, still pleading. Doc, oblivious of the pandemonium and chaos around him, was rocking slowly back and forth, seemingly in a daze, a trance, mumbling inaudibly to the corpse, perhaps apologizing—I don't know—though God knows he had little or nothing to apologize for. And just then a flare shot up overhead and exploded, separating the torn sky into blacks and whites, and freezing everything in my mind as clearly as a camera flash freezes images on film, and from a neighboring foxhole across a still and fragile and flare-lit breath of perhaps ten seconds of almost pure silence came a song, and for no reason I remember that song:

If you're going to San Francisco
Be sure to wear some flowers in your hair.
If you're going to San Francisco
You're gonna meet some gentle people there.

And I don't know, but sometimes when I'm sitting alone in some lost bar or room somewhere and my thoughts slide back, I can almost always remember the music; the faces, sometimes no; but the music, almost always. Maybe it's because the music was always such a shock, always adding so strangely to the overwhelming sense of the absurd: a rock-and-roll war. Impossible!

And as I was sitting there watching Doc and the corpse and listening to the music, out of the corner of my left eye, sliding quickly away, I happened to catch just the edge of something that didn't seem quite right: first, a dim shadow, then a figure; the figure running by under the flare, running along the rim of the hole, running in the wrong direction, running from the wire back toward the interior of the camp. And Strider must have seen it too, because I saw him starting to pivot just as the hole exploded: everyone (me—I can't say for certain about the others) ducking, screaming, trying to make themselves (myself) small; bullets dancing, flying, ricocheting about the hole. And I saw two near-misses zing by Doc—and Doc still rocking and mumbling—then four direct hits, dead thumps, one in the head, exploding it, enter the dead boy's body. And I was holding my helmet on my head with both hands and screaming for God or Jesus or someone to stop it and I'd go peacefully, when I glanced over at Strider again and saw him stand up and clip off a full load into the figure, spinning him (the figure) around and around, gaining momentum and almost balance as he turned, spinning him like a drunk dancing the last dance alone, spinning him away and off into the night.

"Gooks in the wire!" screamed Strider. "Goddamn gooks in the wire!"

And silhouetted now gray against the orange flashes of impacting mortar rounds and the blue dangling drift of flares, I could see them, maybe a hundred or maybe twice or half that many, off to the right, spilling through a broken gap in the wire not fifty meters away: a steady flow surging, then wavering and falling under the repeating sweeps of machine-gun fire, then up and on again, surging on, seemingly undiminished, magically reinforced.

I was crouched down next to Billy watching the charge with a near-juvenile fascination—men of actual breathing and bone rushing headlong toward an almost certain death—when suddenly I heard a scream from behind, a scream not of simple pain or fear but rather of all pain and fear combined, collected and simultaneously released. And I turned and looked back just in time to see Doc, his eyes and mouth wide and filled with the screaming, snatch my M-16 out of my hands. And in dumbfounded amazement, as if from a great distance, I watched as Doc leaped up to the rim of the hole, exposing himself from the waist up, and began firing; standing straight and alone; standing and firing and screaming; screaming between the blasts; screaming through tears and taut neck muscles; screaming: "Come on! Come on! Let's fucking get it on!" Then through the screaming and the firing, the stock of Billy's rifle came up and caught Doc flat across the chest, and Doc flew up and off the rim and tumbled back down into the hole. And there, next to the dead boy, in the dirt and blood and spent shell casings, he lay pounding his clenched fists into the ground, cursing and crying.

And coming on and on, closer and closer; the whole thing fast and flashing: color, sound, movement, fragmented, broken, ripped apart, then rushing, crashing, colliding together and exploding as one—one, final and furious; a spinning black void; the mad hollow laughter of the end.

Then slowly, almost painfully, from above the spit and swirl of what I thought were to be my last moments on earth, there arose the low and struggling churn of an engine, an airborne engine, and as the engine, the sound, the hum drew nearer, the firing grew progressively less and less, until finally there was only a dull droning left to fill the involuntary peace.

"What?" I cried, grabbing Billy's arm. "What is it?"

"Puff," he replied, smiling.

"Puff? Puff what?" I demanded, still clinging.

"You'll see."

And yes, see I did; the effect but not the cause. And only later was I to learn the facts, the facts behind the wrack and ruin wrought by that happy and childish name—Puff. The facts: an AC-47 (originally a cargo plane)—some: the machines older than the men inside—weighted with three electrically controlled and synchronized multibarreled 7.62mm machine guns firing a fusillade of death and destruction at the incredible rate of six thousand rounds per minute per gun, enough reputed firepower to cut down and shred anyone or anything living or standing within the confines of an area equivalent to that of a football field in less than ten seconds.

But the facts were all reserved for later; for me, curled up in a hole and breathing hard, it was only an engine (two engines actually, but at a distance, one indistinguishable from the other) approaching through the dark; an engine (two) tentative and uncertain at best; and the noise, the hum of those engines, coming to my ears not like the trumpets of salvation but rather like a pained and mournful cry of a wounded and dying beast. But then, at that moment, as if to confound the skeptics and dismiss all doubt, the sky lit and the earth exploded. Cords, lengths of what can only be inaccurately described as a red light, came spitting out of the night, sourceless and mysterious; the tracer bullets ripping through the air so fast, ripping into the earth with such frequency as to form an almost unbroken neonlike beam; the beam, bright red and seemingly solid, like some Buck Rogers fix-it-gizmo death ray.

And under the drifting blue of falling flares, I could see the black-clad figures running now, not actually retreating or charging so much as simply scattering, pell-mell, without order or direction, like so many ants fleeing before a boot; the bodies, as if physically lifted, arching through the air in grotesque contortions; the screams; the unmitigated violence; the fantastic chaos; the night, the light, metal, lead, bones, bodies, earth. Then, as suddenly as it had begun, it was over. The noise, the light, the flares, all gone now, all returned into the night; only the dull hum of the engines fading away; then that gone too, leaving only the groans, the high-pitched irate and anguished howls of men dying slowly in the dark.

Holy shit, I thought to myself. I was sucking air fast and trying to control my hands. I knew that I was alive (I could feel my heart beating a mile a minute) but I still needed something more, some further reassurance that we were all in this thing together, that this was, in fact, real and not something that I had dreamed, some kind of human contact—a handshake, a word, something, I don't know. I turned and looked over at Strider, and he had already switched off. He was already back on hold, assuming once again his now-familiar pose (or non-pose, more accurately) of unconcern and nonmovement; his eyes closed; his back resting against the side of the hole; his feet kicked out and crossed; a thin column of pale blue smoke curling up from a newly lit joint held in his hand. I coughed. It was quiet, quiet there in the hole. He opened one eye and regarded me coldly.

"Yes?" he asked.

"Well," I said, still shaking, still trying to breathe. "Is that all?"

"You want more?" he asked.

"No, I mean, is it over?"

"Forever?"

"For tonight."

"And?"

"Yes, well—"

"And so now you think maybe we're brothers or at least members in the same club, so—"

"No," I said. "Not exactly. It's just that—"

"So now you want to know how you acted, how you performed. Shit! An opinion from, say, a brother as to how you compared, measured up."

"Well, since you put it—"

"All right. You lived and you didn't shit in your pants, did you? No. Or shoot off your foot or, more important, anyone else's, so what more could you—"

"Yes, but I was—"

"All right, so you were scared. Big deal. Everyone's scared."

"Even—"

"Yes," he said, taking a long meditative pull off the glowing joint. "Every fucking time."

5

Dawn: the orange slicing through the gray above the palms; the quiet settling from the sheer exhaustion of the flesh; the smoke still clinging to the earth, indistinguishable from the morning fog; now the sky paling: the field, the wire becoming visible; the wire scarecrowed with broken bodies; the field off beyond the wire plowed—furrows of hell; and now brightening yet even more, revealing the full horror of carnage and waste: the bodies bloated, twisted, unrecognizable; here an arm, there perhaps a leg; a boot with a foot still inside; a helmet with a small jagged hole opening outward, sprouting a bloody tuft of blond hair; and immune to it all: the villagers—the very old and the very young—materializing like phantoms out of the fog, moving about, going on forever with their lives. ("Japanese, French, 'Mericans. Same-same. Numbah fuckin' ten.")

"Okay, motherfuckers, bag 'em and tag 'em," ordered a lieutenant with a .45 strapped to his waist. "Let's get this shit cleaned up 'fore the new C.O. gets here."

So, protesting and cursing, we dragged ourselves out of our holes and began collecting our dead. And out across the perimeter wire, the same process—the collection: children gathering up the small silk parachutes from the flares (for silk shirts, Strider said); others collecting unexploded mortar rounds; the old men and women stripping the dead of anything redeemable; a mother, a wife, wailing and clutching a mass of mangled flesh; the wooden carts with high wooden wheels lumbering into place to be piled six high with twisted corpses like some eighteenth-century living nightmare; and scattered about, routing and grunting among the charred hunks of bone and tissue, pigs feeding.

We had not been at our ghoulish task under the watchful and frozen glare of the dead—all with the same repugnant stare imprinted on their faces of universal surprise and uncomprehension; why me, Lord? —for more than half an hour when suddenly our machine guns opened up again. I turned, ran a few ducked meters, heading back for the hole, tripped and decided to remain where I had fallen. And soon the howitzers and mortars too began raining down their own particular brand of hell and destruction upon the fleeing populace out across the wire: old men and women screaming and pumping it back for the jungle faster than you would have thought those fragile old bones could travel; some not even running, petrified, simply holding on to one another; children grabbing up one last parachute; pigs abandoning their breakfast; water buffaloes, some still harnessed to their carts, standing and staring stupidly as the machine guns pumped round after round into their slowly collapsing bodies.

I spotted Strider lying several yards away. I stood

and made a dash for him. I threw myself down next to him. He didn't seem to take notice of my arrival. In fact, Strider, propped up on one elbow, facing the jungle, his eyes shaded by his ever-present sunglasses, never seemed to take notice of anything.

Finally he spoke: "See that kid over there with all them parachutes? Bet you ten to one he never makes the tree line."

"What?" I shouted, horrified.

"The tree line," said Strider, pointing. "Bet you ten to one the little fucker never makes it."

And I looked in the direction in which he had pointed and I saw a boy running. But before the bet could be consummated or even properly considered, the young boy did a forward flip and landed on his back, still clutching a handful of parachutes.

"But why?" I screamed. "Why? They weren't doing nothing! They were just . . . just . . ."

"Don't matter," said Strider. "Can't let the bastards get too close. 'Sides, out here life's cheap."

And later that day the new C.O. arrived—a small man with short jet-black hair and a constant frown—and it all began again. No, not again; at least not again for me; for me it was a first, a beginning. For of the laborious and often futile art of killing—if one can refer to killing (and here not merely killing as so many someones lined up against a brick wall, but rather the hunting to kill, of which there are vast and sundry differences) as an art—it can be said without doubt or hesitation that I was most singularly unproficient and most sorely unprepared. Usually about 0600 (six A.M., civilian talk), after an indigestible breakfast of powdered eggs and animal by-products, we forwarded out into the jungles. The plan, militarily, was for us to hump our way with packs, rifles and ammunition, and other assorted accessories of annihilation, through the hostile and unforgiving green of the surrounding countryside in the hope (here the hopeful being those career officers with their grease pencils and their body-count boards) of luring the enemy into contact and killing as many as possible while suffering an "acceptable" (Christ!) casualty figure ourselves. Somehow the logic behind these operations always eluded me. But then, what did I know? I didn't have a grease pencil.

So we walked, stumbled: hacking our way through underbrush so thick that you couldn't see three feet on either side of you; catwalking along the raised edges of rice paddies (falling in as often as not); wading through muck-filled swamps; nearly drowning fording creeks. And through it all: the fear. The absolute surety that the next step along that one-foot-wide sandy trail will be your last; the certainty of imminent ambush; the pressured expectation of booby traps—exposed, crossing the open fields; surrounded, struggling through the underbrush. Then suddenly, a bird sounding in the trees (a signal?); an animal crashing away through the undergrowth; a burst of automatic-rifle fire; perhaps a grenade; then the quiet, the breathing, the command, the cursing, and then the continuation. The walking. And sometimes we caught them and sometimes they caught us; but still it was always the same, day after day after day—the walking, the heat, the fear. And on occasion the walking and the heat and the fear and the overall feeling of futility and waste became so overwhelming that the squad leaders simply disregarded their orders, invented a firefight, and called in several thousand dollars worth of artillery support while we all sat back and enjoyed the fireworks from a safe distance.

It was on one of these bogus missions that I first met Motown. We had been ordered into a certain sector near an area which was a favorite of those familiar with the countryside: the sacred forest guarded by the holy monkeys.

"Sacred forest?" I asked in disbelief. "Holy monkeys?"

So with Strider taking the point (he was in charge of this particular operation) we—about ten in number, if I remember correctly—trudged off early one morning through the bush and mosquitoes, heading toward what I still didn't believe existed. The sun was up in no time and pounding down unmercifully, sapping our strength. Our helmets cooked our brains. Our heads spun. Sweat poured from our bodies. Our packs became heavier and heavier. Our feet turned to lead. And yet—and this always surprised me, for I was all for calling it quits—we walked. We always walked. And soon the walking became fighting, for we had long since finished with the mere forward movement of feet; we were now all arms and back-swinging branches: fighting through a primeval gloom created by the impenetrable interwoven canopy overhead; fighting along a trail choked with the reaching arms of twisting vines; fighting over monster trees felled by time and weight; fighting under low-thorned branches draped just at a neck-hanging height; fighting our way onward through the massed convergence of ageless doom and decay; fighting on seemingly without reason or direction.

Yes, we walked; one foot in front of the other; walking until I thought that I would drop (one soldier in fact did pass out and we had to carry him); walking, walking, walking; forward, onward, fighting; crashing, cursing, collapsing; meaningless, senseless walking; weary, dragging, sun-drugged, sun-baked, sunburned; following, being followed; mindless, numb, robotic. Then suddenly, up ahead, there was a shout and then a breeze like air conditioning coming down a hallway corridor. Like a veil lifting, we burst through the green latticework of foliage and bush, and there it was—a paradise of sound and color and life. God himself in his first stumbling efforts could not have created a more beautiful setting: cool and fresh and green; shaded by trees the likes of which I'd never seen before; palms twisting up toward the sun, up to unbelievable heights; a few rays of sunlight slanting down through the tops of the trees; the air scented with the clean fresh fragrance of flowers; massive roots shooting up snakelike through the moss-carpeted jungle floor; granite boulders pushing their way up out of the earth; weathered white stone carved long ago into the crude shapes of monkeys and now overgrown thickly with flowering green vines; the sedate murmur of rushing water; the crashing of a great waterfall; water lilies and ferns; frogs croaking; the constant hum of insects; birds and monkeys screeching in the trees; multicolored butterflies (some as large as a man's hand) floating about weightlessly; pineapples, bananas, coconuts, mangoes, oranges. And all of it just waiting there, waiting there for us.

"Not bad, huh?" asked a voice from behind.

I turned around and looked up and then continued

looking up even higher yet. Above me towered an enormous black man: wet, drenched with sweat, glistening; broad-shouldered, solid, shirtless; his Afro frizzed out so fully that a helmet would have been a joke; a small trimmed goatee sprouting from his chin; a gold earring in his right ear; arms larger than my legs, dangling nearly to his knees; two ammunition bandoliers for our unit's light machine gun crisscrossing his chest like rows of shark's teeth.

"Not bad? Shit!" I said. "I can't believe it."

"Oh, it's real," he assured me. "Just watch out for them motherfucking monkeys."

"Monkeys?" I asked, looking around.

"Yeah, man, monkeys," he said, propping his rifle up against a tree and dancing about, scratching his armpits and doing one excellent imitation of a monkey. "Monkeys, man, you know. Gotta watch out for the motherfuckers. They'll rob your ass blind."

He turned and bent. Across the back of his flak jacket was drawn a large yellow-and-red circular target with a small peace symbol in the center for a bull's-eye.

"Want some mushrooms, man?" he asked, turning back around with a handful of dirt and some little white spongy caps.

"Mushrooms?" I asked. (I was still half-dinged-out from the march; my mind wasn't hitting on all fours; I was feeling absent, outside of myself, as though I were only watching again.)

"Yeah, man, you know, psilocybin. These suckers'll trip you out."

"Sounds good," I said, accepting a couple.

"Motown," he said, extending his hand.

"Austin," I said, grasping the huge hand and trying without success to perform a soulful handshake.

"Texas?" he asked.

"No," I explained, "it's just my name."

"Oh," he said, seemingly a little disappointed. "Well, come on, man. I got some smoke and a little music. We can sit over there and get off."

"All right," I said.

He led the way to a moss-covered piece of earth under a large tree. We eased ourselves down to the ground, moaning, with bones popping, and stretched out. It was cool and soft there.

"Well, let's see what they got on the radio," he said, whipping a small red transistor out from under his flak jacket. "They ain't always just too together as far as music goes."

. . . reaching, smiling sweetly.
It's good to touch
The green, green grass of home.

"What'd I tell you?" he asked almost humorously. "Ain't dat some fucking shit! Here we is in the middle of fucking hell with every damn dink and his cousin out to waste our ass, and some lightweight asshole back where it's nice and safe is playing some kinda shit song 'bout green grass and home. Ha! What a motherfucking joke!"

"'Yes, well, it does seem somewhat inappropriate," I admitted.

He turned. His eyes narrowed and seemed to sink back into his skull. "White-man shit," he said, glaring.

"Huh?" I asked, unsure if I had heard him correctly.

"White-man shit," he pronounced again slowly. "Just listen." He turned up the radio. "You think they be playing dat shit for me, for any of us brothers out here. Shit, man. I tell truth: this here's white-man music for a white man's war."

"Yeah?" I asked, trying to be agreeable, not knowing what direction the conversation was headed.

"Damn right!" he said, his eyes narrowing yet even more into a near-disappearance. "They just wants us niggers to fight it for 'em and die for 'em. You think we got anything 'gainst a buncha slopes running round out here? Shit! And believe me, when they finally go to adding it all up at the end, you gonna find one whole helluva lot more of us brothers dead than you white boys."

"Well, maybe so," I said. "I really don't know anything about that."

"Maybe? Shit! You can bet your ass on it!" he said, the excitement and irritation in his voice mounting. "Look at all the brothers getting drafted. Ain't getting no kinda thank-you-ma'am deferments. Ain't getting outta no shit by going off to some sweet-ass little college. Hell, man, they swooped down into my project back home and drafted out nearly every motherfucker I knowed that weren't already in jail. It was like some kinda fucking roundup. Day I went for my physical, weren't but four or five white faces in the whole damn room. So don't be telling me 'maybe' 'bout shit!"

"Sure. Okay," I said, not really caring to discuss race or the inequities of the selective-service system with anyone eating mushrooms and carrying an M-16.

Motown sank back against the tree, breathing rapidly. His eyes twitched nervously. His teeth were clenched in a mad smile of hatred. Suddenly he snatched up the radio and leaped to his feet and began shaking it violently.

"Where'd hell's Eddy Arnold at, motherfuckers?" he demanded of the radio. "Huh? Tell me, where'd fuck's he at?" He stomped and raged.

And quietly, calmly, there came a voice from behind: "Talking to your radio again, Mo?"

Motown paused, one foot lifted, a hand and the radio cocked, ready for a fling, and looked back. Chewing on a blooming sprig plucked from an orange tree, Doc was propped leisurely up against a palm, watching.

"Wouldn't throw it away just yet, Mo. How you gonna know when the war's over?"

"It ain't gonna be," said Motown, lowering his foot and slowly collapsing into an enormous heap of breathing and brooding.

"Yes, sir, Mo, you've really got it tough, don't you?" baited Doc. "Ain't like the gooks were trying to nail us too. Only you, right? A sad situation. A most singular tragedy."

"I got it tough enough, motherfucker," protested Motown somewhat sedately.

"Oh yes, yes. Cry me a river. Only one fighting this whole big nasty war all by his lonesome."

Motown didn't reply. His eyes sought the ground.

"And all those mean old white men," continued Doc happily. "I'sa seen the light and I'sa heard the voice and now I'sa gonna throw off my yoke and be free. Gimme five, Lord."

Motown snapped his head around and glared at Doc. Doc smiled and held the larger man's bitter stare for almost a full minute. Finally Motown broke it off and rose. He picked up his rifle, pocketed his radio, spat sharply on the ground, and then withdrew amid the shrieking laughter of monkeys high up in the trees overhead.

"Rather strange fellow," I observed, watching the figure recede.

"Rather strange, indeed," agreed Doc, settling down next to me. I noticed immediately that Doc wasn't carrying a weapon—not even a pistol.

"What's his story?" I asked.

"Shattered and totally scattered," answered Doc amusedly. Then after a moment's reflection he added quietly, "Like everyone else, I guess."

Doc snapped open his bulging medical pouch and began digging away. He pulled out bandage rolls, bottles of medication of various colors, scalpels, scissors, clamps, comic books, a bag of M&Ms, a toy water pistol which he pointed at me and said Bang, several large medical books detailing surgical incisions and communicable diseases, a can of warm beer, a broken watch, half a sandwich, and a picture of a pretty young girl standing beside a '57 Chevy and smiling. Watching him yanking out all these precious jewels, I was reminded of a squirrel or rodent of some type burrowing into his store of winter goods. And he looked a little squirrelish too: soft brown eyes, a toothy smile, the rapid darting movements. Finally he came up with two handfuls of pills.

"How'd you like it?" he asked, extending both hands. "Up or down?"

"Sideways," I said, pointing to a clump of sprouting mushrooms.

"Ah, the fungi. A most excellent choice."

"Absolutely," I said, already beginning to feel most excellent.

Doc picked out several small white pills and a couple of red capsules and returned the rest to his bag.

"Think I'll get a little sideways myself," he said, taking the whole dose in a single waterless gulp. "A little herb?" he asked, smiling his squirrel smile and producing a ready-roll joint.

"Certainly," I said. "Thanks."

And as I sat there smoking and getting progressively more and more sideways, I was once again struck by the awesome beauty of my surroundings. The explosion of life: the trees—palms and others with jointed white branches disappearing skyward; the animals—monkeys like cautious peasants closing in for a better look at the intruders; the flowers—orchids, white, purple, pink, opening; the voices—the shouts and laughter of the men, high and childlike, swimming naked in the pool under the waterfall. This refuge of peace, the jungle itself, and ofttimes the passing unpeopled countryside in general seemed to have been skirted by time, forgotten by change.

"This is no place for a war," I observed matter-of-factly.

"Is anywhere?" countered Doc.

"Well, no, I guess not," I said. "It's just that it seems so, well, so . . ."

"Peaceful?" suggested Doc.

"Yeah," I agreed. "Peaceful. Peaceful and beautiful."

A white butterfly, almost transparent, eased by in the breeze. A bird, lost in a tangle of twisted vines and knotted branches, shrieked. The monkeys in groups of threes and fours chanced in yet even closer.

"Well, if you think this is peaceful, if you think this is beautiful, just wait till you get to know the people," warned Doc. "Then you'll really be mammothly confused."

"The people?" I asked. "I thought that was the trouble."

"Yes, well, naturally they are," began Doc, a little unsure of his argument. "They always are. But that's only a small proportion—the colonels and the generals and the politicians. Most of the people, the country people, are really beautiful—simple, easy. Beautiful to look at, sure, much more so than your whites or your blacks. But it's their nature that's really so beautiful, and basically quite passive too. What do they want with or care about or know about war? Okay, maybe I'm wrong there; maybe I'm moving too fast. They know about war only too well. But what do they—the average rice farmer or fisherman and his family—want with or care about war? You think they care about the advertised causes of this war: freedom, American-style freedom, or—God save the world—democracy? Hell! Come on! Democracy? Freedom? The right to vote? Shit! They're only terms, school-book terms. Nice neat little phrases with nice neat little pictures. They have no reality out here. These people want only a little rice, a little meat, maybe a water buffalo, their kids, their families, and a little peace. That's all."

"Well, someone sure must want something," I said, listening to the distant whine of a jet edging northward across the sky.

Strider wandered into view about then. He paused for a moment, watching the men swimming and splashing in the foaming pool under the falls, then he turned and walked away alone.

"You know Strider?" asked Doc, rummaging through his medical bag again.

"Well, I've met him," I said.

"Yeah. He's a hard guy to get to know."

"Yes, I've noticed," I said.

"Hard-core. Real hard-core. You know this is his third tour?"

"No, really?"

"Yep," said Doc. "And now he's already short again. I don't know what he'll do if he wants another one."

Doc was no longer looking through his bag. He had forgotten whatever it was that he had been looking for. Instead he turned toward me with a certain amused expression on his face.

"The motherfucker just couldn't make it back in the World," he said.

"The World?" I asked stupidly.

"Yeah. Civilian life. The States. You know, home cooking and mom's apple pie," he explained. "After his first tour he went back home to wherever home was and fucked around or whatever and then I guess he just went nuts, fucking cashews and pecans. He'd go out reconning at night with a hatchet and sneak up on his neighbors' dogs and whack off their damn heads and then leave 'em in his neighbors' mailboxes. Imagine it. You go out to get the mail and there's old Rover—surprise."

"Rather bizarre," I said, looking off in the direction in which Strider had vanished.

"No shit," Doc assured me. "And it probably didn't make him just too overly popular with his neighbors either. Anyway, they finally caught his ass and gave him a choice: jungle or jail."

"Yeah. Well, what about this one?" I asked. "You say this is number three."

And Doc just shook his head and sighed. "The crazy fucker got out and then a week later he reenlisted."

Near the pool under the waterfall, the monkeys were closing in. Some few, the extremely brave or the hopelessly foolish, accepted bits of proffered food from the men. Often this feeding led to wild games of confusion and great shrieks of laughter (from the men) and of panic (from the monkeys) as the monkeys would be snatched up bodily by their long hairy reaching arms and hurled screaming and pinwheeling through the air and into the water. When pursued or trapped, the monkeys would rend the air with terror-filled, ear-splitting cries, and scamper about in frantic, dusty circles, or simply sink submissively into quivering balls of whines and whimpers. The older, larger gray-faced monkeys would sit well back out of reach and watch the men with a weary look of patience like grandparents, removed from immediate responsibility, judging a group of unruly offspring, which, anthropologically speaking, I guess we were.

"Known him long?" I asked.

"Who?" asked Doc, his eyes waxed with a vague and distant gleam.

"Strider."

"Yeah. Since his first tour," said Doc, sliding somewhat out of his trance.

"How many tours you had?" I asked, surprised.

"Three," he said without emotion.

And that shut me up. It confused me. Just a few moments before, Doc had spoken with such obvious sadness, such hopelessness, when relating the facts of Strider's reenlistments that I found this to be flawed and a point in need of examination. But I let it pass. I let a lot of things pass, a lot of things out there—out there where things did not need to make sense, where logic and rational behavior were not required, were often not even expected.

"He's changed considerably," said Doc, remembering. "I knew him when he was still a cherry."

"A cherry?" I asked. Somethings I just couldn't let pass.

"Yeah, a cherry," Doc repeated. "A virgin."

"Strider?" I asked. It was hard to believe. "That guy? A virgin? Come on now. I might look like I just got off the boat but I—"

"No, no," said Doc, checking my outburst. "Not a virgin in that sense, in the sense of someone who has never had a woman. I'm sure he has. Lots of 'em, probably. I'm sure he couldn't have avoided 'em even if he had wanted to. I'm quite sure he could no more have sat in a bar or soda shop anywhere in the world, much less in the good old U.S. of A., without having some hugging whore, no doubt with streaked blond beauty-shopped hair and a poised cigarette just begging for a light, coming up to young Strider from behind and sliding a limp arm loaded down with bracelets and bangles around his young neck and saying, no, probably whispering, 'Honey, I'm gonna turn you onto something good. Light my cigarette.' No, not in that sense of sex and women and getting some, but

73

rather in the sense of killing, of shedding blood. At that game, he was new."

"All right," I said.

"I was there when it happened, when he scored his first kill," said Doc, pulling out another joint and firing it up. "It wasn't like a firefight where everything's happening so fast and you're so busy ducking and diving and praying and maybe getting off a few rounds that you don't have time to look or consider. This was more personal, much more. One on one. Slow motion. It really changed him. It amazed him. It amazed me too. I'll hear those shots—one, two, three—forever. Incredible! Up till then, up till that very moment, I don't think he had given it much thought. Oh sure, he must've screamed, 'Kill! Kill!' and 'Charge!' and all that good shit in boot camp, but I don't really think—"

"All right, tell it," I said, getting a little impatient with Doc's procrastination, and besides, the joint was burning away in his hand most unforgivably unattended.

"Well, okay," said Doc, taking a hit and passing it over. "At the time I was working out of a hospital in Saigon. Strider was there too. He was a guard. I didn't really know him very well, just said hi, and that kinda shit. Like I said, it was his first tour. Mine too. I don't think he had been in-country but a couple of weeks, and never out in the boonies. Okay, so it's lunchtime and me and a bunch of other medics and nurses and doctors are all sitting outside in the sunshine on the front steps, eating lunch. It was a real fine day. Saigon was a beautiful city when they weren't blowing it up. Trees and wide avenues and parks. And the chicks, man! Floating along in those *ao dais,* Jesus! Never seen better-looking women in my life. I knew this one girl—"

"Strider?" I encouraged.

"Right. Anyway, at this time they'd been having a few bombings and shit so everyone was a little on edge, not jumpy, just kinda watchful. So we're all sitting there eating lunch and shitting around with the nurses when this kid—I don't know how old he was; he could've been twelve or twenty; hell, it's just hard to tell about Orientals. Well, so this kid comes pedaling up right in front of the hospital on a red bike. You know it's funny the way you remember certain things: a red bike. And on the back this kid's got a neat little package all tied up with string. So the kid stops and gets off his bike and starts untying this little package. Well, this guard sees the kid and comes up to him wearing a flak jacket and a helmet and carrying an M-16. The guy's ready for battle. He's waving his arms and shouting at the kid in English to move his damn bike. And naturally the kid doesn't know shit about English so he just smiles and goes back to work on the string. By this time we've all stopped eating and we're now into watching. The guard's screaming at the kid and the kid's smiling and working at the string. Then suddenly the guard—not Strider; he was standing a little farther off down the road—the guard jerks up his rifle and points it at the kid, all the while screaming. So the kid freezes. He's got his mouth open and his little package about half-unraveled. Now everybody's real tense. We know something's gonna happen but we don't know what. When suddenly like a bad actor in a bad play, this fucking lieutenant—where do they get those guys, huh? I mean like where the hell do they find 'em?"

"I don't know," I said.

"Me neither," sighed Doc. "They're hopeless. So anyway, this fucking lieutenant comes racing out of the hospital with his pistol drawn, and screaming. Now you've got the lieutenant screaming, the guard screaming, some of the nurses starting to scream too, and everybody stumbling over each other, backing away. General chaos. And now the kid really freaks. All these fucking people screaming and squirming around on the ground, right?"

"It would freak me," I confessed.

"It would freak me too," agreed Doc. "And it definitely freaked the kid. He drops his little package, he had it freed from the bike now, and he leaps back on his bike and tears off. The lieutenant pops off a warning shot and yells out something like: 'Stop or I'll shoot!' A real low-level comedian. Now all the guards have their rifles up, just waiting for someone to tell 'em to fire and everybody else's ducking, thinking the VC are about to blow the hell out of the hospital. So the kid goes flying down this little utility road right in front of the hospital, but it's a dead end so he turns around and hauls it back the other way. Now he's passing right in front of the hospital again, right in front of the guards and right in front of all those guns. Like a moving target in a shooting gallery. And all these guns are pointed at him, following him first down one way, then back the other way. Guns trained on a kid pedaling like hell on a red bike, right?"

"Right."

"Now there are cars and jeeps and bushes and shit

between the kid and the guards. The kid's flashing by in the sunlight. His head's turned back, looking at the guards like maybe if he keeps looking at them maybe they won't waste his ass. I can see his head turned, his eyes popping, rushing by against a background of chain-link fence. There's traffic in the street on the other side of the fence and people standing around watching, wondering what the hell the fucking Americans are up to now. Everything seems sorta frozen—everything: the traffic, the people, the cars. It's weird. It's like the whole city has just stopped. Everybody's focusing in on this kid, waiting. And then finally, as if to break the suspense before someone dies of a heart attack, the lieutenant yells out, 'All right, grease him!' But you see, there's these cars and people and shit all around him and no one can get a clear shot. It's silent. You can almost hear the kid breathing. Things seem to be happening in slow motion. The kid's looking back, not looking where he's going, the guns are all pointed, the lieutenant's screaming, but no one's shooting. Everything's quiet and just kinda holding and waiting to drop. And then up into this void of tragedy and disaster, like a cardboard cutout springing out of a doorway in a fun house, up steps Strider and caps off three single and distinctly separate shots like bam . . . bam . . . bam. And well, it's like a big hand just reaches out and grabs the kid by the collar. It stops him cold. He flies off the bike backward and lands up against a pole. The bike keeps on going a little ways, then it topples down into an open sewer. The kid grabs onto the pole and then he turns and looks right at Strider, then he slides on down the pole and rolls over into the sewer too. Strider's standing there about twenty meters away. He's already dropped his rifle. He's standing there with both arms stretched out toward the kid, just looking. The lieutenant comes running up and spins Strider around and grabs one of his outstretched hands and shakes it and says, 'Good shot. Get the body.' Then the lieutenant turns on his heels and marches back inside the hospital, leaving Strider standing there like a little boy lost at a circus. And he just stood there for a long time with both arms out, his mouth open, looking really dazed. It was like he was appealing to those few of us still left sitting there on the steps to help him or something. And it's that expression that I'll never forget: him standing there watching that lieutenant march back inside, with both arms stretched out, his mouth a little bit open, his rifle at his feet, not moving, just standing there like he was waiting for someone to come along and say, 'It's all right. Don't worry about it.' And I don't know if anyone ever did. And I don't know if maybe he's still not waiting or if maybe it no longer matters to him anymore."

"Not a pretty tale," I said.

"Grim as death," said Doc, shaking his head.

"Well, what was in the kid's little package?" I asked.

"Rice," Doc said with a crazy laugh. "Goddamn fucking rice! The kid was bringing it to his sister. She was working at the hospital as a maid."

"Jesus," I said, handing what was left of the joint back to Doc.

Down by the pool, most of the men were out of the water now, beginning to dress and collect their gear. Strider, having recently emerged from the forest wall, was walking about among them, talking. Overhead, from out of the swaying trees, chirping birds swooped down in long effortless parabolic arcs.

"A beautiful place," I remarked.

"Beautiful," agreed Doc.

"Peaceful. Real peaceful," I said with a certain un-earned satisfaction.

But before Doc could comment on the quietude of our surroundings, the quiet itself was shattered by the sharp popping of an M-16 firing somewhere up ahead. Men, naked or half-dressed, scattered, scrambling for cover and grabbing up rifles or pants according to preference. Above the pool, to the right of the falls, halfway up the rocky trail leading to the top, a monkey, helmeted, wearing a flak jacket no less, was clipping off random shots in our direction with a stolen rifle.

At the first shot I rolled to the right; at the second Doc rolled to the left. Then, assessing the situation, Doc leaped to his feet and raced off into the heat of the firing. A bullet ripped by overhead, slamming into the tree under which Doc and I had been sitting. I, void of courage or caution, stumbled up and ran after Doc. I didn't want to be alone.

Men were crouched behind the huge rocks and the felled trees, laughing and cursing. No one was return-ing fire. I could see Doc hunched down behind a boulder with Billy. I ran up and joined them.

"Cover me," commanded Billy, moving into the open.

"Cover you?" I cried. I had neglected to bring along my rifle.

A round struck the rock behind which Doc and I were now hiding. Pebbles pinged down upon my helmet—at least I had remembered to bring that. Another round impacted less than a meter away, kicking up a small shower of dirt. I began to wonder if perhaps I was being targeted. Three more rounds in rapid succession landed in our general vicinity, then the forest fell silent. Doc and I waited tensely for a long minute, then Doc stood up and eventually I inched up next to him.

The monkey had spent his clip and evidently had not had advanced infantry training: he didn't know how to reload. Finally, after pointing the rifle and squeezing the trigger several times to no avail, the monkey gave up and tossed the rifle off the cliff and down into the pool below. His compadres who had opted for the treetops at the initial outbreak applauded his sensibilities and sent up a loud chattering chorus. The monkey, still in battle dress, stood up triumphantly and danced about, spinning and leaping.

One of the men had twisted his ankle running for cover. Doc went over to assist. We had taken fire and no one had been seriously injured. Everyone felt good. Several of the men began laughing and joking about "Killer Kong."

Suddenly there was another burst of rifle fire. And again there was a mad scramble for cover. I dived down alongside the length of a moss-covered tree. This time it was Billy. Peeping cautiously over the side of the tree, I watched as he capped off a short burst at the dancing monkey. The animal spun around once and then nose-dived into the pool below. In the flak jacket, he sank immediately.

Doc ran up, shrieking and waving his arms. "What the hell do you—"

Billy turned. Doc fell silent. With an evil smile spreading slowly across his lips, Billy ejected his spent clip and slapped in a new one. Then there was an awful silence as Billy chambered the first round. He aimed up into the trees, paused once to look at Doc, and then emptied the clip. Doc turned away. Monkeys began falling from the trees, screaming and shrieking. The jungle echoed with their anguished cries of terror and dying. Billy emptied two more clips and three more trees of monkeys before he finally satisfied himself or lost interest, and left off the killing.

"Bad!" began Billy, strutting. "'Bad! Real bad! Baddest fucking monkey in this fucking jungle! Real bad!"

Doc came back and slowly began to collect the contents of his medical pouch.

"Bad, Doc!" called out Billy, still strutting. "How'd you like that shit, Doc? Bad, huh? Real bad!"

"Yeah," said Doc, not looking up.

"Aw, come on, Doc. Just having a little fun," said Billy, seemingly surprised at Doc's coolness. "What's wrong with that?"

But Doc didn't answer him. Instead he simply turned and walked away.

"Just having a little fun, Doc!" shouted Billy angrily, his voice echoing off the walls of the waterfall. "Just a little fun! . . . fun! . . . fun!"

6

And yet, we walked: hard red clay, centuries packed, blistering young and tender (and some not so young and tender) feet; deep brown mud, shining, nearly impossible to traverse; foul-smelling, black-watered rice paddies, alive with disease, peeling strips of dead skin from feet too long submerged; soft white sand, paradisiacal, yielding gently to heavy heels; folding disappearing green, booby-trapped, fooling feet finally and forever. Yes, we walked: circling, backtracking, sidetracking, stumbling, fumbling, falling, no matter. Irrespective of roads', paths', trails', non-trails' colors, conditions, or final destinations, we walked.

"Saddle up! Moving out!"

I put out my cigarette and looked wearily at my sixty-pound pack.

"Gonna 'ave to get me some new feet," lamented Motown, massaging his size-eleven foot. "Just look."

Motown extended a foot black on top and almost white on the bottom.

"Most sorely abused," I said.

"You got that right," agreed Motown, gingerly slipping a wet sock over his foot.

"All right, ladies, move it!" came the voice of encouragement again.

And like a spineless disjointed snake, the long line of men, some fifty strong, stood and shifted itself forward.

This particular march of which I now speak—write— was taking place some ten days after the Great Monkey Massacre of '69. ("Bad! Real bad!") During the elapsed and intervening days we had actually done very little, mostly local stuff: check this trail, spoil that well, burn these huts, shoot those chickens, destroy a little rice. Our mission on this bright and sunny day as I understood it (which I probably didn't) was to lay an ambush for a select group of VC tax collectors and propaganda officers who, along with a sizable entourage, were scheduled to be passing a certain point at a certain time. How such accurate and valuable information could have been obtained was not questioned by me; later it became self-evident.

So we walked: sweat pouring; wet patches where skin touched cloth forming on the backs of our shirts; equipment, supplies, garbage—packs, helmets, Coke cans, candy wrappers—being dropped along the trail; the air thick with marijuana smoke; troops talking, shouting, laughing, joking, cursing; some playing radios; some singing along; troops tripping over roots, crashing headlong and fully weighted into the undergrowth. A herd of enthusiastic elephants could not have been less secretive. I was hoping the ambushees were deaf.

Finally we arrived at the said ambush site and deployed into the jungle along the trail. What had been only minutes before a noisy rabble of teenage boys acting like teenage boys now dissolved wordlessly, soundlessly, professionally into the high grass and the dense thickets of bamboo. It was as if we had never existed. The jungle surrounded us completely and took us to its heart.

The quiet was appalling. I could almost hear myself sweat. Mosquitoes thundered in my ears. I was sure they would give us away. The trees usually so alive with bird sounds fell silent. Complete and utter silence. I half-expected someone (myself) to scream or cough or whistle just to break the tension. It was unbearable. But no one did. I almost began to pity our adversaries. It didn't seem fair. We had them dead to rights. They never had a chance.

Only, as it turned out, they had a far better chance than I had suspected; they never showed. We waited. We sweated. We listened with ears straining. But nothing happened. Finally, after several hours, with the sun already folding into a bright orange sky-glow in the west, the officer in charge of the operation, a young captain, decided that the whole thing was bogus and ordered everyone back onto the trail. We came out barking like a pack of hungry dogs. The injustice of it! The indignity! I, too, proclaimed in strong and heated words my bitter disappointment at the missed chance for murder and mayhem, although secretly I was greatly relieved. And I suspect that many of those other gallant young hearts who complained so loud and obscenely were also quite relieved. Billy cursed (but for real). Motown said that he needed some new ears to go with his new feet. Strider was silent. Doc was stoned.

On the trail within a tight circle of extreme excitement were the two skinny Vietnamese guides who had brought us to this most unproductive end and who with shaking hands and heads and half-sentences were now trying to explain what had gone awry. Twenty or thirty soldiers towered above them, looking down coldly. Perhaps there would be no ambush, but a couple of murders might suffice. After all the walking and all the waiting, tempers were high, nerves were frayed. There was a general demand for blood, any blood. And it was blood in triplicate that we eventually got.

"Waste 'em."

"No, wait! Me numbah—"

"String the little fuckers up!"

"No, no, me numbah-one friend numbah-one GI!"

"You number shit!"

"Anybody got any rope?"

"Just shoot 'em."

Safeties were clicking on and off. Radios were playing again. Coke cans and beer cans were brought out of packs and drunk hot. Boots were removed. Helmets were dropped. Joints were lit. Laughter filled the air. A festive, near carnival atmosphere prevailed.

"Hey, Bobby, gimme a hit off dat motherfucker."

"Pass it down."

"What is it, bro?"

"You got it."

"Yeah."

Suddenly a shot rang out. A young soldier, dark, Chicano maybe, drinking a Coke, spun. Both hands reached up for the throat. All voices and movement stopped. Blood like from a ruptured water main spurted out between the fingers. The soldier staggered and crashed with brown eyes frozen into the open arms of another, and together they tumbled into the high weeds.

Another shot and another. First, countable in ones and twos, then like an entire string of firecrackers going off, the jungle was ripe with death. I dropped and rolled off the trail. Men screamed and shouted, pointed, pulled, ran, collided, cursed. It was impossible to tell where the firing was coming from. It seemed to come from everywhere and nowhere at the same time. In blind hell-struck terror, sweeping arcs of fire burst off into the jungle, killing and wounding friends and fellow soldiers. Chaos punctuated by confusion. Finally someone stood up and pointed into the air and shouted, "The trees! The trees! They're in—" A round caught him in the stomach, sitting him down abruptly. He sat in calm wordless amazement with his legs thrust out straight, holding his stomach. After a few stunned seconds he pulled his hand away, examined a cupped handful of his own blood, and then quietly toppled over sideways.

I looked up. High up in the trees, strapped to the thicker branches, snipers fired down with immunity. They looked like a flock of migratory birds up there—birds come home to nest.

From down the trail, coming toward me, I could see Billy running, his head down. He lunged from side to side as he ran, as if he knew instinctively where the next bullet would or would not land. Little red puffs of dirt kicked up about his heels. (Billy always amazed me. I'll not go so far as to say that I liked him personally, for I didn't, but still he amazed me. Maybe it was that boyish and innocent look that always threw me. He seemed to actually enjoy the war—the walking, the waiting, the rain, the mud, the blood. Only once did I ever see him upset, emotionally moved. Things just didn't seem to touch him. But then again, I don't know, maybe they did. He was always something of a puzzle to me—a puzzle with a piece missing. Sometimes when we—Strider, Billy, Motown, Doc, myself, and others—would be sitting around and the complaints would start [there were always complaints—food, weather, death] he would exhibit a profound reluctance to join in, and if pressed on some certain grievance held in common, he would simply shrug his shoulders and say something like, "Ah, it ain't so bad." Which always led me to ask myself, "So bad as what?" Maybe there was something dark and sinister in his past that made everything else in comparison seem bright, some tragedy unknown. I didn't know, and I never found out.) Just as he passed me, he looked down, his eyes wild. A stiff volley of fire cut across his path, effectively curtailing his advance. He spun and doubled back. Another barrage halted his retreat. He threw himself down into the weeds across the trail from where I lay.

"Damn," he said. "Who's in charge of this shithole operation?"

"Hell if I know," I answered, shaking my head.

Three rounds cut through the conversation, impacting on the trail. We both covered up.

"They oughta be shot," shouted Billy into the flying dirt.

"They probably have been," I shouted back.

"Dammit, ambushed on an ambush," laughed Billy. "What a piece of shit!"

Suddenly a large object crashed to the earth on the trail between us. It landed loud. I thought I was dead.

After a few seconds of not being dead, I looked up. A sniper perched directly overhead looked down empty-handed. An awkward old bolt-action rifle with a cracked wooden stock lay on the trail. "Gone, sucker." Billy smiled, turning over on his back and raising his rifle. Then he paused and lowered his rifle and laughed. He reached out onto the trail and snatched up the old rifle and pointed it at the sniper (he was young; you could see it—the youthfulness—in his face; he was that close) and the boy (the sniper) closed his eyes and turned toward the tree trunk, hugging it with his face buried in the bark. A second, two seconds, three, then a loud shot—much louder than that of an M-16—rang out. The boy went limp and then flopped over. And like an acro-bat, like a child on a gym set, caught up in the tangle of rope which secured him to his branch, he dangled down headfirst, swinging slowly back and forth, back and forth.

"Hey, this thing's heavy," observed Billy, turning the rifle over in his hands. Then he heaved it into the bushes.

Time was expanding and contracting. It was hard to mark it precisely. Probably only about fifteen minutes had passed since the first shot. But it seemed much longer. It was getting dark. The night was coming, filtering down like the shredded leaves and violently torn twigs from the trees above. The fire from the trees continued murderously. Our position was unten-able. We had to move; even I knew that. Men at random would stand or come up onto one knee and fire off a couple of quick bursts, and then, almost inevitably, they'd go down. It was better to lie low. Young men, boys, were dying all around. Some went quietly where they lay, others with loud protests, defi-ant and unrepentant. Next to me, only a few feet away, a boy lay jerking in soundless spasms. Eventually he stopped jerking. He never did cry out. Farther up the trail I could see Doc working over a young lieutenant with a chest wound. The lieutenant was trying to look stoic. Probably a point of honor. He died anyway. Next to the lieutenant, two of Doc's patients with bandages wrapped around their heads, covering their eyes, comforted each other blindly and shared the contents of a canteen. And nearby, hidden partially in the high elephant grass, a body, faceless, lay alone and unattended. Finally the captain in charge of this misbegotten fracas roused himself up and screamed, "To the clearing, men! Follow me!" And with a wave of his arm, he was off. He must have been practicing that move forever, I thought to myself. It almost made me laugh, it looked so ridiculous. The gallant captain leading his valiant troops. Onward! Hurrah! Victory! Only now the proportion of valiant troops left to follow was severely reduced. Nearly a third of our original number was either dead or dying.

So follow we did: no music now, simply running; a gauntlet of death, an obstacle course of dying; hearts pounding, lungs bursting; vaulting bodies crisscrossed along the trail; dodging the spinning wounded; every man for himself; wholesale panic; wild cries and animal screams; firing blindly up into the trees and running; running like rats trapped; running; mad, crazy, insane.

And now, up ahead, even more insane: Doc and Strider standing in the middle of the trail, arguing; bullets zinging through the air; bodies twisting and twirling and falling around them; and they, standing and arguing.

Doc, frantic, pushing: "Go on! Go on! Get outta here!"

And Strider, calm, waiting: "No. You come too."

And the bullets banging at their feet and the men running by, and I, pulling up next to them and crouching down, firing up into the trees and hoping, praying to be included in whatever it was that protected them and kept them there, alive and standing.

And Doc, his hands flailing the air: "I can't! I can't! Can't you see?"

And Strider, calm, looking off: "Yes, I can see. Now come on."

And I, looking up, not believing yet still firing and hoping.

And Doc, wild, excited, pointing: "What about them? Leave 'em? Huh? Do we just leave 'em?"

And Strider, calm, looking down, considering, then stopping the next passing stampede of fleeing soldiers: "Pick 'em up."

The men, bunched, cowering, darting quick covert glances up into the trees, screaming: "What? What? Let's go! Move it! Shit!"

And Strider, calm, placing the muzzle of his M-16 under the chin of the tallest and loudest: "Pick 'em up." Then to me: "You too."

And now running again: crouched, complaining, carrying the clumsy burdens, cursing; the wounded flopping, being bounced about, more dead than alive; but still, maybe, maybe a chance, at least a chance; and Doc picking up his pouch and running now too; and Strider following; running with our burdens, our brothers; running through the long green tunnel; wondering: would they do this for me?; the tunnel, dark, smelling old like something dead and forgotten and wet; then slamming into the sunlight, the last of the sunlight, into the clearing.

In the clearing stood the captain, his helmet off, his blond hair blowing lightly in the breeze, marshaling his troops into some semblance of order, into a tight circle. The clearing was only about as large as the infield of a baseball diamond, completely surrounded by trees. Through the trees on one side were rice paddies and the beginnings of a village—huts and hedgerows. On all other sides were only trees, dark and stretching away into a green blackness. It was quiet now; only an occasional shot, not directed at us anymore, coming from behind us.

I deposited the body that I was carrying on the ground where Doc indicated and then took up a position along the perimeter next to Billy. All about, soldiers lay wounded and exhausted. Moans and whimpers could be heard everywhere. Someone nearby was praying. I didn't turn to see who. Instead I reached for my canteen and took a long steady drink. The water was hot but wet. It tasted good. Behind me in the center of the circle I could hear radio static and Strider's voice rising above the static. He was talking with the captain.

"This is as bad as the fucking trail," said Strider emphatically. "Let's at least cross through those trees and into the paddies. We can call in the choppers. It's gonna be hell here when night comes."

"We will be calling in no choppers, Sergeant," said the captain with equal emphasis. "We are not here to run, to retreat. The word is not in my vocabulary. We are here to attack or, failing at that, then at least to make a stand. Here. Here to the last man."

"We'll all die then," said Strider calmly.

"You're not afraid of dying for your country, are you, Sergeant?" shouted the captain, gripping his rifle high in front of his chest with both hands. "Sergeant?"

But Strider was already walking away.

"Not long now," said Billy, unwrapping a piece of chewing gum and putting it into his mouth.

Overhead the skies had blackened to the color of slimy mud. Night like a living thing came creeping out of the trees. A surprisingly cold wind pushed in across the clearing, stirring the tall grass and the tail-ends of bloody bandages. It soon began to rain. And there in the rain and the darkness and the quiet and the cold, we lay waiting, wondering what death would be like.

The first mortar round fell at the edge of the clearing, exploding like an orange flower opening. The second exploded within the perimeter itself, taking off the top of the young captain's fair head. The third and the fourth landed far off to the left. Before the fifth fell we were up and running again.

Out of the clearing, through the trees, across the paddy fields and into a bamboo thicket, we ran. And this time we didn't even need to be told about the wounded; we simply picked them up and ran.

With no officers left living, Strider took command. He established a new perimeter in the bamboo and made contact with our fire base. Things were looking dim. We couldn't be evacuated until dawn. We would have to hold our position and make do as best we could. And as it turned out, as best we could was not overly superior. We got our collective asses kicked.

Flares lit the night into jagged half-shades of dangling disaster; through the high grass they came: swarming, wave after chanting grinning wave, grinning death, like insects—ants—little men: skinny, black shorts, a rifle, a blade, an alarming smile, bloody eyes, faces distorted; a helicopter gunship overhead now: circling, a spotlight sweeping, fields lit, red tracer bullets streaming; artillery fire from the fire base zeroing in, the rattle of gunfire, grenades, high-pitched screams, obscene shouts, mud, rain, blood, fire; fire burning in the grass, the wet grass—fire cooking the dead and the dying; the stench of human flesh burning; gunmetal heating in the cold rain, hissing like snakes; the howls of the dying, the burning; the gunship exploding: metal, fuel, a body in flames falling from four hundred feet, arms thrashing the air and falling; then the line breaking, the perimeter overrun: screaming, cursing, crying, retreating farther; butchery, machetes, the wounded, mutilation; a sanctified slaughter; and all, all happening fast yet feeling slow.

I crawled away. Most of the fighting had died down now. The troops were scattered. Only a few, too brave or too afraid, were still firing. I had spent all of my ammunition. I had nothing left. I crawled away like an animal, to sleep, to hide, to die. I was past resistance. I was exhausted. I had seen too much. It was time to shut it down, to forget. I lay facedown in the mud and buried my face in the crook of my arm and thought: Well, this is it.

Then I went to sleep.

How long I slept, I know not. I know only that when I awoke it was quiet and I was cold. I groped about for my rifle, found it, and clung to it. I lay still, breathing the earth air and feeling the suction of the mud along the length of my body. After a while I lifted myself up onto one knee and looked around. I could see nothing, hear nothing; only the wind through the grass. I lay back down and rolled over on my back. The sky was clear now; the stars were out. Then like the fine-tuning of a radio, across the night I began to hear them: the cries and pleas of the wounded. Someone calling alternately for his mother and a medic. Someone else pleading to be shot—"Help me, kill me! Help me, kill me!" And another simply calling out different names at random. I lay there in the damp darkness and listened, frozen in the impotent terror of helplessness, my own and theirs. There is so little that one can do when it really comes down to it. Fragile little insignificant specks lost in a gallery of absurd misfortune. I listened.

In the background could be heard the constant night hum of insects and birds. Then soon the humming and the chirping became something else: giggling, it seemed. It was. They had returned. Swishing through the grass I could hear them. Giggling at first and then laughing openly as they moved; blurred figures in black against the moonlit sky. And when they would stumble upon one of the wounded, they would shriek like little children at play, calling over their friends to marvel at the wonder that they had found. And again like children, after a few minutes of taunts and examination, they would become bored and a single shot would ring out and then they, in high spirits, would move on, looking for more and finding more.

Dawn came quickly after that. With the sun, the VC, like the mist in the morning, vanished, leaving only a trail of naked and mutilated bodies mirrored horrifically in the black still waters of the flooded paddy fields. And soon, from out of their secret spots, the survivors began to emerge: bedraggled, bloody, muddy, blank stunned stares, grizzly hard faces, matted hair, weaponless, falling forward with robotic awkwardness, finding a friend or just someone familiar and embracing.

Strider ran about trying to organize what was left of the men, handing each a rifle (which some promptly threw down) and telling everyone to sit and wait, the choppers were on the way. I had to admire his effort, his resiliency. Doc moved about offering cigarettes and readjusting bandages. He no longer carried his medical pouch, maybe he had lost it or perhaps he had used up all of its contents during the hellish night. Billy and Motown sat under a large banyan tree smoking and cursing and more or less standing watch. Of the fifty or so men that had started out so jubilantly the morning before, little more than half of that number now sat breathing in the sunlight.

Soon three helicopters came whipping in from out of the west. Strider popped some smoke and two of the choppers, after sweeping the tree line with machine-gun fire, sank to earth. Overhead the other one (a gunship) continued to circle protectively. In the first load Strider ordered the severely wounded and those who appeared to be borderline breakdowns. I waited with Strider and Doc and Motown and Billy and several others for the next run.

Doc came up and sat down beside me. He offered me a canteen of water. I accepted and drank. He offered me a cigarette. I accepted and smoked. And together, in silence, we stared out at the awakening countryside.

The sun, still low, not yet above the trees, cast long cool shadows over us. A water buffalo with a small half-naked boy sitting astride its back crossed the paddies well out of gunshot range. A line of Buddhist monks with shaved heads and flowing orange robes walked in single file along a path leading toward the village that we had sighted through the trees the day before. And from that village, small cooking fires now sent narrow columns of smoke spiraling up into a new morning labored heavily with the laughter of children and the beating of rotor blades.

7

Two days later the sun was out and the sky was clear and we were loaded into helicopters to reap revenge. If anyone had bothered to ask me (which no one did) just how much revenge I was intent on exacting, I would have been forced to confess, very little, and I imagine that most of the other men in my company would have expressed a similar disinclination toward retaliation. We wanted only to rest, to be left alone. But the high command, from their vantage point of safety and comfort, felt hard the sting and humiliation of defeat, so we were loaded up and bidden farewell.

"Kick some ass, men!" shouted a one-star general flown in especially for the occasion. "Kick some ass for America!"

"Your ass, motherfucker," mumbled Motown under his breath as he hopped up into the chopper and took a seat next to me.

"Gonna be a bad day," observed Billy, speaking to no one and to everyone. "I can feel it."

And true, there was a certain feeling in the air: a highness and at the same time, a contradicting dullness; a seemingly foregone conclusion, an acceptance of the unacceptable.

"Can't be any worse than last time," offered Doc, his hair blown wild across his face.

"There it is," agreed Motown. "Tell it."

"Told," said Doc.

"Hey, man, got any go-fast?" asked Billy, leaning across Motown and me, addressing the Doc, shouting into the wind.

"Sure," said Doc, searching through his pouch.

"Well then, pull that shit out," encouraged Motown.

"Pulling shit," said Doc, smiling. He produced a green bottle, shook out a handful of small white pills, and passed them around.

I took three and felt immediately worse.

Strider, having a few final words with a new lieutenant (there were so many new lieutenants), stood with his handsome face of frozen fatalistic calm cocked into the wind. Finally heads nodded and he ran and jumped in and we were off.

And so reinforced and reequipped (our company was almost up to full strength again), we swirled out of a scattering cloud of red dust and into the cool embrace of blue skies: fifteen to twenty helicopters trailing each other in double file like disciplined schoolboys changing classes, walking erect yet with their heads bobbing and weaving at different heights; undulating through a suspended nonexistence of whipping blades and rushing wind. A beautiful sight if one could disregard the purpose.

The flight was only about a fifteen minute hop yet it seemed much longer: the bad jokes and the sweaty palms; the upset stomachs churning with a rotten breakfast eaten too quickly; the clenched teeth and the gripped weapons; the hope that nothing is forgotten and the regretted assurance that something always is; the exposed bodies like rocks in a mad sea just waiting for the wrong wave; and the feeling—bad; a bad, bad feeling; a feeling of worms and hollow eye sockets.

A village came quickly into view along the right side of the chopper. According to Strider, it was the same village that we had first seen through the trees three days before. Maybe it was; I don't know. They all looked the same to me.

We circled around to the west and landed. We leaped out screaming and snapping off quick-fire rounds into the tufts of elephant grass and the mounds of anthills. We fanned out, keeping low and firing. It was terrifying—moving across the open fields. With so much firing and noise it was impossible to tell whether we were under fire or the only ones firing. Finally the choppers lifted and spun away. There were shouts of cease-fire. There had been no return fire. We stood up feeling a little stupid and greatly relieved. We were breathing. We were still alive. It was hot and it was quiet except for the cackle of the radios and the command chopper circling high overhead.

We separated into three groups as was prearranged. And soon, with heavy-artillery fire slamming into the far end of the village to prevent the villagers' escape, we began the sweep. Our group moved out in single file along a narrow dirt path leading directly into the village. One of the new lieutenants took the point. I was with Motown in the back of the column. The sun was blazing down unforgivingly. After advancing less than fifty meters there was a sudden explosion and a scream. The lieutenant had tripped a mine and forfeited a foot. He lay on the ground, on his back, with his eyes wildly searching the trees and the faces before him, and crying, crying up at the faces and the trees, crying, "Never even got to see one of the little fuckers! Oh, Jesus . . ." Someone called in for a dust-off and we waited, then he was gone and we were on our way up the trail again, feeling the numbing anger of hopelessness and frustration.

"Brother-man might be right," said Motown.

"Brother-man?" I asked.

"Yeah. Brother-man, Billy-boy. He might be right."

"How so?"

"It might be a bad day."

"Well, it sure as hell isn't starting out too fine," I said.

"You got it, my man."

"No shit?"

"No shit."

The bull's-eye with the peace symbol on the back of Motown's flak jacket swished and swayed in front of me. I liked to watch him walk, the rhythm. I had not known many black guys before. It was not that I was prejudiced; it was just that I had not had occasion to meet very many. That's one thing about war—it's a great leveler. Death is notably unselective. After a few meters of silence Motown picked it up again. He loved to talk. Doc said that he'd talk to a tree if no one else was around.

"You understand now," he said, "that this ain't exactly my style."

"Yeah?" I asked. "What's your style, Mr. Mo?"

"Well, let's say a long low ride in metallic green, some long and lovely ladies—ah, chocolate!—some fine threads, something with some sparkle, and maybe a couple of large closets full of some smooth smoke."

"Sounds good," I said. "Can you arrange it?"

"By Tuesday, I expect."

"What's today?"

"November."

There was no breeze. There were no birds. There was heat and there was fear and stupidity and carelessness and selfishness and ignorance and a false sense of bravado that only those tortured by the prospects of an immediate and futile death can appreciate. And as I walked I thought: Yes, I'm wrong; there's yet a lot more to all this living business.

A low black cloud of smoke could be seen now swelling up over the village. The cries of women and children and panic-stricken animals could be heard. And like a nightmare exposed to sunlight, it started quick, snowballing: a few random shots at the head of the column; childlike enthusiastic shouts from behind; a few more shots and a few more and more; coming fast now; the men in front infected, running forward; those behind urgent, pushing; all hurrying down the trail; and no fear now, no concern for mines or legs; a game; certainly unreal; someone's radio playing loud, screaming: *Well, come on! Come on! Come on! Come on!*—Janis Joplin; and then up over a small rise and the entire village—dried grass huts, a small muddy creek, a dirt path, fields of bamboo, paddies of rice— breaking into view; the men wild, running up and over the rise, firing blindly on full automatic and laughing; flesh flying away from flesh; the air raw with death, bitter with dying; the grass huts exploding into orange flames; people running from the flames; the soldiers waiting; the radio again: *Take it! Take another little piece*—; a woman with her hair on fire; a soldier waiting; water buffaloes, cows, cats, dogs dead, dying; ARVN scouts dropping rifles, chasing chickens, ignoring the chaos, laughing; huge clay jars filled with rice and water shot up, bursting open; kids grabbing for mothers; mothers grabbing for kids; a mother shielding her child with her body; *Break it! Break another little bit*—; a small multicolored shrine shattering; fire everywhere; everything burning; faces blackened by smoke; eyes, teeth insane; children abandoned, crying; women being pulled into the undergrowth, crying; legs and bare breasts; an old man holding up his pants with one hand and looking, his mouth open; two small children crawling away into the bushes, into the flames; *Hava! Hava 'nother little piece*—; a child's sandal in the middle of the trail; a toothless old woman laughing and clapping her hands; the command chopper circling overhead; the creek gone red; bodies bumping against the banks.

"We gotta stop it!" I screamed. "We gotta—we gotta do something! I mean—Holy shit! Jesus Christ!"

I turned to Motown. He stood on the rise. I stood next to him. His M-16 was pointed at the ground. He hadn't fired a shot yet. Neither had I.

"We?" he laughed, his teeth large and white. "Hell! Go 'head on, hero. Ain't nothing you gonna stop but a bullet in the back. If you ain't gonna do no shooting, better just sit your ass down and shut up."

"Yes, but—I mean—but wait!" I screamed, and stopped and looked: and blood and legs and—and sometimes I don't know, sometimes I wonder (not a milligram of mercy, not a cup of compassion), and sometimes I'm stupid and sometimes I'm utterly dumbfounded by what I see, but mostly I just live in a slow state of abstracted amazement, a perpetual disbelief, and sometimes—

"Touch and tag, man. Touch and tag," said Motown, turning and looking down at me. "Just playing games."

"What?" I cried.

"Look at that cat over there," he laughed, pointing. "Who-ee! Get some for America! Shit, man."

"What?" I cried again.

"Bring me a flag, sing me a song," he said, and smiled. "Yeah, I'm a regular Yankee Doodle Dandy."

And fire and—hell, I don't know how else to say it anymore: the forgotten graves and the toppled tombstones and . . . and nothing, nothing anymore.

Then suddenly there was a noise, movement to our right. Motown dropped. I spun and fired off half a clip. The bushes shredded: leaves and twigs and a hand and a scream—and God, too far, too fast, and no foundation—a child's scream.

There was a moment of silence. I stood panting with my ears ringing. Motown looked up from the ground, his eyes big then small. He picked himself up and began dusting himself off. He shook his head and continued to look at me.

"Might look 'fore you leap next time," he said, walking over to the bushes.

My knees went weak. I sat abruptly.

"Looks like you've scored. Big kill," said Motown, pulling the small hand, followed by a small body, out of the undergrowth.

It was about three feet long; black hair to the waist. Small. So small. A little girl.

He dropped the body into my lap.

"Welcome to the club," he said grimly.

Her heels dug two small ruts across the sandy trail.

"How does it feel to be a warrior?" he asked.

She bled. My pants turned wet and spread dark as I held her. Her little head turned. Her eyes were big and brown and looked hurt, not physically, but rather sad, as if someone had stolen her doll or something.

"Still alive!" I cried. "She's—"

"Not for long," said Motown, turning his back.

"Call—"

"Call? Hell!" he laughed bitterly, spinning quickly back around. "You win! No contest!"

And how heavy she was. How small and how heavy. And Jesus, that face, that face upturned and small and beautiful and confused, that face that I would see so many times in so many places, that face turning, rolling back to haunt so many of my broken and sleepless nights.

Up the path now came Strider. His face was smeared black and streaked with sweat. His eyes, burning red, held an alien stare of wild desperation. He looked at me, then at the dying child that I continued to hold.

"I'm finished," he said, turning toward Motown.

"Sure ain't as advertised," Motown agreed. "Think I'll sue."

"I'm leaving," he said calmly.

"Leaving?" asked Motown in half-joking astonishment. "Where for?"

"For? . . . can't . . . gotta . . ." he sputtered and stopped. He looked down at the ground; his eyes were blank.

Most of the shooting had stopped now. The fires were settling slowly to coals. Two soldiers were kicking an old man with half-interest. Another soldier was barbecuing a cat at the end of a bayonet. A baby sat in the sand next to the body of a naked woman, crying. The command chopper was edging down into a clearing scattered with bodies.

"I'm through," said Strider, dropping down into a squat position. "I'm tired. So goddamn unbelievably tired. Committing crimes in the name of justice, making war in the name of peace. I quit."

"Quit?" asked Motown, shocked at Strider's sincerity. "Quit? Hell, man, you can't just quit. You can't just walk away."

"That's exactly what I'm gonna do," said Strider, looking out over the ruins below. "I'm gonna just walk away and let it be."

"Crazy," said Motown, turning toward me. "The man's gone crazy. Ain't nobody just ups and walks away."

"No?" asked Strider. "Just keep watching my feet."

A collection of men with their faces, like Strider's, smeared black and streaked with sweat, began filtering up the rise from below. Doc and Billy walked side by side at the head of the group. The men behind moved slowly with their heads bowed, shuffling their feet through the sand. Billy was laughing and gesturing and waving his rifle wildly about. He was making little popping noises with his mouth like a child imitating the firing of bullets.

"—and pow! pow! pow! You should've seen the whore spin! Like a fucking top, I tell you! Just like a motherfucking top!" concluded Billy with a broad smile as they reached the rise.

"Graphic," sighed Doc. "Real graphic."

Billy and Doc and two others whose names I didn't

know stopped at the top of the rise. The rest of the men passed on down the trail without a word toward the LZ, where hamburgers and Kool-Aid were being flown in by chopper for lunch.

"Ain't you guys gonna eat?" asked Billy.

No one said anything; no one even looked at him.

There on the rise it was quiet. There was a slight breeze now. I held the child and I thought: Did I do this? And quickly a voice inside my head answered: Yes, and all alone. Doc came over and looked at the child, then moved away. Her eyes were closed now and she was still. Except for the blood, she might have been asleep.

"The man's gone crazy," said Motown after a moment. "Completely crazy."

"Which man?" asked Billy, giving me the eye.

"This man," said Motown, pointing down at Strider.

"Strider, have you gone crazy?" asked Doc, dropping his medical pouch and himself down onto the ground next to Strider.

"I've been crazy," said Strider.

"He's been crazy," echoed Doc with a marked lack of concern.

"Yeah, I know," agreed Motown. "But now the man's talking crazy too. He says he's leaving."

"Leaving? Leaving all this?" asked Doc, sweeping his arms open wide across the vista of horror and destruction below. "I fail to understand why."

"You can't leave," said Billy in a tone that sounded almost hurt.

"That's what I done told him," said Motown, exasperated.

"Strider, you can't leave," repeated Billy, looking down.

"Yeah, why not?" asked Strider, his eyes fixed on some lost spot on the horizon.

"Well, because . . . because . . ." began Billy, and then he stopped. "Hey, why can't Strider leave?"

"Why can't we all leave?" threw in Doc cheerfully.

"Well?" asked Strider, looking up at Motown.

" 'Cause they'll slap your fucking ass in fucking jail for fucking ever when they catch you," said Motown, exasperation now boiling over into disgust.

"Yeah, 'cause they'll slap your fucking ass in fucking jail for fucking ever when they catch you," translated Billy.

"Yeah, well, they've gotta catch me first," said Strider, rising.

And this profound observation brought an immediate and prolonged silence to our little hilltop. In fact, so studious was this silence that at first we didn't hear him, and then we did.

"Twenty-one, twenty-two." He came up from behind us, puffing and wheezing, cursing and shouting and counting. "Twenty-three, twenty-four." We all turned to watch. "Twenty-five. That's twenty-five, goddammit! Right there! Twenty-five!" he shouted, pointing down at the little girl still in my lap, still looking like she was only sleeping. He was overweight and a lieutenant. His flesh looked soft and his hands were small. "Count 'em. Gotta count 'em for the colonel," he laughed, his voice quivering. "All right, goddammit. Can do. That's twenty-five, twenty-six, twenty-seven." And on down the hill he ran, counting.

"Yeah, baby, you count 'em," said Strider, watching, "you count 'em all and when you get through with them you can start in on our side, then you can get yourself a big scoreboard or something and write all the names and numbers up on it and then you can stick it up right in the middle of Washington fucking D.C. and then maybe you'll be through with it. But don't count on me, Jack, 'cause I'm already gone."

Then without a further word Strider turned and pushed an opening in the foliage and disappeared behind a closing wall of nodding branches. And for several seconds we all stood in stunned amazement, silently looking at the spot into which, through which, Strider had vanished. And then slowly, as if by mutual yet unspoken consent, the others, one by one, turned and disappeared through that same opening and closing, working fast now, working like a giant mouth chewing and swallowing and never giving back, until at last there was only Motown and myself left alone on the rise as before.

"Well?" he asked, slinging his rifle over his shoulder.

"All right," I said, and I struggled up to my feet.

Motown stopped and looked at me. I stopped too, stopping in the middle of rising, and I looked back at him.

"Ah, you can leave her," he said.

"What?" I asked, still stopped, still halfway between up and down.

"Her," he said. "You can leave her. She'll be all right now. She's dead."

"Oh, yeah," I said. "Sure." And I put the little girl down in the grass and I picked up my rifle and followed Motown through the self-sealing wall of hungry green.

8

It was the beauty and the horror of it all that always struck me blind, and still, even now, leaves my pen hanging: the paramount paradox: the flat green stretching out to the horizon, broken only slightly by an occasional cluster of trees; a swath of pale blue crowned by low-hanging white puffs of cloud; reflective pools of water; white geese feeding; a large bird turning in slow effortless circles overhead; palms, so sturdy, so well-designed; short, stubby cedar trees; flowers, orange and yellow and pink and purple; bamboo thick as flagpoles, cut and stacked; wooden shacks reinforced with flattened empty beer cans; orange and yellow temples and shrines; thatched huts; smoke and silk, creeks and canals, rice and rain; and the people—the people, unconquerable; the people, corruptible, killable, but not conquerable, not the spirit, not in a thousand years; the spirit, timeless: peasants up to their knees in paddy muck, bent double under a scorching sun, planting rice; a man standing in a swallow-bottomed wooden boat, poling a load of green vegetables down a winding muddy creek; an old man squatting alone in a field, burning incense, lost in thought; small boys herding water buffaloes homeward at dusk; a young woman sleeping on the ground under an umbrella; an old woman, her teeth blackened by betel nuts, gathering twigs for a morning fire; a child with a cane pole fishing; and death—death, swift and sure, slow and subtle; death everywhere: a paradise of incomparable color and beauty and mystery, lost in a maelstrom of death and senseless violence.

But wait; I'm wandering, falling away from the story, losing the sequence.

So freed now from our immediate past, yet still damned by our immediate future, we walked. Behind us we could still hear an occasional shot fired or grenade tossed. The feet dragged, the sweat poured, the eyes fell vacuous. No one spoke.

At the head of our defecting column (defecting not to the other side, simply away, away from war, killing, or so I thought, hoped) was Strider, followed by Billy, Doc, Motown (he had jumped ahead two places), then the two other soldiers from the rise whom I had never seen before that day and would never see again after the next, and myself. Within a hundred meters or so of entering the jungle, we came upon a narrow sandy red trail and we followed it as it twisted away from the village. Where it led, at the time, I neither knew nor cared. I simply walked, mindlessly following the man in front of me. If he had walked off a cliff I would have been only one short step behind. I was in a blur. My mind, my thought process, was severely clouded by the mayhem which I had just witnessed, and in which I had so unwittingly and so foully participated.

Finally, after walking for more than two hours, we stopped at the edge of a clearing for a short marijuana break. The guns could no longer be heard; the air had lost its bitter taste.

"Well, where the hell are we?" asked Billy, taking his rifle apart, cleaning it. "Where the hell are we going?"

"An opportune line of questioning," observed Doc. "Most sagacious."

"Yeah, Strider, what's the fucking deal, man?" asked Motown. "Where're we going?"

"To the sea," said Strider.

"And just what the hell are we gonna do once we get there?" demanded Billy, unimpressed with the brevity of the answer.

"Well, I don't know about you," said Strider, "but I'm going swimming."

"Oh, Jesus Christ," sighed Motown. "Another shit-hook operation."

"Well, Mo, you can always go back," suggested Doc.

"And you can always gnaw on this, motherfucker," said Motown, pointing to his lap.

"According to the map," began Strider, pulling a folded sheet of multicolored paper from a flap pocket on the side of his jungle fatigues, "there's a—"

"Hey, where'd you get that map?" demanded Billy.

"I've had it," said Strider, spreading it out before us. He smoothed out the creases, folded down the upturned corners, and dusted off the specks of dirt. It was just a map, perhaps a little more worn than most, but still just a map like a million others—green places, blue places, red places, little lines, dots, numbers, and X marks—but to him, from the way that he handled it, almost caressed it, it seemed to be something more, much more.

"How long you had it?" asked Doc.

"Awhile," he said.

"Nice map," said Motown.

"Right. Okay, look here," said Strider, pointing at his map. "There's this little string of villages here that runs up along the coast here, about two or three days' march away. They're pretty well isolated by this little spit of land sticking out here. See? I can't see as how they'd be of any strategic value to anybody. There's nothing around the place that's worth anything. I think we'd be safe there for a while, at least until we can figure out something more permanent."

"No strategic value, huh?" mocked Doc. "Like the one we just left?"

Strider ignored the question.

"But what are we supposed to do once we get there?" asked Billy.

"We're not supposed to do anything," explained Strider. "We can do whatever we want. As for myself, as I've said, I'm going swimming."

"Now, wait a minute, chief," interrupted Motown, hovering over the map and casting a dark shadow over all of South Vietnam. "Let me get this straight in my mind. The plan is we gonna follow this here fucking trail that we're on now for two or three fucking days till it's gonna run sure enough right smack dab up into these here little villes, where we gonna bag down and just generally cool ourselves out and let everything be everything. Am I right, there? Now, is that the master plan?"

"Unless anyone's got any better ideas," said Strider, folding up his map. "Well?"

And the response was snowlike in its unity and silence.

As our daylight was fading, we voted (for from here on out we voted on virtually everything; it was all very democratic, although in truth Strider was still very much in control) to camp where we were for the night. I lay down in some high weeds and immediately fell into a sweaty, dreamless sleep.

The next morning after a very quick breakfast of the two cans of cold C-rations that one of the two soldiers whose names I didn't know happened to have with him ("Just in case," he said), shared among six people (Strider refused his proffered portion), we, astonishingly ill-equipped as we now became painfully aware, struck out again.

By unanimous consent we had agreed earlier that every man would take a turn walking point. The young innocent-faced kid who had contributed the two cans of C-rations for our morning's breakfast had volunteered himself for the first shot, so to speak, at walking point. And so with a smile and a beckoning wave, he turned and headed down the trail. The sun as yet had not fully risen, the breeze blew cool, and the trees fairly roared with life. As we walked I thought to myself: This will be a good day; this will be a good new beginning. And as usual, I was wrong.

The day dragged slowly on. The birds ceased their screeching. The sun rose higher. We had been on the trail now for almost three hours. My feet became heavy. My back started to hurt. I began to wonder when we'd stop for a break.

When it actually happened, or maybe finally happened, I was not overly surprised, although I did wonder to myself, why?—not why it happened, but rather why it happened to one and not to another: was it all

113

in the luck or unluck of the draw, the toss of the dice? Random selection for random violence?

The explosion ripped through the tunneled green quiet of that tree-lined morning with all the hell and fury of an indifferent god exhibiting his base indifference. The boy who had been walking point now lay thrashing and bumping against the earth, his leg torn away at the knee. Doc was kneeling next to him, administering morphine; he later tied a sort of tourniquet above the boy's bloody stump. There was little else that could have been done. For all practical purposes the boy was already dead, just waiting to die. Strider, who had been second in line, only a few paces behind the boy, stood nearby, nursing his face where he had caught a few fragments of shrapnel. Billy went on up the trail a little way to have a quick look around. The rest of us stood well apart from the boy, in silence or talking softly. There was nothing that we could do. It soon became apparent that it would take some time, so we all sat down. After quite a few uneasy minutes—I don't know why—I got up and went over and knelt down next to Doc. I guess that I was just curious or bored or afraid or something.

Doc was holding the boy's hand. Doc's eyes were cast skyward with the persecuted look of an overworked and underpaid clerk. The boy was passing rapidly in and out of consciousness. Doc noticed my arrival and turned toward me.

"Here," he said, thrusting the boy's limp hand into mine. "You stay here. I'm gonna take a look at Strider."

"Stay here?" I squawked. "But—"

"That's right," said Doc. "You stay here and do what you can."

"But what can I do?"

"All right then," said Doc, "just stay here so that when he opens his eyes again at least he'll see someone, at least he'll know that he's not alone, not yet anyway. Okay?"

"All right," I said.

"Good," said Doc, and he moved away.

Everything was quiet: the voices hushed, the air still. The boy's hand lay cold and damp in mine. He didn't move; his eyes were shut. Doc and Strider, like two figures out of a silent movie, were in a wordless tussle, with Doc reaching up for Strider's face and Strider keeping him at arm's length. Motown and the other soldier whose name I didn't know sat in the shade, hunched over, throwing occasional uneasy glances in the direction of the boy and myself. Time ticked on. Billy came back from his reconnaissance and fell asleep without saying a word. Motown lit a cigarette; the smoke rose in an unwavering column. The other soldier got up and went behind a tree and unbuttoned his pants and squatted down. Finally Strider relented and Doc cursed and dabbed a little medication onto the cuts. And still time ticked on. Billy woke up, looked around, and went back to sleep. A bird called. The shadows of the trees pulled slowly across the ground. Motown lit another cigarette. Doc came over and looked at the boy and then went away. Strider took off his boots and began to check his feet for jungle rot.

Suddenly the hand tightened, the body jerked, and the eyes jumped open wide.

"Christ!" the boy screamed. "What now?"

All eyes spun in his direction. Doc hurried over, bringing his medical pouch.

"How's it going there, ace?" asked Doc quietly, his hand rummaging around in his bag.

"Oh God!" shrieked the boy, looking at the spot where his leg should have been. "Oh Jesus God!"

Doc gave the boy another injection and then turned his sad and knowledgeable eyes on me.

"A little longer," whispered Doc. "Just a little longer."

The boy bumped against the ground once and then with liquid eyes looked up.

"Oh Jesus," he cried, "I never thought it would be like this. I thought I'd live forever. But hell, I didn't even make nineteen. I've always wanted to—"

"Yes," interrupted Doc. "But sleep, sleep now. Tell me later."

The boy closed his eyes and was out again.

"He can't last much longer," sighed Doc. "There's no way to stop the bleeding, no help. He's lost too much blood. I'm surprised he hasn't shocked out already."

"Yes," I said, watching as the boy's face grew gradually paler and paler.

"If this had happened back there," said Doc, gesturing with his head back in the general direction from which we had been coming since yesterday, "a chopper could've had him out of here and on an operating table in twenty minutes. But here—this is hopeless. This whole thing's insane. You can't leave. You can never leave."

"Yes?" I asked.

"Yes," said Doc. "But then what's the alternative, huh?"

Suddenly the boy lunged up again and screamed:

"It's blue! It's goddamn blue! I thought it would be black! But it's blue!" And then, wide-eyed, frenzied, he collapsed. Dead.

I was startled, taken aback. The violence and the futility of the struggle. Perhaps—I don't know, I just look and listen—but maybe no one wants so much, so hard, to live as when he's young and dying. His whole life like an uncashed check blown by the wind, slipping away before him, slipping out of his grasp.

"Blue?" I asked. "What did he mean, blue, not black?"

"Who knows?" said Doc, closing the eyes. "I've heard 'em say a lot of strange things just before they go out."

And as I looked at that heap of wasted flesh, that mass of missed chances, I thought: A dead body is a sad and lonely thing; it leaves so little to the imagination; it is exactly what it is: nothing, gone, finished.

"Okay," said Strider, standing up. "Let's pack it. Gotta move."

"Leave?" I cried, spinning around. "Leave now? Just like that? What'd you mean? Aren't we even gonna bury him?"

"You think he cares?" asked Strider, looking down at the body.

"Well, no, I mean—" I started and stopped. "Yes, well, maybe it doesn't matter to him much now, but it matters—"

"All right," said Strider, holding up one hand. "You do it. And the leg too." He reached around with his other hand, slipped a small collapsible shovel out of his pack, and threw it down at my feet. "Keep it," he said. "You'll probably wind up burying all of us anyway. Fucking new guys. Shit!"

I dug a shallow grave while Doc constructed a crude cross with the words IT'S BLUE in capital letters on it. Doc and I lowered the body, with the half-leg across the chest, down into the hole. I covered him over with dirt—dirt hitting the exposed body, the face: awful. Doc hammered in his small cross.

"All right," said Strider. "That's it. Let's get the hell outta here. We've already lost half a day."

"And a whole man," I said.

Strider shot an icy stare straight through me.

"And?" he asked, his aggravation and the strain of the day audible in his voice.

"And, well . . ." I sputtered. "Someone should say something."

Everyone stood stone-still for nearly a full minute. The sweat rolled down my back. Strider's eyes had me nailed; mine searched the faces of the others for confederation. Finally Strider laughed and turned and said: "All right, Doc, say something."

"What?" asked Doc.

"Say the poem," said Strider.

"Which poem?" asked Doc innocently, knowingly.

"You know, goddammit! The one by that Brit guy," said Strider impatiently.

"Kipling?"

"Whatever."

"Well, it's not really a poem," said Doc. "It's a chapter heading in—"

"It rhymes, doesn't it?" demanded Strider.

"Yes."

"Then say it for shit's sake and quit fucking around!"

"Well, all right," said Doc. "Since you put it so nicely."

Doc ran his fingers once quickly through his hair, pulled his shirt straight, tilted his head up and began:

> Now it is not good for the Christian's health
>   to hustle the Aryan brown,
> For the Christian riles, and the Aryan smiles
>   and he weareth the Christian down;
> And the end of the fight is a tombstone white
>   with the name of the late deceased
> And the epitaph drear: "A Fool lies here,
>   who tried to hustle the East."

"All right, Christian?" asked Strider, turning his iron-cold gaze upon me. "You happy now, asshole?"

"Yes," I said, feeling the warm satisfaction of tradition preserved.

"Good," said Strider. "It's your turn to walk point."

"Mine?" I cried. "Mine? But I—"

"That way, asshole," said Strider, pointing down the trail. "I'll be right behind you."

And ahead of me the trail bloomed bright and sinister with poppies and orchids and tripwires.

Now walking point: the jungle rising thick and solid on both sides of the trail; the branches of the trees overhead like the fingers of old men, twisted and intertwined; underfoot, the soft decaying carpet of the jungle floor giving way to the weight of the boot; and constantly, the fantastic fright, the unreal sense of being outside of one's own body, merely watching.

My eyes were glued to the ground, searching for something, something elusive and nonexistent; nonexistent that is until in a flash and a bang it takes you out and leaves you haunting the wind. Perhaps it would be a telltale wire seen half a second before the foot found it, maybe a mound of freshly turned earth, anything that looked just a little on the off-side of right. I walked and looked.

And as I slowly, very slowly inched my way down the trail, I thought to myself: Fool! How long have I been kidding myself? Bathing in the soft waters of self-pity? Fool! Do I not really want desperately to live? Do I want to end up like that boy back there? A nothing. A gone nothing. Do I never again want to feel a summer's rain cutting through the lingering heat of a long hot day? Does not the sight of something as simple as a bird in flight somehow affect me? What of the smell of a wood fire, coffee in the morning? What of a woman's kiss, a child's smile, a friend's handclasp? What of palm trees silhouetted against an evening's sky bright with lightning? What of cats crouching in shadows, old dogs sleeping in the sun, seashells, bells tolling in the distance, a crumbling stone wall, a pond buoyed with lily pads, the even breathing of a girl asleep? Fool! What of yesterday? Fool! What of today? What of tomorrow—tomorrow packed with promises, dripping with dreams? Fool! Fool! Yes, I know, I'm wrong, wrong again. I want it all, all forever.

And thus was I so preoccupied with my thoughts of the future that I nearly misplaced my present. I was watching the ground and thinking, entirely missing the rest of my surroundings. If it was not on the ground or six inches above it, then I didn't see it.

The gloom of the jungle had set in tight, the vegetation had thickened, the path had narrowed and soon began making abrupt blind-angle turns like those found in an English maze garden. Several times I lost my way entirely and was promptly steered onto a corrected course with a sharp rebuke from Strider. "Asshole!" And yet further still my mind wandered. I began making plans and imagining lives to be led. And in all truth, I didn't see them until it was too late.

I was thinking and walking, my eyes following the ground—all right, guilty; I was daydreaming—when I turned a blind corner and ran hard into something black and solid coming from the opposite direction. I bounced off and landed most unprofessionally on my bewildered ass. There then followed a pause of perhaps three seconds of breathless silence with everyone looking. I, being on the ground and being too confused to respond properly, did what I do best: I ducked; I rolled over onto my stomach and covered up. Then Strider and the man behind him—the other soldier whose name I didn't know, although now, thinking about it, I seem to recall someone calling him Jim or maybe they were only saying "him," I don't know—opened fire. The trail at that point was too narrow and the angle too severe for more than two persons to stand abreast. The firing was fast and intense; the air screamed, a body in black flopped down next to me—I could see this out of the corner of my eye; I was afraid but still I couldn't stop watching—followed by another in green. There was moaning and shrieking, cursing and crying, bullets and bullets and then no bullets. When the guns had finally stilled and someone had reached down and grabbed me by the back of my collar and commanded, "Up, asshole," the color patterns which presented themselves on the ground spoke clearly of the result. Red—predominant; black—clustered; green—a smear. Three VC, who had happened along the trail coming from the opposite direction and whom I had blind-sided into, now lay in a bloody heap. Slightly off to one side the other unknown (Jim or him) lay with a bullet hole centered cleanly through his high young forehead.

"Good scouting, ace," said Strider, looking down.

"Well, I didn't—" I began.

"Didn't, don't, and never will!" spat out Strider, his upper lip slowly curling with scorn. "Billy, check it out up ahead. Motown, close it off behind. And you—you—you just bury him, shithead! Still got the fucking shovel, I hope."

"Yes," I said, reaching over my shoulder. "I have it right—"

"Great! Use it! At least you're good for something," said Strider, shaking his head and starting to curse.

With no excuse, no defense, I moved back down the trail and found myself a suitable spot and began to dig. And as I dug I could hear Strider and Doc up the trail talking together as they searched the bodies of the VC.

"This isn't quite working out the way you planned, is it?" asked Doc, his voice almost humorous.

"I don't make plans. I only react to situations."

"Right," said Doc.

Silence. Only a running stream somewhere nearby.

Then after a moment, Doc again: "You know, it's still probably not too late to turn back if we wanted to."

"It is for me. As for the rest of you, you can do

whatever you think is best. I'm not forcing anyone to come with me. In fact I don't want anyone with me who doesn't want to be with me."

"Right."

Silence again.

Then Doc again: "But say we did go back and left you out here all alone, what would you do then?"

"Exactly what I'm doing now. I'd just keep on going until something stopped me."

"Right," laughed Doc.

Then the sound of metal clanking together—rifles, I later learned; three AK-47s which, along with two belts of ammunition, were parceled out among Strider and Billy and Motown; Doc (under protest: "All right, but I'll only use it for self-defense"; and Strider: "That's all I'm asking") was already carrying the M-16 of the first soldier to die that day and would soon be carrying another—and bodies being heaved into the undergrowth.

And then Doc again, his voice still light, still humorous: "Well, okay, let's get this cat in the ground and get the hell out of here. No telling who might've heard all that damn shooting."

"Right," said Strider.

9

The next day broke cold and gray and rainy. We had slept the night before under some huge leafy trees which were now collecting the rain and channeling it down directly upon our heads. The chill in the air held an ominous note, but then everything every day held an ominous note if one cared to look for it. Having had virtually nothing to eat—we had plenty to drink though; we filled our canteens at practically every creek and rivulet we passed—except a few dry mouthfuls of cold C-rations for the last two days, we were most understandably hungry. We fanned out looking for something, anything, to eat. After a futile fifteen minutes of stomping the bush, which produced only a cluster of small bitter berries, we were on the verge of abandoning our search when Billy—logical, home-grown, and ever-resourceful Billy—spotted it: a lone coconut tree almost hidden behind a thick rising wall of foliage. We first tried climbing the tree monkey-style, which failed miserably and almost rewarded Motown with a broken back. We then tried to free the coconuts with rocks and nearly sustained some sub-stantial head injuries as our missiles fell victim to the laws of gravity and came plummeting back to earth.

Finally we gave up these more peaceful approaches and opened fire. Coconuts and palm fronds fell like the rain. And, all in all, except for the occasional lump of lead found rattling around in a coconut's center, it was quite an enjoyable breakfast.

So now with the hot pangs of hunger at least temporarily subdued, we moved out quickly, not caring to linger in an area where our presence had been so loudly advertised. Billy was walking point. (I had been banished from that position and was now relegated forever to the rear.) Strider had taken up his usual position directly behind whoever, if not himself, happened to be the point man. Motown and Doc and I followed in that order.

The rain by this time had eased somewhat but the hard chill still held fast in the air. The trail, awash now in low spots, had become a deep sucking mud-filled rut, strewn with broken branches and collapsed trees. The going was difficult. Our boots were heavy and caked with mud.

"Lovely weather for a picnic," observed Doc as he stomped his foot down loudly into a large mud puddle.

"Yes," I agreed. "Couldn't be more perfect."

"It really is so refreshing to get away from the mainstream of things and get a good feel of the countryside," said Doc.

And although I couldn't see Doc's face, I knew that he was smiling.

"Enchanting," I said.

"Reminds me of a field trip I once took through the hills of North Carolina during my scouting days," said Doc.

Doc, as they say, could talk some shit, and talking

anything—nonsense, shit, call it what you will—was far better than dwelling on the improbable state of our deteriorating affairs.

"Scouting?" I asked, repressing a snicker.

"Yes," said Doc. "Short pants, funny hats, merit badges—the works."

"You were a Boy Scout then?" I asked.

He stopped abruptly and spun around. I bumped squarely into him. He gave me a look (part of his act) of waning tolerance and then proceeded on. I followed, lengthening my distance a pace or two.

"Yes, of course, a Boy Scout," he said. "And I was pretty good at it too."

"I'm sure," I said. "Did you ever get to become the leader of your pack?" I asked.

"Troop!" he snarled with comic scorn. "Troop! In my day, sir, we called them troops!"

"Oh," I said. "Rightly so."

A moment of silence presented itself and passed.

Doc continued: "No, in fact, my scouting career was most unjustly nipped in the bud."

"How so?" I inquired.

"Well," said Doc, "on one memorable outing to a singularly loathsome spot not long after I had won my merit badge for honesty and clean living, they, the screws, you know, the high idiots in charge, caught me with two fifths of vodka and three cartons of cigarettes."

"And they, the screws, wouldn't believe you when you tried to explain that you, honest and clean-living you, had only brought the . . . the extras along for medicinal purpose, eh?" I asked, picking up the lead.

"I lied till I was blue in the face," sighed Doc.

"So they, the screws, made you resign your commission, huh?" I asked.

"The bores insisted upon it," replied Doc.

"Well," I said, "I think you're well rid of them. They sound like an insufferable bunch of assholes to me."

"They were," agreed Doc, "and I told them as much."

In front I could hear Motown's radio softly whittling out a song. Doc lit a joint and passed it back. I took a hit and returned it with gagging thanks, then promptly stumbled over a fallen limb.

And so we walked: talking, casual, careless, onward, onward to the sea. It was easily past noon now but still there was no sign of the sun. I was hoping that we would soon stop for a break and maybe some more coconuts. The trail had straightened itself out somewhat by this time and the underbrush alongside had thinned. The coolness of the day and the relative dryness of this particular part of the trail made the walking considerably less laborious. It was not enjoyable by any means, but it was not too bad. As we topped a small rise we passed several flowering bushes. Doc stopped next to one and plucked a small tuliplike yellow flower and inserted it into the camouflage webbing around his helmet. He looked rather rakish, I thought. Motown, whom I could see bobbing along in front of Doc, seemed to be doing a little dance of sorts—two steps forward, one step back. From what I could judge, everyone seemed to be in a vastly improved mood, perhaps sensing that at last we were nearing our journey's end.

Suddenly, in front of me, Doc pulled to a halt, rammed for the earth with one knee, and made a quick flicking hand motion for me to do likewise. I did.

Along the trail I could see that everyone else had adopted a similar posture. Billy and Strider were huddled together at the head of the column, poised, peering into the undergrowth and whispering in hushed tones. Soon their conference broke up and Strider slipped back to have a word with Motown. Motown (the radio silent now) nodded and Strider returned to where Billy, who had not moved two inches, still knelt, staring straight ahead with a look of feline intensity. The message in due course was relayed to Doc, who then condensed and simplified the matter for home consumption. "Looks like trouble," he said. Well, hell, I thought, I could've guessed that much.

Strider then motioned us all forward. We slithered up without cracking a twig. Once up with the others, I could hear Vietnamese voices coming from the other side of a high hedgerow. The voices seemed drunk; there was shouting and laughter and something that sounded like a chant. Strider, his eyes calm, almost bored, signaled for everyone to pop in a fresh clip.

So with clips in and safeties off, we waited and watched and waited. It seemed like an eternity; it seemed like two eternities, back to back, shuffled and stacked. I could almost hear myself sweat, almost feel the hair growing on my head. I was beginning to wonder what the deal was, whether this was as far as I'd ever get, when suddenly, simultaneously, Strider and Billy burst through the hedgerow. Motown and Doc shot through right behind them. So that by the time I had worked my way through the thicket and clambered up to my feet and dropped my rifle and my helmet, it was already too late—the scene was already frozen and the laughter was already dead.

And now like a drunken sailor crashing a baby's funeral, I came with wild eyes and waving arms, spilling out onto the stage: and first, the stage itself, as if created, built, constructed especially for this one-time only, one-shot performance—a circular clearing of mud and sand with an irregular circumference of about twenty meters, surrounded by rampant vegetation shooting up thick on all sides, dark and green and smelling old and forgotten; and the time—mark it Fall '69; and the place—somewhere lost Vietnam; and the characters, the players—Billy and Motown and Doc and Strider, standing, weapons pointed, ready; and me, stumbling and stunned; while across the sand and the mud and a light sprinkling of rain now, across a maximum distance of maybe five meters (everyone was pushed back as far as the foliage and the circumstances would allow) stood and knelt and lay seven figures (five ARVNs, or so I was led to believe by the uniforms that they wore, and two obviously not)—two of the ARVNs standing, rifles pointed, smiling (almost everyone was smiling, everyone except the two who were obviously not ARVNs and who had no reason to be smiling, and myself, who knew not even enough to smile); another ARVN, unarmed, his rifle only a dash away, standing with hands open, extended in a gesture of friendship and greeting, smiling, seemingly relaxed although with quick and darting eyes; and yet another, this one standing too, clearly caught with his pants down, his pants literally around his ankles (the only one of the lot that I could see who had even the vaguest of reasons to be smiling), smiling, one hand cradling the moonlike brown and upturned face of a young Vietnamese girl kneeling in the mud before him, the other hand holding a black .45-caliber revolver, with his rod rammed down the young girl's taut throat; and the final ARVN of the group, all but out of the picture, lying in the mud on his stomach, both hands tucked under his body, his head turned, looking up, smiling a smile of embarrassed apology; and last, finally, the two obviously-not (Vietnamese girls)—one, on the ground next to the prone ARVN, naked, with the top of her head gone and something fleshy hanging half out of her mouth; and the other (already mentioned), kneeling in the mud, her face cradled, her mouth crammed, her eyes shut, her hair matted and caked with mud, her cheeks bulging and streaked wet with tears or rain, her nose bleeding, her forehead smeared white with a clinging creamy substance, her shirt torn open and pulled down off her shoulders, her waist small, her ribs protruding, her breasts firm, her fists clenched and oozing mud between the fingers, her arms with elbows locked straight down at her side, and all, all with the pistol pressed tightly against her smooth left temple.

And here, between these two groups, in the middle, center stage, no-man's land, I stood half-erect like some half-wit or worse, out of place and out of time, looking rapidly in stunned incomprehension from one group to the other until finally someone (Doc) called my name ("Asshole") and I stooped down the rest of the way and picked up my rifle and then scurried into line beside him. But again, it was already too late. The situation had already deteriorated from whatever it had been before into a scene that was now primed for disaster. And yet strangely, there was still something here that was almost intramural and collegiate, some sense of fraternity and men among men in which one could almost take comfort—comfort, if you were a male of the species. But in truth there was no comfort. There was only the blinking and the breathing and the two groups like opposing firing squads stretched out into two lines facing each other, smiling and whispering in hushed undertones.

"What's up?" I asked, panicking, stumbling. "What the hell's going on?"

"Shut up and smile," said Doc, smiling. "And when the shit starts, go for that joker over there on the far left."

"The left?" I cried, not smiling worth a damn. "Oh Jesus!"

Slowly one of the ARVNs—one of the two with the rifles in hand—pulled smiling out of the line and began circling away to the right. Then Strider shouted something loud and harsh-sounding in Vietnamese, which sent a visible wave of shock rippling through the ranks of our allies; and whether it was what he had shouted or whether it was because he had shouted it in Vietnamese, I don't know; but the immediate and most evident result was that the smiling, circling soldier stopped circling and smiling and turned about sharply. And unfortunately for him, or perhaps, more accurately, unfortunately for them—his friends, his compadres—they were now positioned directly between him—one of the two with the rifles—and us.

"If I have to smile much longer I'm gonna break my fucking teeth," lamented Motown, smiling.

"It won't be much longer now," smiled Strider. "They just fucked themselves up."

"Well, hell then, let's take 'em out," suggested Billy

with a smile of placid goodwill spreading amiably across his handsome face.

"Wait," said Strider, still smiling. "Watch that cat in the back there. If he goes for it, they lose."

And, needless to say, he did and they did. Big.

The soldier in the back stood for a moment longer debating the air and then lunged out from behind his companions and opened fire. He clipped off two or three shots and was promptly recycled for dirt. The other soldier with the other rifle did a little better, getting off a full half-dozen well-directed rounds, one of which came so near to my head that I felt it pass. His contribution and effectiveness, however, were abruptly curtailed by the combined efforts of Doc and me, which reduced him to a tangled heap of blood and tissue and backward-bending bones. The ARVN in the middle with the congenial manners and the out-stretched arms tried, but failed, to reach his weapon; he never made more than two steps. A quick burst from Motown caught the man in mid-stride and sent him cartwheeling wildly into the undergrowth. The soldier with the .45 and the interrupted blow-job, seeing that all was obviously lost, his friends flopping about like fish on a wooden pier, turned (his pants still around his ankles) and managed to stumble away, fleeing, a few feet in the direction of the tree line before Billy, still smiling, stitched him neatly up the back.

It didn't last long but it was loud and close. I stood there with my ears ringing and my heart pounding and my knees jumping and a dark patch in the front of my pants spreading noticeably, gasping spastic lungfuls of the sweet and bitter air and thinking: Alive, alive, alive . . .

Doc turned and looked at me. He winked and laughed. "You okay?" he asked.

But I didn't answer him. I felt no need, no desire, for I was alive and that was enough.

Overhead, like restless souls, the trees pushed and swayed together in the wind; a leaf spiraled down; a wild something somewhere shrieked and then scampered away; a small trickle of blood coursed across the ground, rammed up against my boot, then ran on.

Then over to the right, out of the corner of my eye, I saw her—a ghost, a statue, like something from which the life and the breathing had passed; like something in which they (the life and the breathing) had never existed—still kneeling in the mud, the body rigid, the mouth open, the eyes shut, the mud oozing slowly between the locked fingers of the fists.

And we hadn't moved yet either; we were all still standing right there, still in line, breathing and looking and maybe praying or laughing—I don't know.

Then after a further moment of silent observation and reflection, I coughed and spoke. "What about her?"

"What about him?" countered Billy, stepping out of line.

And yes, there was yet another one alive, forgotten, overlooked, obviously overshot. The ARVN who had been lying on his stomach next to the dead girl now looked up (still on his stomach, his hands still buried beneath his body) from a congealing pool of blood and brains, and smiled an uncertain smile.

"Nix him," said Motown. "Nix him and let's roll."

"What's his problem anyway?" asked Doc, walking

over to where Billy now stood towering over the smiling man with the muzzle of his M-16 inserted into the man's ear.

"Well," laughed Billy, jabbing the smiling man with his rifle, "it looks like this sucker was trying to get a little head and the bitch there chomped his wang off."

"That's what that is?" asked Doc, pointing at the lump of loose flesh hanging half out of the dead girl's mouth.

"Looks like it," laughed Billy.

"Nasty,'" said Doc, and he turned and walked over to where the other girl, the kneeling girl, was still kneeling.

"So what do we do with him?" asked Billy, turning toward Strider.

"Nix him," repeated Motown. "Nix his ass and let's roll."

"Yes," agreed Strider. "He's finished, finish him."

"Right," said Billy, smiling at the smiling man.

Motown and Strider and I moved away, leaving Billy to his task. Strider lit a joint and we sat on the ground and smoked it and waited. It was only a short wait.

"Say thank you, shithead," said Billy, smiling. "Say thank you."

The smiling man looked up and smiled at Billy.

Billy gave him a swift kick in the ribs.

"Say thank you, shitface!" shouted Billy, his mouth starting to twitch. "Say thank you!"

The man smiled.

Billy kicked him.

"Say thank you, you goddamn gook!" screamed Billy. "Say thank you!"

The man smiled again.

Billy kicked him again.

We smoked and waited.

"Say thank you, goddammit!" screamed Billy, bending down and grabbing a handful of loose hair and wrenching the man's head around. "Say thank you!"

The smiling man looked up and smiled and silently moved his lips.

"What?" cried Billy, wrenching the man's head around farther. "What? What the shit did you say, you godda—"

"Thank you," the man said in a whisper. "Thank you," he repeated, louder.

"Yes," said Billy, straightening up and breathing easier again. "Yes," he said, and smiled. "You're welcome." Then he blew the smiling man's brains out.

And still the girl knelt. Doc was trying to talk to her now but you could tell that he wasn't really getting anywhere. True, she had opened her eyes and shut her mouth, but that aside, she remained mostly as before: in the mud, on her knees, looking somewhat, somehow like an oil painting of an Early Christian martyr— the look of distance and serenity for which the terrible cascade of events of the immediate past could not account.

"But what about her?" I asked again.

"Yes," said Strider, already moving toward her. "What's the score, Doc?"

Then Strider and Doc going fast, switching on and off, good-cop/bad-cop, speaking mostly in Vietnamese though occasionally slipping back into English: and sometimes it was harsh (sounded harsh) and sometimes it was soft and sometimes there were cigarettes (to smoke)—she declined—and smiles and sometimes there were threats (but only threats; they never touched her; they were only going for the reaction, the answer) and sometimes there were tears. Finally after about twenty minutes Strider removed his own shirt and draped it around the girl's shoulders and helped her to her feet.

"Okay," said Strider, "somebody"—looking at me, meaning me—"find a pole or a branch or something and strap the other one to it. We're taking them with us."

"Where?" I asked.

"To hell," muttered Motown, turning.

"To where we've always been going," said Strider. "To the sea."

"And the girl?" asked Billy, still smiling, and now looking at the girl.

"She says she's from a village up ahead," explained Strider. "So's the other one, the dead one. They're sisters, she says. From the way that she described her village, it sounds like it might be one of the ones on the map. She says it's on the coast, only another couple hours' walk. So we'll take 'em home. They might be of some use to us."

I returned with a sturdy length of bamboo about six feet long, and using some strips from the uniform of one of the dead ARVNs, Billy and I lashed the dead girl's wrists and ankles to the pole and then lifted the pole up onto our shoulders. It was a grim sight: naked, half the head gone, dangling there like a great slab of meat—bagged game.

Doc and Strider made a quick search of the bodies (nothing), picked up the loose weapons—there were four rifles this time; the pistol was thrown away—and distributed these, one to a person, to everyone but to me. (Presumably the thinking was that for me one rifle was more than enough.) Then we seemed ready to go.

"Okay," said Motown, "let's book."

He turned and headed down the trail.

"Hold it," said Strider.

Motown stopped and looked back.

"Let her walk point," said Strider. "If there's any shit down there she'll find it first."

"Or sidestep it," I said. And I knew that I should have kept my damn mouth shut but I also knew that I never would, never could.

"Yes?" asked Strider, his eyes wearily seeking the tops of the trees.

"Well," I said, "she's probably not just too overly fond of us after what our comrades-in-arms did to her and her friend, her sister, and she might decide—"

"What the hell are you talking 'bout, asshole?" demanded Strider. "We just saved her ass!"

"Did we?" I asked.

And Strider just looked at me for a moment and then he began to laugh, laughing a laugh that was high and rising and sounded pained and unsure, laughing until the very trees and the jungle itself seemed to be laughing too, laughing at me and my question, laughing but still offering no answer.

10

I guess by this time we must have looked a little rough—all except Billy, that is; he always looked good, neat. But the rest of us were a mess: our hair hanging loose and going off in all directions; a couple of days' worth of beard and mud on our faces; our uniforms spattered heavily with blood and soaked with sweat; our eyes red and pinned from too much smoke and too little sleep; our entire general appearance one of hungry animals—which was exactly what we were. With Doc and Motown now carrying the blown-apart young girl (we had exchanged meat for metal earlier— they had decided to trust me with the extra rifles after all; the walk turned out to be considerably longer than the two hours first estimated), and with the other young girl, in Strider's shirt, leading our motley procession, yes, we must have been quite a sight to see.

That's why when we passed the man on the trail—an older-looking man with deep hollow eyes, wearing a conical straw hat and black shorts, pushing a flimsy bicycle with wobbly wheels, weighted down with a huge bundle of harvested rice—and we didn't stop and he didn't stop (he didn't even bother to look or look away but just kept right on walking, pushing his bike),

I was somewhat surprised. Not even a nod or a wink. Nothing. He just kept on walking. I, in fact, being the last in line, turned and watched him disappearing down the trail, hoping that once past the others, he would turn and I could smile and maybe communicate something somehow, but he never did. Not once. He just kept on keeping on. Amazing, I thought. And yet maybe it wasn't amazing at all, maybe it didn't even matter anymore. It certainly didn't seem to matter to him, so why should it matter to me? So I just kept on walking too. No think, Strider had said, no think or it'll drive you nuts.

With the gathering darkness now closing heavily on the heels of the dying day, we peaked a rise, rounded a rocky slope, then forded a clear-water creek and were there. Not much. Ten to twelve huts thrown about in a seemingly indifferent fashion, silhouetted black against the spreading gray of the sea. A light shone here and there; a small open fire burned near the village's center. Doc and Motown set the dead girl down near the fire. Several villagers who were squatting about the fire immediately rose and came over and looked at the body and then scurried quickly away. We stood for a minute talking, trying to get our bearings; then Strider and Doc and the other girl walked across a clearing and into one of the huts. They returned a short time later with a man and a woman—the man was old and walked with a stick; the woman was squat with broad shoulders and stubby legs. The party advanced, ignoring Billy and Motown and me. We stepped aside—we had to or the old guy would have walked straight through us. With the aid of his stick, he lowered himself to the ground next to the dead girl and stared into what was left of her once-pretty face. The fire behind him rose bright, sending sparks and ashes skyward. Finally, after what seemed like a long time, the girl, the sister, the one still with the breathing, approached and placed her hand lightly on the old man's shoulder. After a moment more, he rose. He then turned and swept his old and blinking eyes across our young and dirty faces, stopping, looking into each face, each set of eyes—not a hard or bitter look, not even a sad, but rather simply puzzled—and then, with the girl and the older woman in tow, he slipped back into the night and was gone without uttering a word.

Later, a couple of other old men came and picked up the body and took it away.

"Well, all right," said Motown after the body had been removed. "You tell me. What's the story?"

Doc dropped into a squat position next to him and lit a cigarette.

"Well, Mo," said Doc, "the story is that those guys that we took out on the trail back there were apparently some sort of renegades or something who had been operating out here for the past year or so. Some really bad cats, according to Pops there. Selling weapons and whatnot to Charlie, dealing in anything for a buck or piaster. They've been extorting the shit out of this little ville and half a dozen others like it up and down the coast here. First it was money, then livestock, then rice. Finally, when the folks couldn't or wouldn't come up with anything more that was worth having, the boys went and offed up with the old man's—who also happens to be the headman—the old man's daughters which, as you know, we have just succeeded in rescuing—well, one, at least, anyway—from a fate dark as death. So now we, us, the bright and the brave, are the heroes, the saviors, what-have-you, of this here nice little ville, and tomorrow they, the people, to show their appreciation, are gonna throw some kinda big *sheen*-dig and clambake in our honor."

"All right. Okay. Good deal. I like," said Motown. "But what about tonight?"

"Tonight," laughed Doc, slapping Motown on the back, "tonight, my friend, we eat rice and sleep on the beach."

And so we did.

I woke up early the next morning. The skies were gray and overcast. Spread out along the beach next to me, the huddled black shapes told me that the others were still asleep; it also told me that one, besides myself, was not. I scarcely needed to guess who that might be. I stood up, shook the sand off my shoulders and back, and walked down to the water's edge. And sure enough, standing there alone, fresh from his morning swim, with only a short checkered cloth wrapped around his waist, was Strider, staring out at the sea, and seeming to be strangely at home, strangely within his element—the uncertain pallor of a new day, the peaked howling of the wind, the relentless exploding of the surf.

"Looks like it might rain," I observed, coming up quietly behind him.

"Maybe," he said and shrugged. He didn't turn around.

"How's the water?" I asked.

"Wet," he said, with his back still turned.

"Well, anyway, this seems like a good enough spot to hide ou . . . hang out for a while," I said, correcting myself, yet still knowing that I hadn't been fast enough.

"And?" asked Strider, quickly spinning around, his face flushed with anger or by the wind.

"Well, yes, you know," I said, "and so like I was just kinda wondering how long we were planning on being here."

"You got someplace else you wanta go?" he demanded.

"No," I said. "It's just that—"

"Good!" he snapped, already turning, already two steps down the beach. "Then we'll be here as long as it takes!"

"Right," I said, and thought: Jesus, you just can't talk to some people in the morning.

But that wasn't it and I knew it; it was something else, something more, something deeper and more profound. It was as if Strider believed himself to be somehow personally accountable for the acts of not only himself but also others, others over whom he could have had no possible influence or control; as if the acts and resulting conduct of one man were the natural extension of the forces and conditions which encompass and embrace the lives of all men, and propel them ever onward in their vain and mostly idiotic enterprise of living, of being alive, or maybe it was vice versa or maybe it wasn't any of this. But then, I don't know; I do know, however, that whatever it was that stroked or stabbed at his soul, it certainly seemed to cut directly against the grain of his "no-think" philosophy.

So I just let it lie; it didn't matter; I couldn't change it. I turned back toward the village and walked on. And as I walked, I watched the morning coming on: the sun breaking hazily through the clouds—the rays slanting in across the water; a cock, his breast red and black and pushed out, poised on the trunk of a fallen tree, crowing; a mangy dog barking, cowering, backing away; people talking in hushed voices in dimly lit bungalows; the sound of sweeping; a man in raggedy shorts dipping collected rainwater out of a huge red clay jar with a small plastic bowl and then pouring the water over his head; birds tweeting in the trees, crickets in the grass; a water buffalo standing peacefully in a large open field; the women already outside their bungalows, already working—cooking, washing, hanging clothes on a wire strung between two trees; the children laughing, looking, pointing; one child, alone, flying a bright yellow kite; the palms heavy with coconuts; flowers everywhere; an old woman draping a sweet-smelling jasmine garland over a branch of a bush and then kneeling and praying before the bush; a small girl, too young to understand, watching the woman, then imitating her; the morning cooking fires trailing smoke, mingling with the morning mist—a breakfast of rice and fish; a narrow wooden footbridge arching over the creek we had forded the night before, and in which now, on the banks, young boys with cane and string sat fishing; jungle flowers floating down the creek, swirling around in the current; wooden boats with colorful prows pulled up onto the beach, upside down; nets hanging or being mended; fish drying; an old man, stooped, walking along the beach, collecting the refuse from last night's tide; a water well with young women clustered about, whispering, casting covert glances in my direction; chickens and cats and ducks and sea gulls; bungalows raised up a couple of feet or so on stilts; thatched roofs and, in some cases, thatched walls too; unfinished weathered wood; swing-out shutters; glassless, screenless window openings; a small Buddha shrine in front of each bungalow; rubber sandals outside every doorway.

After breakfast—a bowl of rice with small pieces of fish mixed in and covered over with a foul smelling, yet quite tasty black sauce—I sat and waited for the others to wake up. And soon, like the return of the dead, one by one, they came dragging themselves up from the beach.

" 'Morning," said Doc, flopping down beside me with his bowl of rice.

" 'Morning," I said.

"How'd you sleep?" asked Doc, shoveling in a huge mouthful of rice. He was using chopsticks. I had been using a spoon.

"Like a crab," I said.

"Well, tonight it'll be better," Doc assured me.

"How so?" I asked.

"They're gonna give us some bungalows today." Doc smiled. "And a housegirl." He winked. "Each."

"Most considerate," I said.

"No shit," agreed Doc, shoveling in another mouthful.

An old woman wearing a straw hat walked by with two large straw baskets suspended from the ends of a split bamboo pole balanced across her right shoulder.

In the baskets were small packets of something tied up in green banana leaves. Doc engaged her momentarily and received a toothless smile and one of the banana-leaf packets. One was offered to me but I declined.

"It's a kind of sausage," he said in reply to my curious stare.

And true, he unwrapped the green leaf covering and produced a plump red sausage.

"Quite good," he said after taking a bite.

By now the clouds had mostly burned off and, contrary to what I had surmised earlier (I'm hopeless when it comes to the weather), we seemed to be heading for a beautiful day. As Doc and I sat and talked, a small group of village children ventured in cautiously. Doc gave them what was left of his sausage. Their faces lit. They fell eagerly about his feet. And soon, like a magnet and bits of iron filings, we were encircled; with Doc, the magnet, talking and smiling and making comical faces, and the children, the iron, alternately staring in wide-eyed awe or shrieking with high-pitched laughter.

"Well, what's happening, cats?" asked Billy, approaching, stepping over the heads of the children, and dropping down in between Doc and me.

"Not much," I said, moving over a bit.

"Get the fuck away from me, you little beggar!" cried Billy, brushing a small child's hand roughly off his arm.

Doc and I just looked at him and said nothing.

"Phew!" snarled Billy after a quick sniff into his rice bowl. "What the shit is this shit?"

"Well, you got some fish," began Doc a little wearily, "and some rice and—"

"Yes, yes, I know that. But what's this shit?" demanded Billy, pointing. "This black shit here?"

"That's *nuoc-mam* sauce," replied Doc, smiling.

"Well, what the hell's that?" asked Billy, his face dropping a shade paler. "It smells like goddamn rotten fish."

"Well, yes," laughed Doc, "that's just about what it is. They make it by—"

"Spare me, Doc. Spare me, please," sighed Billy, closing his eyes and heaving his bowl over his shoulder; the eyes of the children went dark and disturbed. "I don't even wanta know."

After a while Strider and Motown joined us too and we all sat together and smoked and waited, and in a half-hour or so the old man—the headman—and an entourage of equally aged men appeared and approached. Strider and Doc stood up and nodded and bowed and then went with the old men to squat on their heels in the sand in the shade and talk. In another half-hour or so, they—Strider and Doc—returned (the old men peacefully plodding away in the opposite direction, rocking with that wonderfully animated rhythm and sway of the old, the aged, who have lived full and useful and vigorous lives and damn well mean to continue for some time yet, thank you very much) and said that, yes, they—the old men, the city fathers—had moved out several families, combined several households, and that they—the evicted—had been, yes, yes, more than happy to surrender their hearths and homes to us to enhance our stay.

Well, all right, we thought, and proceeded on.

So we moved; well, no, not actually "moved," since

we had no place to move from except the beach, which was not ours to possess but was rather a resource held in common by mutual consent, and we could just as well have said, while we were at it, that we were leasing the air too, but we didn't; we just arrived (the bungalows vacant, clean, and waiting), arriving like the monsoons perhaps or maybe a plague. And still, and yet, the bungalows (mine, at least; we each had one of our own): not much, a room raised on stilts: thatched roof, bamboo and thatch walls, windowless window openings, a wooden floor, a wooden door, a bamboo bed, a bamboo table, two bamboo chairs, a small piece of a broken mirror, a kerosene lamp, and a picture of Jesus hanging from the cross. And that one, the picture (no frame, nothing; a simple sheet of thin paper hanging straight and loose against the wall, over the bed; two small nails, one in each upper corner), where they had gotten it, found it—it was new, you could tell, or had been meticulously preserved for just such an occasion, opportunity—and why it was there in the room, I'll never know.

By midday I was settled into my new abode. As I have said, it was not much. I tossed my helmet onto the table, dropped my rucksack onto the floor, propped my rifle in a corner, kicked my boots across the room, and flopped down heavily onto the bed. I was home. I woke up several hours later (the sun, I thought to myself upon waking, it must be the sun that makes me want to sleep so much, the sun and that same impulse that drives the ostrich's head underground: "If I'm sleeping then I'm not thinking") and stumbled out onto the small porchlike appendage attached to the front of my bungalow. There, beside the doorway in a neat little pile, was a somewhat used straight-edge razor, a bit of soap, a frayed cotton towel, and a small plastic bowl. A hint, no doubt. I must have stunk like a dog and looked like the devil. So I took the hint and the razor and the soap and the bowl and the towel and the piece of broken mirror from the room and found a large clay jar beside the bungalow similar to the one that I had seen earlier that morning and went to work. In a short while I was good as new, or almost, and went out looking for the others.

They were not overly difficult to locate. I just followed the music—Motown's radio. I found them very much as I had suspected: sitting in the shade, smoking from a long-necked bamboo pipe, and working diligently on a large bottle containing a light greenish liquid.

My friends, I thought, looking at them sprawled out upon the ground in their various stages of repose, undress, and intoxication. Then I thought: No, wait a minute, "friends" here is too strong a word, too much implied. Or maybe it's not strong enough. Our exact position in relation to one another was nebulous at best. We were like people lost in a storm, shipwrecked on an island, infected with the same disease. But then, I don't know. Human relationships in general have never exactly been one of my strong suits.

"Ah, far-wanderer," hailed Doc with a beckoning wave of his arm. "Come and rest yourself, for you have traveled far and must have much to tell."

"Right," I said, and seated myself on the ground next to him.

"My friend here, my guide, perhaps," said Doc, indicating an old and wrinkled fellow with a shaved head and a penetrating stare, whom I had not noticed before, "will prepare for you a little medication to help ease your mind and free your soul."

"Right," I said again, and watched.

His friend, his guide, was busying himself with a long wooden stick on which, at one end, boiled a large black bubble with the consistency of road tar on a hot afternoon. He held this stick, the end with the bubble, over a small candle flame and turned it slowly in the air. After the bubble began to smoke, he took the stick and crammed the smoking bubble down into a very small hole at one end of the bamboo pipe and then fired the hole. His eyes never left the bubble or the hole.

"Opium," said Doc, taking the first hit to show me how it was done. "Beautiful," he exclaimed with a smile. "Gone!"

And it didn't take long—about three solid hits—before I too was gone. Really gone. Far away and fading fast; drifting, lifting, falling, floating, flying; the colors too bright, the sounds too far away, the weight too heavy. Gone.

After a couple of hours of being gone—actually more than a couple; one loses count and concern—I came back and it was dark and I was alone. Where the others had disappeared to, I knew not—and here, "disappeared" is the right word, for one moment it seemed as if I had friends about me and there was music and sunlight, and then the next I found myself waking up alone in the dark with the dew settling on my skin. Across the way in the center of the village where the night before there had been a fire, there was again a fire—only this one was more like a bonfire, blazing up and shooting wild. I rose and made my way with much sideways dancing for it. Around and about the fire, seated cross-legged on a series of straw mats spread out upon the ground, was a group of older men. In the center of this group was the headman—I recognized him now; I had seen him twice before already—and on either side of him, two to a side, sat Doc and Motown and Billy and Strider. There was an empty space next to Motown. I approached and fell within the circle of light from the fire.

"Here comes our delinquent boy," cried Doc. "Sit. We have saved you a place. Dinner is about to begin."

"Dinner?" I asked.

"Sit," encouraged Doc.

The old man smiled and nodded so I smiled and sat.

"What's happening?" I asked Motown, after apologizing for having stepped on his hand.

"Why, hell, man, we gonna get fed and fucked," he said with a smile.

"Yeah?" I asked, still not wholly together.

"Yeah," he said. "Just look at dat one on the end there. The tall one with the tits. Ain't she summuh!"

And in front of us, on the other side of the fire, sitting on straw mats similar to our own, with hands folded, legs and feet together and tucked up to one side (almost like a relaxed kneeling position), attentive, serene, ghostly in fact, like glimpses caught of something unreal, were perhaps two or three dozen young and beautiful girls. It had been a long time. The girls were dressed in *ao dais*, in sarongs, in jeans; their eyes flickered magically between the peaks and valleys of the flames; their hair was long and silky and blew gently in the breeze; several wore silver, several more necklaces of seashells—they all could have been sisters. ("I don't care what you say," Doc had said, "they're a beautiful people." And Doc knew whereof he spoke.)

In and out of the darkness, skirting along the outer reaches of the light, ran a steady stream of older women and children carrying large trays heaped with food. The trays were presented first to the headman, who took a small helping or not, according to his desires, and then the trays were passed along to one side or the other. It was all grand and wonderful and all like a dream.

And the food—Jesus Christ! They began with clams (there were three different types) and chunks of coconut and bits of raw fish in a tasty sauce; then came the salads—lettuce and tomatoes and cucumbers and onions and carrots and green peppers, topped, unbelievably, with Kraft blue-cheese dressing (no doubt stolen from somewhere or, on second thought, perhaps a gift from the good people of the United States; we give such unusual gifts); there were also several localized versions of meat salads (one that I personally favored was made with thin clear noodles and tiny baby shrimp); next came the soups—there must have been six or seven different offerings, from a thick gumbo to a clear chicken broth; this was followed by a flood of entrées—duck in orange sauce, roast suckling pig, whole chickens stuffed with rice and barbecued, thinly sliced beef covered with a thick rich gravy (I was later informed that this had probably been water buffalo—delicious!), lobsters, clawless, of the variety found in warm waters, some weighing several kilos, and prawns ranging in size from nearly as large as the lobsters to no bigger than half the size of the nail of your little finger, all to be dipped in a dozen different and delicious and hot sauces, and fresh crabs, steamed, and fresh fish, maybe as many as ten different species cooked in as many as ten differing styles; and curries—chicken and beef (maybe buffalo again) and shrimp; with dozens of local dishes whose names (and in some cases, contents) I never did discover; with vegetables—baby corn and snow peas and bamboo shoots and mushrooms and more; and always the rice (mountains of it)—steamed and fried; and afterward, after all this, plates of sweets and platters of fruit—mangoes and bananas and papayas and oranges and pineapples and you-name-it (and some that you probably can't); all drenched and drowned with endless pots of hot tea and endless bottles of creek-chilled French champagne (I noticed all the bottles were dated some twenty years back) and Russian and Polish vodkas (the Vietnamese could adapt, no doubt; they had had plenty of practice) and American—Jack Daniel's—bourbon; and finally, topping it off and rounding it out, long thick Cuban (I was no longer even surprised anymore) cigars and a few thoughtful passes of the opium pipe.

And at this point my memory eases somewhat; try as I might, the details are fogged and obscured. I can remember quite clearly up to a point—the point at which someone lit my cigar (Motown, in fact) and I said, "Thanks"—but then, after that, it all sort of falls in patches. I remember the sequence roughly, but that's about it. The moon, however, I do remember: the moon was full.

So the sequence, more or less, maybe, I think, was this: the women and children came and cleared away the trays and plates and platters and what-have-you and Motown and I shared a few more pipes and drank some more champagne (or it may have been vodka by now) and the old man, the headman, stood up and made a little speech (it was all in Vietnamese; I understood not a word) and then the music began (four or five young men—some of the few that we ever saw in the village; the rest dead, gone, fighting for one side or the other, who knows—sitting in the grass, shirtless, directly behind us with drums and tambourines and cymbals) and the girls stood up and the fire burned bright and the air felt cool and the girls filed out from behind the fire (the girls beautiful and lithe) and began to swing and sway to the beat of the drums and the beat picked up and the cymbals crashed and the girls moved faster and the music moved faster and the girls moved faster still (and it was as if the girls who were dancing and the boys who were beating the drums and the cymbals and the tambourines were somehow making love through the music) and then the girls started shrieking and clapping their hands and lifting their legs high up into the air and spinning and shouting and spinning and shouting and soon you couldn't tell if the girls were following the music or the music was following the girls and then Motown got up and pulled me up and then he let go and I fell back and a few of the old men laughed and helped me up and

dusted me off and shoved me out into the spinning
and shouting and Motown and Doc and Billy (I didn't
see Strider) were already dancing (a sort of square-
dance operation; a do-si-do, I guess is what you'd call
it) and so I started dancing too (although not really
dancing much, just sort of jumping up and down in
place like a hyperactive child) and the music was banging and I was jumping and the girls were spinning and
the fire was blazing and the old men and even the old
women and children were standing around in a circle
and smiling and clapping and smiling and Doc turned
and shouted something at me and I shouted something
back at him and it was all spinning and spinning faster
and faster and louder and louder and then suddenly
out of the crowd, out of all that spinning and jumping
a hand reached out and touched my face and I
turned . . .

11

I awoke the next day sweating from the heat and the excesses of the night before. I looked around the room. The room was clean and orderly and smelled of incense. It looked as if my uniform had been washed and my boots shined. My hands were shaking; my head throbbed. I pulled myself up and fumbled into my pants and stumbled out into the bright and piercing sunlight. I blinked a couple of times and brought the world into rough focus. It was late. The shadows from the huts and the trees were stretched out almost to the water's edge. Birds were singing. Women were bringing in the day's wash. Children were playing in the surf.

"G.I." A voice thin and girlish from below.

I looked down. Squatting on the ground next to a small smoky fire, stirring a big black-bottomed pot, was a girl. This must belong to me, I thought. She was small and brown and had eyes that lit up her entire face. I was surprised that I had chosen so well—what with the drinking and all. Then I remembered: No, it was she who did the choosing; and then: Yes, I guess that's the way it usually is, war or no war.

"G.I.," came the voice again. "G.I."

The girl motioned to me to come and sit. There was a wooden bowl, a straw mat, and a steaming cup of brownish liquid. I sat on the mat as the girl ladled out a bowlful of whatever was in the large pot.

"Eat," she said, and handed me a spoon.

I did and it was delicious. And as I ate, I studied the girl. She had long black hair and deep brown eyes. Her cheekbones were high, her nose and her mouth were small, and her teeth were straight and white. Her body, what I could see of it (she wore a long flower-patterned sarong; I remembered nothing of it from the night before), was smooth-skinned and compact; her breasts rose small yet firm. Hmm, I thought, taking a sip of tea, hmm.

A bracing breeze kicked up from out of the sea and sent the pale blue columns of smoke from the nearby cooking fires wafting before it. Fishermen wearing hats sat on the overturned hulls of their beached boats, laughing and smoking cigarettes. Several huts away I could see Strider sitting on the top step of his bunga-low, alone. Off to the west a jet shrieked away un-seen. Across an open field an enormous white goose with wings outspread honked and charged into an unruly pack of black and brown puppies. Along a dirt path that ran in front of my bungalow and off into the jungle, two young girls, both wearing sarongs, both barefoot, one with a flower tucked behind her ear, walked; they stopped and exchanged a few words with "my girl" and a few shy smiles with me.

"Sisters?" I asked on comic impulse after they had passed.

"Yes," she said, neither smiling nor looking up. "Everybody sisters."

The sky was paralleling now on toward night—pink and orange and purple. Palms were silhouetted black against the brilliant sky. Crickets were frantic in the bush. Jungle birds from the trees behind the huts were calling out to one another, filling the air with their long and looping crys. A dog, a bicycle bell, children.

"More?" asked the girl, ladling out another bowlful of what tasted like a sort of combination vegetable and seafood stew.

"Thanks," I said, and continued eating.

She had a long stick in one hand with which she was aimlessly raking the coals of the fire into a neat little pile and then scattering the pile out again. This game went on in silence for quite some time.

"How do they call you?" I finally asked. "If, say, I should need you in the heat of the day," I continued, not really knowing exactly how to proceed (was she my girlfriend or my maid or what?), "how do I gain your attention? Yes, yes, I know. Just put my lips together and blow. I saw the movie, too. But I guess what I mean is—"

"Me speak only *ti ti*," she said; her head was bowed, she was talking to the earth.

"*Ti ti*? " I asked. "What the hell's a *ti ti*?"

"*Ti ti* same-same little bit," she explained, holding out a gapped space of air between her index finger and her thumb—the universal sign of a "little bit."

"Oh, all right," I said. "Let's try this then: name you?" I asked, pointing.

"Name me: Anh," she said, still stirring the fire, still talking to the earth.

"Good! Excellent!" I exclaimed. "Definite progress!"

She didn't respond to the praise. Perhaps she did

not understand, but I rather suspected that she understood a good deal more than she was letting on. She
was going to be a tough nut to crack. Her body and
her services, as I soon found out, were apparently
mine for the asking but her mind and her heart I could
tell were going to be an entirely different story. ("You
may be able to own a kite," the old opium man said to
me one day out of the blue; he spoke beautiful English
but hardly ever used it, "but you can never hold the
wind." Not exactly profound, but I understood what
he meant.)

"Name you?" she asked quickly; her eyes darting in
my direction and then away.

"Name me?" I asked, a little surprised. "Name me:
Austin."

"Austin," she said, letting it linger in the air. "Austin good name."

"Yeah?" I asked, pointlessly flattered.

"Yes," she affirmed.

She put down her stick and picked up a long-handled
wooden spoon lying nearby and gave it a couple of
quick turns around the black-bottomed pot.

"You no eat?" I asked. There was plenty left in the
pot.

"Soon," she said. She laid aside the spoon and
picked up her stick and began prodding the fire again.

The shortness of her last answer disconcerted me
somewhat. I was trying to be generous and she had cut
me off. Although, in truth, I really don't know what I
was expecting. Salaams and curtsies, maybe.

"Where do you come from anyway?" I asked a little
pointedly.

She stopped messing about with the fire and looked

up and I realized how incredibly imbecilic my question must have sounded.

"Me from Vietnam," she said, eyeing me suspiciously; she was probably wondering if she had picked the idiot of the group.

"Yes, yes," I persisted, trying to hurry along, feeling as stupid as my question. I never could make conversation. "What I mean to say is, you come from this village? From down the road? From over the next hill? From where?"

"From here," she said. "From there." She pointed to a small hut across the way in front of which an old woman was squatting in a manner similar to hers, tending a fire also similar to hers.

"Very nice," I said.

"Yes," she agreed.

She was a real little beauty. Eyes, lips, nose, sculptured, molded; with the kind of skin, color and texture, that some American girls spend their entire summers trying to obtain. Her feet and hands were marvelously small, and when the sunlight hit her hair just right, it appeared so black as to be almost red at the roots.

"Tell me, Anh," I said after a while, "why me? I mean, why you choose me?"

"Choose?" she asked. I could tell that she was being evasive, stalling for time. "Me no know 'choose.'"

"Choose," I explained, picking up her arm and pulling it gently toward me, "you know, choose—pick, select."

"Oh," she said, and let it drop.

I picked it up again.

"No," I said, "come on, tell me. I wanta know. Why you pick me?"

"Me no know," she said with a quick glance.

I continued to look at her.

"Me no know," she said again, stirring the fire again. "Maybe me like you."

Silence.

"*Ti ti*," she added and then she stood up and walked quickly up the steps and into the bungalow.

Her abrupt departure and the succeeding silence left me in a ponderous mood. I picked up the stick with which she had been stirring the fire and began to stir it myself. *Ti ti*, I thought. Well, I guess a little bit's better than none.

Under my encouragement, licks of fire danced up from the glowing red mass of coals, and soon the contents of the pot began to bubble and smoke. "Damn!" I said to myself when I realized that I was ruining what stew was left in the pot and generally filling the air with a foul smell. I snapped the stick in half and tossed both lengths under the bungalow and left the smoking mess behind. I crossed the little grassy village center and walked on down to the beach, where, in the last lingering shot of sunlight, bobbing in the surf like the children whom I had seen earlier, I could now see Billy and Doc and Motown.

"Come on in!" cried Billy, waving his arms and smiling.

"The water's fine!" encouraged Doc.

"I would!" I called back. "But I don't have anything to wear!"

"So who the fuck gives a fuck!" laughed Motown,

jumping up high above the waves, huge and black and naked.

And so we (Strider too, sometimes, ofttimes, if the truth be known, coming down off his perch or platform or cross or whatever it was that he was on and joining in) spent our days and nights loose and loaded, playing games, aimless mindless games, games that had no real meaning but also did no harm: swimming (finally the good people of the village appalled at our lack of modesty and decorum furnished us with some shorts) and sunning ourselves and eating (tons) and drinking (Strider organized, built a little bar of sorts, really just a weathered plank painted green and nailed between two chunks of palm with a few other chunks of irregular size along one side for barstools, behind which a small black monkey from somewhere—one day he was just there—on a long leather leash raced about and shrieked while a young village boy whom Strider had trained opened bottles—the villagers had plenty, they said, and gave freely—and mixed our drinks and smiled) and smoking (I was up to seven bowls a day now, no problem) and laughing and joking and dancing (Motown's radio) and singing and bedding one (I: only Anh; and an amazing thing here: she always prayed before we went to sleep—kneeling on the bed, knees tucked up, hands together, palms touching, fingers extended, three bows; "for a good fuck," Billy said), two, three, four (Motown) girls a night; and Doc teaching the children English and the children in turn trying to teach me Vietnamese (a hopeless case); and Billy going out with the fishermen, fishing with grenades (you should have seen their faces—Billy's too—coming back with all those goddamn fish); and waking up at dawn or dusk or whenever and gathering at Strider's Bar, as it soon became known; and the talking and arguing (all day, all night) and the conversations and the debates and the plans—all without beginnings or reason or end.

Thus life and living continued; days into weeks, with the weeks rolling over on top of one another like kittens in a wicker basket. Confused, happy, wild days of laughter and sunshine balanced against the lusty and absurd nights.

"This shit's hard to take," said Motown, smiling with one hand draped over the shoulder of some "new young thang" while the other hand slowly turned a glass of whiskey and rainwater on the green surface of Strider's Bar.

"Life's a bitch," I agreed, raising my glass for a salute.

We both laughed and then drank.

Yet, as it is with most things, there was a definite and defined time limit to our merriment, to our salad days, a period beyond which there could be no possible extension, and that time, date, arrived one bright clear morning as we sat in the shade nursing the last of a bottle of good American whiskey. We had been up all night and were crashing fast. Billy and Motown were in the midst of a fine argument—about what, no one knew nor cared—when suddenly Doc stood up and pointed.

"What the shit!" he exclaimed.

We, as one, all turned and looked and saw, much to our disbelief, two young village boys with ten or twelve

162

wristwatches dangling off each of the boys' arms like bracelets, walking out of the jungle, carrying a large color television set.

"Let's check this shit out," said Strider, standing up too.

Strider and Doc questioned the boys at some length in an attempt to learn the source of their newly acquired wealth, and finally, after much haggling and a sworn promise that they could keep the watches and the television set ("Swear God?" "All right, all right" "Raise hand"), the boys agreed to lead us to the spot from whence such opulence originated.

So with the boys acting as our guides, we set out half-drunk with rifles and helmets and packs and all, through the rapidly rising heat of a blue morning. And a pretty good little hike it was too: through the jungle, across a river, up around one side of a steep rocky slope, then down the other side and into a festering fog-shrouded valley, until finally, wide-eyed and sweating alcohol, we found ourselves standing neck-deep in a clump of thorny bushes, peering through a part in the undergrowth at the tangled and still-smoking wreckage of a U.S. Army Chinook helicopter.

"Fuck!" exclaimed Motown, roundly summing up my own surprise and astonishment. "Wonder if anybody's still kicking in there."

"Don't know," said Strider, pushing aside the branches, "but we'll soon see, won't we?"

"Lead on, McDuff," applauded Doc, bowing the way clear.

"Cram it, comic," said Strider over his shoulder as he stepped out into the clearing.

The Chinook lay like some enormous dead bug at a severe angle with its underside exposed. The little wheels like legs jutted up hopelessly into the air. The rotor blades were deeply embedded in the earth or else snapped off clean and scattered about. The glass in the cockpit was completely shattered, and out of one of the window openings dangled a loose and bloody arm. Along one side, the side facing us, ran a wide jagged gash as if opened by a gigantic can opener. The entire machine, position and all, reflected a sad attitude of utter submission and surrender.

We approached the craft with understandable caution. It might very well have been booby-trapped (it certainly looked ominous enough) or it might have just suddenly exploded on its own (it was still smoking and the air hung heavy with fumes of leaking fuel) or there might have been any number of unknown persons bent on any variety of unkind designs secreted about in the surrounding foliage. We therefore split ourselves up into two groups, with Billy and Motown in one, and Doc and Strider and myself in another, and proceeded to reconnoiter the area. After finding nothing we regrouped on the far side of the clearing, about twenty-five yards away from the chopper.

"All right," said Strider, "let's see what we've bought."

He then turned to the village boys, who, during all this time, during our reconnaissance, had been happily squatting on their heels, very much amused at our caution. He said something in sharp-toned, rapid Vietnamese which immediately brought the boys to their feet. They advanced and then led the way on toward the helicopter. They stopped in front of the jagged slash in the chopper's side, held a brief conference among themselves, and then scrambled in through the hole. We followed. Coming as we did from out of the brilliant sunlight into the gloom of the helicopter's interior, it took a few seconds of blinking for the eyes to adjust. But once they did (the eyes: adjust; adjust and then spring open wide again like the eyes of so many Tom Sawyers and Huckleberry Finns gaping at bandit's gold), what we saw was truly amazing: crates stacked upon crates, crates strewn about, crates whole, crates splintered; and inside the crates (some of it already spilling out)—everything! It was like some type of flying garage sale or flea market. There were color television sets and stereo components and watches and tapes and records and cases of whiskey and cases of beer (Budweiser) and boxes of canned goods (spaghetti, peaches, corn) and cartons of cigarettes and hundreds of pairs of blue jeans and shirts and tennis shoes and cameras and power tools and surgical supplies (clamps, scissors, syringes, scalpels, pills and bottles) and toys (little trucks, model-airplane kits, space guns, dolls with blond hair) and appliances (toasters, blenders, mixers, and mashers) and automotive parts (carburetors, cams, batteries, tires, and hundreds of cans of oil) and more and more, until finally sitting down and drinking a hot beer after an hour or so of wild ripping and tearing at crates and boxes—well, it just didn't matter anymore because it was all unbelievable, all too fantastic.

"Well, fuck me!" cried Billy, standing on top of a color television set, holding a space gun and a beer. "This is like Christmas in July—or whatever the fuck month it is."

"Look at this!" exclaimed Motown, thrusting out a record. "James Brown! My main man! Get down! I can live!"

"Hey, Strider, what is all this crap anyway?" asked Billy, jumping down off the television set and crossing over to where Strider sat fingering a couple of watches. "I mean, you know, like it all looks brand new. What's the fucking deal, huh?"

Strider sat silent for a moment. The air in the chopper was stale and hot. The beer was making me feel a little sick.

"Well," he said finally, looking up then looking off, "I don't really know for sure but I've got a pretty good idea that ain't none of this shit here exactly kosher."

"Fuck kosher!" interjected Motown. "What I wanta know is how we gonna carry all this shit back and where the fuck is we gonna put it once we get it there?"

We all turned to Motown; but Motown, as was to be expected, wasn't holding his breath, waiting for an answer, any answer. In fact, he was already lost again in the record pile.

I sometimes thought that Motown saw things, reacted to events much more naturally than I did, or maybe he just expected less from them—events, life; call it how you wish—so that he was very seldom surprised or disappointed; "go with the flow," I guess, but then, I don't know. I do know that he was often able to ferret out avenues of the obvious much more readily than I could or could ever hope to. Some things just pass me by. Whereas I tend to approach a problem or an act or an action from the point of view of watching and waiting to see how things develop, he always went right to the meat of the matter, a sort of "screw the reason; what and where are the results?" But then, as I have said, I don't know. Perhaps he was just simple—not simpleminded, but rather basic, uncomplicated; and simple fun, simple pleasures were all that he sought. Limited returns for limited investments: food, drink, sex, laughter, friends—good times. I don't know, and the more that I think about it, the more it confuses me, so I'll give it over and press on.

At some point during all of our ripping and tearing, Doc had managed to slip away unnoticed. Managed? Ha! As if stealth were needed. The earth could have moved, the sky could have fallen, and for a while there we never would have known it—we were so absorbed with our boxes and crates. But now Doc was back in our midst to report that the crew, what he could find (he had found three), was all dead, and all, strangely, had no insignias of rank (they all wore simple flight suits) or dog tags or any papers on their persons to give the slightest clue as to who they were (had been) or where they had come from.

"All right. Okay," said Billy. "I'm sorry as dog shit on a hot afternoon that they're dead. But what can we do about that now? Maybe they were on some kind of secret mission or something. Who knows? What matters now is—"

"Secret mission?" snarled Strider. "That's rich."

"Right," agreed Billy, pacing on. "But what matters now is, like the Mo said, what are we gonna do with all this crap now that we've got it?"

We waited.

"Well," said Strider after a moment, "we'll claim

167

the liquor and the food and the cigarettes and what medical supplies Doc can use and whatever else anyone wants to carry, and give the rest of it to the village."

"Give! The village!" protested Motown. "But hell, Strider, this shit could be worth a fucking fortune! Cameras and color television sets and—"

"It could be," interrupted Strider, dropping the watches back into the box and standing up, "but it's not. Not here. Here it's just a lot of deadweight and sparkle."

"Beads for the Injuns, huh?" I asked.

And Strider just looked at me for a moment, the way that you might look at a drooling beggar with only a dime in his cup, and then he smiled and said, "Speaking of deadweight—"

"All right," I said, already rising.

"—I hope you brought your shovel."

While Strider and the others shifted through the spoils that had so unexpectedly fallen into our hands, I endeavored with much heavy breathing and cursing to wrestle the bodies out of the chopper and into the sunlight. And this was no small task either—stiff bodies (two of which, the pilot's and the copilot's, were forever fashioned into sitting positions) and narrow passageways. I then planted these three anonymous victims of what misbegotten enterprise, at the time, I knew not, in three shallow unmarked graves and returned to the helicopter. Back at the chopper the others had already completed the separation of the goods and were now waiting next to a small mountain of plunder for the return of the village boys, who had been dispatched posthaste to enlist a platoon of able hands to help with the transportation. We clearly had more provisions than we alone could conceivably have carted away in ten or even twenty trips.

"A heap of shit." Motown smiled, sitting atop his private mound of crates and boxes which in size almost equaled twice that of our communal goods.

"A heap," I agreed.

And soon, like a mad stampede of game show contestants called onto stage, the entire village came hurtling out of the jungle—old hags and dogs and young girls with babies straddling their hips and old men with sticks who could move with amazing speed and little children, some of whom could barely walk. They shot past us without so much as a nod of recognition and made straight for the helicopter, from which soon arose an excited chorus of shrieks and laughter.

"I thought they were supposed to be helping us," complained Billy, watching the mayhem.

"Well," said Strider, "let them have their fun. We're not going anywhere anytime soon. We can wait."

So we waited, drinking warm beers and watching. In a steady and seemingly endless stream, like ants swarming over an insect's body, they came and went, taking everything that was not nailed down, and even a few things that were—an old man struggling a few meters with a large color television set and then setting it down and resting and smiling; a child rolling away an automobile tire; an old woman pumping down the trail (there was a trail now) with eight or ten cameras dangling from her neck and shoulders; and ox carts and wheelbarrows and bicycles loaded up and pulled or pushed or ridden away.

And who could blame them? Certainly not me. Their lives, by Western standards, which admittedly were the wrong standards by which to judge but still one must use what one knows, were grim enough, totally devoid of luxuries and sometimes even lacking in necessities.

Finally after almost an hour, Strider flagged down the headman, who was dashing by with a hair dryer in one hand and an oil filter in the other, and persuaded him to restore some semblance of order to the chaos. The headman, after much shouting, assembled his people about him, and after a little further shrieking and shouting, he drafted fifteen or so very unhappy young girls out of the crowd to act as our porters and then released the rest of the populace back to their busy business of pillage.

And so it went: the young girls, resigned yet still visibly frustrated, with our booty piled high on heads and shoulders, twitching it down the trail; Motown lugging away his own goods, sweating (and his goods, I thought, seemed somewhat unrealistic, considering the circumstances—a color television set, stereo components, records, and the like; and all with no electricity in the village; "A nigger can dream, can't he?" he had responded briskly when I questioned him about his selection); the rest of us carrying little or nothing (I pocketed only a watch—a ladies' watch, gold and sparkling with tiny diamonds around the face—which I later gave to Anh, who in turn said that she gave it to her mother); with the archway of trees swaying and rustling overhead, and with the sunlight flashing through between the leaves, giving a strobe-light effect to the progress of our caravan.

We had already made half a dozen trips back to the village and had returned once again to the crash site where we were loading up the girls for another trip when suddenly a shot rang out from the wreckage. The villagers who had been inside the chopper or milling about outside panicked and scattered like birds. I immediately, as I am wont to do at the least and first sign of danger or violence, hit the ground. Strider looked at me, shook his head, and moved on toward the helicopter.

"Come on," he said.

We deployed ourselves about the jagged slice in the chopper's side. Strider and Motown took up positions on one side of the gash, with Billy and Doc and I on the other.

"Ready?" asked Strider with a wild glint of something indefinable in his cold blue eyes.

"Ready." Billy smiled, holding up a thumb.

Strider lunged through the opening first and was followed up quickly by Billy and Motown. There was a tremendous crashing about of crates and boxes and much loud and obscene shouting.

"Hold it!"

"Fuck you!"

"Get the gun!"

"Look out!"

"Wait!"

"Fuck him!"

"Somebody get the goddamn gun!"

Then there was a sharp and resounding smack. Then there was silence. Doc looked at me, shrugged his shoulders, and calmly lifted himself up into the chopper. I followed.

Inside, sprawled out among the broken chaos of cargo, lay a man with his head resting against the far side of the helicopter. He was obviously a European or an American. After a moment, after my eyes had adjusted once again to the gloom of the interior, I could see that the man was wearing the same type of nondescript flight suit that the other three men whom I had buried had worn. I could also see that his right arm was bleeding. Doc was examining the man's arm as Strider, on one knee and holding a revolver, talked with the injured man.

"Awright," the unfamiliar voice was saying in a slow and weak Southern drawl. "Help me up."

"Waving a goddamn pistol around like some kind of fucking toy!" snarled Strider. "Hell, you could've killed someone!"

"Awright," the wounded man agreed again, his eyes swimming inside his head. "You're right, of course. Now help me up."

"You're damn right I'm right!" continued Strider relentlessly. "Do we look like goddamn gooks or something? Huh? Do we? Look at my eyes and tell me—"

"Leave off on him, Strider," interjected Doc. "He's hurt pretty good. He's got a ripped-up arm and his foot's all fucked up."

"Awright," said the injured man again—agreeing with what, I didn't know.

"Well, I just don't like some fucker waving a fucking pistol around in my fucking face," said Strider, calming down a bit. "It's like . . ."

And as Strider continued his condemnation of events, I observed the person to whom the criticism was directed. The man looked to me like an accountant or a professor. He was small and frail—not sickly, simply delicate. He couldn't have been more than five and a half feet tall or weighed more than a hundred and twenty pounds. His hands were small and smooth, perhaps one would say even feminine. His head was bald and fringed with thin white hair. His skin was pulled taut across his skull. He wore wire-rimmed glasses, behind which burned green intense eyes. And flickering across his face was a constant gray-toothed smile, as if he were on the verge of laughing at some deep and dark inner secret or joke.

"And it's bad enough," concluded Strider, standing up, "to have half the goddamn country out trying to nail our ass without having Americans going for it too."

"I'm sorry," said the man.

"Yeah, you're sorry all right," agreed Strider, turning the revolver over in his hands.

"Yes, I'm sorry," repeated the man with a sigh, and then his body went limp and his head flopped over to one side and he was down for the count.

"We've gotta get him back to the village," said Doc, examining the man's rolled-back eyes, "so I can clean up his arm and try to patch up that foot."

"Yeah, yeah," said Strider, still stewing over the indignation of having nearly been canceled by one's fellow countryman. "Okay," he said. "You, asshole"—me; I knew it—"fix up a stretcher or something so we can get this man back to town."

"Awright," I said, smiling, trying to imitate the injured man's deep Southern drawl, which was even more pronounced than my own.

But Strider seemed less than amused at my mimicry and regarded my exit with cold and scornful scrutiny.

With the help of several villagers—they did most of the actual work; I merely explained with hand gestures and words that they couldn't understand what it was that I needed—we constructed a crude litter of sorts. I then returned with my litter to the helicopter and entered once again through the gash in its side.

"Done," I announced.

"Okay," said Strider, "let's get him out of here."

So gently, we lifted the injured man up. Strider and Billy each took a leg, Doc and Motown each had an arm, while I supported the head. In this manner, we had gotten him almost to the door when Motown stumbled slightly against the shattered remains of a color television set. The man moaned and then suddenly his head shot up out of my hands.

"My hat!" he cried, reaching for his head. "Where's my hat?"

"Your hat?" asked Doc.

"My hat!" he cried again, struggling to free himself. "I must have my hat!"

"Somebody find his fucking hat," sighed Strider, shaking his head in disgust.

Billy dropped a leg, the one with the injured foot—it bounced once against something hard and the man let out a scream—and returned to the spot where the man had first been discovered. After a little cursing and a little shifting about of the crates and boxes, he proclaimed victory. He brought the hat back to where we now stood with the injured man like a partially stretched animal skin suspended in midair.

"Here you go, pop," said Billy, squashing the hat—a battered tan bush hat soaked round with sweat, with the brim turned up and a blue patch on one side with red lettering on it—down upon the man's head.

"Okay?" asked Strider.

"Awright," said the man, visibly relieved.

"Okay," said Strider, "let's move."

We transferred him as gently as we could out of the helicopter and down onto the litter. Strider summoned over four village girls to carry the litter back to the village.

"A hat," exclaimed Motown. "Big fucking deal."

"Yes," I said. "A hat."

Motown and I stepped back off the trail and allowed the litter and the girls to pass. Motown pinched one of the girls. She turned around and smiled. I looked down at the man—he was already out again—and then my eyes caught a passing glimpse of the red lettering on the blue patch on the man's hat. The patch read: SORRY ABOUT THAT, VIETNAM.

"Sorry?" I said, speaking to no one. "Ha! Sorry."

And as I continued to watch the man being borne away down the sun-filtered and jasmine-scented trail and then on out of sight, I couldn't help but wonder if that flippant phrase might not have a broader and more meaningful application, standing not as a merely whimsical expression of unfelt personal sorrow but rather expressing the unspoken (the never-to-be-spoken) regrets that one nation might offer to another nation for a job sorely botched, and even more, perhaps (although the wording might need to be changed slightly) the apology of a nation (the first) to those, her sons, who went, who stood in line and signed the forms and said, "All right, I'll go, take me, but I'm remembering that I could've caught that night bus to Montreal"—the unalterable epitaph of the dead; the lame lament offered with a backhanded pat and oyster eyes to the crippled, the blind, the forever forgotten; the shrugged shoulder to those many abandoned and cast adrift on the surging seas of betrayal, deceit, sham, and pretense, lies and broken promises.

Then I thought: Naw, I'm drunk; I'm reading too much into too little; it's just a joke, for God's sake.

So leaving it at that, I kicked a stone and spat on a leaf and followed the others on down the trail.

12

"He says his name is Comfort, if you can believe that, Colonel Comfort," reported Doc a few days later. We were all sitting around Strider's Bar drinking and smoking and feeding green bananas to the little bar monkey. "He claims to have something to do with psych warfare in this sector."

"Winning hearts and minds and fattening his own wallet," laughed Strider.

"It's a nasty job," declared Doc, "but someone's got to do it."

"Yeah," said Strider.

In the village now the roosters and dogs were just waking up, and in the air was already the morning smell of charcoal fires and fish frying.

"Well, what were those cats doing around here anyway?" asked Motown. "I mean like there ain't been a fucking thing happening around here since we been here."

"He says that they were on a mission—" began Doc.

"What kind of mission?" interrupted Strider.

"I asked him that and he said, 'Don't ask.'"

"Huh," grunted Strider.

"Anyway," continued Doc, "he said that they were on this mission, whatever it was, and ran into some real heavy weather—kind of a monsoonlike thunderstorm was the way he described it—and were forced to try to make an emergency landing."

"Some landing," snickered Billy, extending his hand, palm up, toward Motown.

Motown slapped it.

"A thunderstorm?" I asked. "But it hasn't rained anywhere near here for more than a month!"

"So our colonel lies," said Doc, signaling the young bar boy for another bourbon and rainwater.

"What kind of shape's he in?" asked Strider.

"Well, not really as bad as one might suspect—considering his age and all," said Doc; the tone of his voice brightening somewhat. Doc loved to talk about his work. "I was able to more or less fix up his arm. It's all right. It was really nothing more than a good healthy scratch, but his foot seems to be fractured. All I could do there was just tape it up and brace it with a few strips of bamboo."

"Is he gonna be able to walk?" asked Strider.

"Soon. With a stick," said Doc. "And he's already talking about when we'll be going back."

"We?" asked Billy, his glass halted halfway to his mouth.

"Yes," answered Doc. "We."

"Well, it was to be expected, I guess," said Strider.

"Perhaps," agreed Doc.

"Has he been asking many questions—questions about us?" asked Strider.

"Surprisingly few," said Doc, lighting a joint. "Surprisingly few."

So we let it—the conversation, the concern—lie. (What more could we do?) We sat and smoked in a gloomy and meditative silence as the blue smoke from the joint drifted up and vanished like so much lost time and wasted effort. The morning blew out of the sea a lazy shadow of pale lavender, and the clouds, a deep and dangerous mix of purple and orange, held all suspended and shaded for some few and fragile moments before the sun finally broke out over the horizon, dissolving the mounting day into hard and very real yellows and greens and blues. The conversation soon picked up again and wavered irresolutely between baseball and blow-jobs. Conversations of this nature—sports and sex—always bore me, as this one soon did, so I bade my companions a fond adieu.

"See y'all later," I said, standing up and stumbling a bit. We had only been at it for about ten hours now.

"Yeah," called out Motown over his shoulder, "go on and take it to the house, you legless honky."

"Screw you, bro," I said, and staggered off in the direction of my hooch.

And as I trudged away through the knee-deep, dew-soaked grass sprouting up along the path that wound its way up to my bungalow (I was having great difficulty in navigating this trail), I thought to myself how very pleasant it is to be drunk at dawn—you had to work at it, true; anyone could be smashed at sunset, but at dawn, ah! now at dawn, that was different, that took patience, fortitude: the feeling of freedom, of guiltless irresponsibility; the knowledge of the somehow rightness of it all: the cool melting away of night; the fulfilled promise of a new day; the mist rising phantomlike out across the paddy fields; the gentle sea-scented breeze; the light smacking of waves some-where; the people smiling (no doubt laughing) as one labors along; the birds singing; the dogs with wagging tails; and finally there, almost at my doorstep, my foot in fact already on the first step, there in the fork of one of the lower branches of a fruit tree, a calico cat winking at me, seeming to be signaling, if not outright approval, then at least a benign acquiescence.

But then, I don't know; maybe I'm just a romantic fool (a fool period, I'm sure some would say) and perhaps none of this—this account, this confession, this whatever—really matters at all; matters, that is, to anyone except me (a voice screaming in a hollow box in a wall-less room), and who saw it, felt it, was there, and so now, in my own feeble and grossly inadequate way, must here try to set down and capture the feel-ings and the facts so that perhaps somehow, someone might understand and will be able to derive some meaning and intelligence from it all, so that in the end, all will not have been for naught. Maybe. Jesus! It gets harder with each day, with each line; if I had known in the beginning that it was going to be this difficult, if I had known that it was going to be this painful, personally, to me, to recount and recollect these events, I assure you that I never would have begun; I simply would have gone on drugs or maybe have gotten myself a real job somewhere; but then (now), since I have already come this far, since I've already inflicted this much punishment upon myself, I might as well push on and wind it up and be done with it. Dammit!

So with my right foot on the first step, I winked back at the cat and mounted the few remaining steps and passed through the already open door and into the room. Anh was busying herself with nothing of particular importance that I could see, so I commanded her to stop. It was making me dizzy watching her—all that hustling and bustling about in front of my already blurred vision. She stopped and looked up and said something in rapid Vietnamese and then continued with her frantic arranging and rearranging. It was often difficult for us to express ourselves clearly; her English was rudimentary at best, and my Vietnamese was far worse ("Huh?"). I sounded more like a stuttering idiot drowning in a vat of molasses than someone trying to speak a language. We were, however, able to communicate through our own private system of point and touch. We also did a lot of smiling.

"Quit!" I commanded, waving my arms about like a football referee. "Cease! Halt! Immediately!"

"What you want, lazy dog?" she asked, looking up again and smiling. This was one of our favorite expressions. We were both "lazy dogs," and we always said it with a great deal of tenderness and affection.

"I want you, now, immediately, to stop all this rushing around," I said, lurching after her, trying to grab her and hold her still in one place.

"Rushing?" she asked, sidestepping as I plunged headlong into a wall and nearly through it. "Me no know. You sit. Me get food."

She turned and rushed out the door and down the steps and was back again in half a minute with a tray of food.

"Sit," she said again, indicating a straw mat on the floor in the doorway. "Sit and eat."

I did as I was directed. It was easier than arguing.

On the tray were two large prawns, almost as large as lobsters, in a curry sauce, a large bowl of the inevitable white rice, and half of a small watermelon. And in spite of the fact that I was severely drunk and quite fatigued, I managed to wolf it all down with no problem.

"Thank you, lazy dog," I said with a burp of appreciation after I had finished.

"Chinese man?" she asked in response to my burp.

"Yes," I said.

I stood up to stretch myself and look about. The sun was full up now, the birds were still singing, and I had just had a wonderful breakfast.

"All right, little girl," I said in a lordly manner, for I was indeed feeling rather like a lord if not a king. "We now to bed."

"You bed," she countered, swiftly removing the dishes and bowls. "Me wash clothes."

By this time we had stored our uniforms and boots and things and were now going about in blue jeans and T-shirts salvaged from the helicopter. And with our tire-tread sandals—a gift from the villagers—and our tennis shoes and sunglasses, I thought that we all looked extremely sporty.

"Well, I'm terribly sorry, my dear," I said, "but I'm afraid that you don't seem to understand or to appreciate your precarious position here. You see, lazy dog, I'm in charge here and everything that you see I am master of"—a wide sweeping gesture of the hand; I spun around and almost fell down—"and I hereby command that you finish with whatever it is that you are about and prepare yourself at once for a good bedding." I was smiling like a cat; sometimes when I'm under the influence of heady drink I truly believe myself to be wonderful.

"You command shit," she said in the sweetest voice with the dearest smile.

"What?" I stammered. "What did you say?" I was stunned. I knew that she had been picking up some of the lingo of late but I had not realized how far her education had progressed.

"You command shit," she repeated. She spoke these words so softly and with such a total lack of malice that I could only laugh. It was like listening to young children in a schoolyard learning to curse without understanding the meaning or the intent of the words.

"Oh, lazy dog, lazy dog," I said, and laughed again.

"You wait. Me wash clothes," she said. "You sleep. Me come bed later."

And with that she was out and gone. I stood alone in the room for some minutes with my mind reeling from the drink and the smoke trying to think. The heat and the light of the new day, like something almost fluid, poured into the room, washing through the thatch roof and the thin bamboo-and-thatch walls. Across the way I could hear Motown's radio playing a tinny, high-pitched Vietnamese song. I was already starting to sweat; my eyelids were heavy and my stomach was full. I stripped off my clothes and threw them down onto the floor and flopped down naked upon the bed, intending to wait for Anh, and immediately fell fast asleep. I awoke sometime later with a start and found, much to my surprise, for it seemed as though I had but closed my eyes for a moment, that the room was now dark and cool, and through the open window to my right I could see the bright pinlights of stars revolving through the cloudless skies of a tropical night, and I could hear the crickets in the fields and the quiet laughter of the villagers in their huts. And pressed up tightly against me, almost desperately it seemed, with her light and lovely naked child body, was Anh, her face faintly illuminated yet still visibly reflecting an innocence and trust even as she slept. I kissed her lightly on the tip of her nose and she opened her eyes.

"Good morning, lazy dog," she said with a smile.

"Good morning," I said. "Good morning."

And soon, just as Doc had predicted, the colonel was up and walking about again with the aid of a stick—an elegant hand-carved affair of blanched wood given to him by one of the village elders. He could be seen almost every morning now with his bush hat— SORRY ABOUT THAT, VIETNAM—and his walking stick making his way slowly along the beach alone. We would often be, as was our habit, winding up an enjoyable evening—morning—of liquor and lies at our little bar when he would come pegging up into view, and upon sighting him, some jolly member of our crew, usually Billy or Motown, would invariably hail this solitary figure, and always the response would be the same: a darting rat-eyed glance, a sneer (no words), and then a quickening of his pace. "Maybe he don't like us," Motown once sagaciously suggested. But in actual point of fact I think that it was not so much a case of mere dislike as a case of almost painful contempt. He ignored us, avoided us, acted as if we did not exist. And if perhaps you happened to be so unfortunate as to encounter him on a one-to-one basis, say, coming around a blind bend in a broken trail somewhere, and offered a mild good-day, he would stop and stare and then begin to curse. The only one of our little group with whom he was known to have had anything even vaguely approaching a conversation was Doc, and that—the conversation—was always in private and always for a very limited period of time.

"The man ain't right," observed Motown one bright morning after the colonel had passed.

"Not by a long shot," said Doc.

"For sure," added Billy.

"What do you guys talk about," I asked Doc, "when you have your little chats?"

"Well, not much really," conceded Doc. "Although he does seem to be greatly concerned that, quote, 'the gooks got the goods,' unquote. He seems to take it almost as a personal insult."

"No doubt," said Strider. "Has he ever said exactly what they were doing with all that crap?"

"Only that they were transporting it," answered Doc. "He dropped a vague and rather mysterious hint a few days ago that it was all top-secret, all highly classified. He spoke of an Operation Highroad."

"Highroad? What's that?" I asked.

"Nothing, I don't think," explained Doc. "I think that he just made it up on the spot to try to sound official."

"No shit," laughed Strider. "Some big-deal secret mission, huh? TV sets and blue jeans. Bullshit on that noise."

"Yeah, well, that's the story for now," said Doc. "I think that's one reason he doesn't like to talk too much. He knows his story doesn't hold water. He's not really a very good liar."

"Well," said Strider, twirling one end of his mustache, "it's pretty damn obvious what those clowns were doing."

There was a moment of silence and a general nodding of heads.

"What?" I asked.

"Well, asshole," said Strider, "figure it out for yourself: a chopper full of that kind of crap in the middle of fucking nowhere."

I thought for a moment. I had long held a private suspicion. I now offered it publicly.

"Black market?"

"Bingo." Strider smiled. "They were probably ripping off some government warehouses or something down in Saigon or Danang or Cam Ranh or somewhere and moving that shit up the coast to unload it on some locals or maybe they were gonna ship it out to Hong Kong or anywhere. Who the fuck knows?"

"Ah," I said, and began nodding my head too.

"Some kinda low shit," sighed Motown.

"Truth, justice, and the American way," Doc suggested.

"Shit," said Motown, not smiling.

"For sure," agreed Billy. "Low shit."

13

It must be something similar, I thought to myself, to what a parachutist feels when he finds himself drifting toward high-tension wires—waiting, waiting, closer and closer, all the pulling and twisting to no avail. Or maybe not; I don't know. Jumping out of airplanes has never been exactly my idea of a good time. But regardless, the day approached and was there. We had been fully forewarned—if forewarned is the right word—that we (according to the desires and the wishes of the colonel, as transmitted to and through Doc) would all be leaving that next morning. We were to be his bodyguards, I suppose. His foot was much better now, he said. That night, before the morning of our supposed departure, we sat and drank at our little bar as usual, although the mood was somewhat more subdued; in truth, it was almost somber. Even the little monkey was less than playful. Dawn arrived and we were still sitting and drinking and looking around the bar from face to face. There was a hint of rain in the air, I remember. Watery, deep blue clouds hung low on the horizon. There was no wind. All was still and quiet.

"A no-show," said Billy hopefully. "Let's call it a miss."

We waited.

Closer, closer, I thought.

And soon, like a bad dream, the colonel, with his bush hat cocked at a rakish slant on his bald head and his walking stick stabbing the sand, came bustling up to where we were sitting.

"Okay," he said with no preliminaries. "Let's go."

"Go where?" asked Strider innocently.

"Back," answered the colonel, his eyes narrowing sharply.

"Have a drink, Colonel, and let's talk," suggested Doc.

"Fuck you and your drink!" snarled the colonel. "Now, off your asses and let's move!"

"A rude sort of a son of a bitch," whispered Doc into my ear.

"Exceedingly," I agreed.

We all sat and stared back quietly at the hot little man sweating in the new morning sun.

"Okay," said the colonel, his hands on his hips, one hand, his right, resting on the butt of his revolver—Strider had given it back to him earlier, a .38-caliber Smith & Wesson, I believe it was, in a leather holster strapped onto his belt. "I said, let's move it, goddammit!"

And this surprised me somewhat—the pistol—because I had thought that they—officers—all carried .45s, at least the ones whom I had seen (noticed) did, but the colonel had a .38, although maybe they could choose their own personal sidearms if they were on secret missions or running hot goods up the coast.

"Move it, goddammit!" the colonel repeated.

"Well, there's the road," said Strider, pointing to a sandy trail winding off into the jungle. "In about five or six days you oughta come to somewhere—or maybe not."

"What?" demanded the colonel, his face turning red, the blood vessels popping out on the side of his head.

"The trail," said Strider calmly. "Hit it."

"I gave you an order, soldier!" screamed the colonel. "Now, move!"

"An order?" Strider laughed. "An order? Here? There are no orders here. You must be kidding or crazy. How do we even know that you're who you say you are? You could be fucking anybody—no insignia, no papers, no nothing. And by the way, Colonel, if you are a colonel, which I doubt, what were you guys doing flying around with all that crap in the chopper?"

"You're asking me? Me?" shrieked the colonel, his body shaking with anger or fear. "What are you doing here? That's the question!" he screamed, pointing at Strider. "What are you doing here?"

"We," said Motown, standing up suddenly behind the colonel, rising up like a volcano out of the sea, "we live here. And now what's we wants to know is what's you doing here?"

The colonel turned around and looked up at Motown towering above him. He swallowed a lump in his throat and licked his lips.

"I don't have to answer that," he said, looking off toward the sea.

"You don't have to," agreed Motown with a friendly smile, placing his big hand on the colonel's small shoulder, "but if you don't, I just might break your fucking neck."

After a moment of further consideration and silence, the colonel cleared his throat and then in an unsteady voice spoke again:

"We were on a highly classified and secret—"

"Shit!" laughed Strider. "Doc was right. You ain't no damn good at lying."

Motown removed his hand from the small man's shoulder and sat down again.

"Colonel, or whatever or whoever you are or think you are," said Strider with a sigh, "we ain't going anyplace with you or with anybody else, now or never. This is our own little piece of somewhere and we like it and we'll stay here until we, not you, not anybody else, but we, we are damn good and ready to leave. You see, it's our lives now."

"Tell it," encouraged Billy.

"We're taking it upon ourselves—our own lives. You understand? We've had it with you and your kind and all of your self-serving little shit wars. No more! Not for us! So you can just hit the trail like I told you before or you can shut the fuck up!"

"Amen," declared Motown.

"And may God have mercy on our souls," added Doc.

The colonel's mouth flopped open but he said not a word.

"And now I'm going to bed and to sleep," announced Strider wearily.

He stood up and headed off toward his hooch. We, as a group, excluding the colonel, all stood and followed.

"Hold it, goddammit!" shouted the colonel from behind us before we had advanced more than three meters. "Just hold it right there!"

We turned, and there in front of us was the colonel with his .38 pointed in our direction. A cold chill coursed down my spine. I, being the last to join the group returning to our bungalows, was now the one closest to the colonel and the pointed pistol. Strider, the leader of our movement, was at the back of the pack.

"You aren't going anywhere but to hell in a hurry!" threatened the colonel. "None of you!"

Behind me I could hear Strider starting to curse. He pushed briskly past me, pushing me in fact to one side—out of his way and also out of the way of the pistol—and stalked up to where the colonel stood.

"Fuck you!" said Strider, drilling his index finger into the colonel's chest. He stood at least a head and a half taller than the colonel. "I'm tired and I'm going to sleep! Understand? No more shit from you! Either get it together or get the hell gone!"

Strider stared down at the colonel silently for a moment with the .38 leveled at his stomach, then turned and continued on toward his hooch. The others followed.

But I, for reasons unknown to me even now, stood yet for a moment longer, and there I found myself watching in frozen and speechless horror as the colonel slowly raised his revolver to shoulder height—I couldn't believe that he'd do it—and aimed it carefully at Strider's back—I couldn't believe that anybody would do it—and pulled the trigger.

Click!

The dull snap tore through my brain louder than the loudest scream.

Strider and the others stopped and spun around. The colonel's eyes darted wildly from the pistol to Strider and back to the pistol again in a confused panic. He pulled the trigger half a dozen more times as he stumbled backward, reeling like a drunk.

Click! Click! Click! Click! Click! Click!

"Okay!" declared Strider. "That does it!"

He pushed his way up to the colonel again, and with a downward sweep of his hand, snatched the clicking revolver out of the colonel's grip. He then grabbed the colonel by the shoulder with his free hand and brought his other hand, the one now holding the revolver, up and across the colonel's face. The colonel spun around once and landed in the sand in a bewildered heap. Strider broke open the pistol and flung it down at the colonel. (Doc, as it was later explained to me, had taken the liberty of removing the colonel's bullets from his pistol the night before as he slept, and replacing them with some sand-filled duds of his own manufacture.)

"Okay!" shouted Strider, his face flushed with anger. "You wanta leave, huh? Huh? Look at me, you son of a bitch! All right then, get the hell outta here 'fore I kill you myself, you wormy bastard!"

The colonel, as if in a dream, sat on the ground examining the pistol.

Strider kicked him.

"Awright, awright," he said, pulling himself up with the aid of his stick. "Awright." He had lost and he knew it. He reached out for his bush hat, which had been knocked off his head by the blow and now lay at Strider's feet.

"Sorry about that, Colonel," said Strider as he pinned the colonel's hand to the ground with his foot. "Leave it."

"But the sun! Good God, man," whined the colonel, looking up, his hand still trapped beneath Strider's foot. "I'll need it! The sun!"

"Yes," agreed Strider thoughtfully. He reached down and picked it up. "But I'll keep it," he said, placing the hat on his own head.

"Damn you!" cried the colonel, straightening himself up and leaning heavily on his stick. "Damn you all! I'll be back! You'll see! Mark my words!"

Billy, who like the rest of us was now standing next to Strider, took a step forward and kicked the walking stick out from under the colonel's hand, sending him reeling once again to the ground.

"And I'll take this," declared Billy, reaching down for the walking stick. "Real fancy. I like it," he said, turning it over in his hands. "You know, pop, for such an old cat you sure got a helluva lot of hate in you. You oughta cool out."

"My stick!" shrieked the colonel, crawling on his knees toward Billy. "My stick! Gimme back my goddamn stick!"

Billy stopped the colonel's advance with a sandal on the colonel's shoulder. "Stick it up your ass, old man," he said, and then he flipped the colonel over on his back like a turtle.

We all stood still, watching silently as the cursing little man struggled painfully up to his feet again, bracing himself this time against the edge of the bar.

193

Several of the villagers who had been attracted by the commotion were now also standing around and watching.

"Come here! You! Come here!" shouted the colonel, motioning wildly to one of the young village boys. "Come here and help me, you son of a bitch! Help me!"

The boy, handsome with large girlish eyes, looked at the colonel for a moment, then at Strider, then at his friends; he shrugged his shoulders and then they, the villagers, all walked away together, talking.

"White-man shit," observed Motown. "You tell 'em, little ace."

The colonel stood there braced against the bar, watching them walk away. "Oh, you'll die! You'll all die!" raged the colonel. "All of you!" Then he turned and began limping away. "Ali! Die! Die!"

"Let's kill him," suggested Billy calmly. "Let's do him now."

"No," said Strider, turning back again toward his hooch. "There's already been too much of that."

"But he'll come back," protested Motown. "You heard him."

"If he can. If he doesn't die first," agreed Strider; his eyes, his entire face, looked incredibly tired.

"You'll die! You'll all die! All of you!" the colonel continued to scream as he retreated farther down the trail. "All! Die!"

"Let me kill him, Strider," begged Billy. "Come on. Let me kill him."

"No," said Strider firmly. He turned around and looked at the man hobbling out of sight, still screaming. "What'll happen, will happen. We'll leave it at that. Fate. He's still one of us, regardless. An American. At least we haven't gone that far yet."

"You're wrong," said Doc, shaking his head sadly. "You're dead wrong. We've gone further than that, further than simple murder. And besides, he's nothing like us. He's no countryman. He's worse, infinitely worse."

"Maybe," said Strider, resuming his trek homeward. "Maybe you're right."

And he was.

14

With the colonel gone now from our sight, his presence removed from the present, we, with the exception of Strider, immediately began to make some quite pleasant rationalizations about the colonel's situation and to discount his long-term chances for survival.

"Hey, man, like he's an old cat with a fucked foot, right?"

"He's got no water."

"Only one canteen."

"And no food."

"None."

"And he's got no hat."

"Maybe his brain'll boil."

"Maybe he'll get wasted by some gooks."

"Maybe he'll get his ass eaten up by a tiger."

"A tiger?"

"Maybe."

"Well, who'd believe him anyway, even if he did make it back?"

"They'd think he had cracked."

"Yeah."

"I mean, five guys in a little ville drinking and getting stoned and screwing all night and all day."

"Living like kings."

"Like fucking kings!"

"Come on, who'd believe it?"

"I wouldn't."

"I still don't."

So we soon settled once again back into our effortless routine of careless debauchery and easy living and forgot all about the colonel and his threats of reprisal. We thought that we were safe, beyond the touch of man or God, and that we, logically, could and would live forever. And why not? We were young and strong and stupid. It was some scant two weeks later, however, that we learned how fraught with error this assumption was, and how vulnerable both externally and internally, both from within and from without, we actually were.

It was night, a strangely soundless night. Deviating from our usual custom of staying up all night (it was cooler) drinking and smoking and talking and then sleeping away most of the day, our little bar had thinned out early, and sometime shortly after midnight we were all in our own bungalows asleep. I know this to be fact because afterward I polled the members of our tribe and found that they, like myself, were all in like postures of peaceful repose.

So I was asleep. I recall vividly that I was dreaming a weird sort of dream in which I found myself on an uncomfortable and antiquated train in the company of goats and chickens and sheep and a score or so of foul-smelling, dark-skinned, Spanish-speaking peasants in colorful and impractical dress traveling backward through vanishing, forward-fleeing mountain terrain at an excruciatingly slow rate of speed, and each time this ever-retreating train backed itself to a stop I tried to disembark, but was halted by a conductor with an exaggerated mustache who (the cockroach!) would demand a large sum of local currency from me (I had only dollars) before I could exit, and in the dream I remember we were stopped (it was night) at some lost and hopelessly forgotten dream depot and were deep (the cockroach and I—"No dollars!") in the midst of laborious negotiations for my release (I thought that I almost had him) when suddenly shooting erupted. I fell immediately out of my dream, out of my dream night, out of my bed, my real bed, and into a real night ripped with gunfire, explosions, and screams.

"Holy shit!" I screamed to myself, still half-dazed. "Is this real or what?" And then seeing Anh, also screaming, standing naked in the middle of the room as bullets tore through the fragile walls of the hooch and swarmed madly around and about her head, I concluded that the situation was most horribly and definitely real. I made a flying tackle at Anh, knocked her to the floor, and somehow managed to get her stashed under the bed. She was still screaming. This is it, I thought; this is real! I made my way on hands and knees across the room to where I thought my rifle and gear had been stowed. Anh had put it somewhere to get it out from underfoot. Where exactly, I knew not; in fact, I had not a clue. Rifles and things of that sort had ceased for some two months now to be a part of my life. My rifle was not where I had thought, or hoped, it would be. I crawled back across the room to the bed and shouted underneath it, imploring Anh in God's name to shut up and tell me what she had done with my rifle. It was, however, utterly hopeless; she

198

was quite beyond herself with fright, still screaming. I was panicking myself. No weapon; bullets everywhere. Jesus! What's a poor boy to do? I set off again around the room, still on hands and knees, still with bullets ripping through the thin bamboo-and-thatch walls. I went down one wall and then across another. Finally in a wild flash of orange light as the hooch next to mine (Motown's) burst into flames, I caught sight of my rifle and helmet and pack squirreled away under a small rickety table in the corner opposite me. I scurried up to my gear, slapped a clip into my M-16, spun my helmet onto my head, and kicked open the door (which I later realized was an act of totally unnecessary and demented adrenal excitement, as the door could have been opened quite easily with a simple twist of the latch), and then saw that I was as naked as the day that I was born. I threw myself back down onto the floor, crawled over to where I had left my pants and, lying on the floor, on my back, somehow was able to squirm into them. I then picked myself up, made a mad dash for the open door, and went flying out of the door, into the dark and off the porch, and nearly broke my young fool neck.

There was shouting and shooting and screaming and fire everywhere. I didn't know what to do, which way to turn. Should I run or stay, shoot or hide? Were the shadows real or not, friend or foe? People were darting about helter-skelter, dogs were howling, babies were crying. I was lost and twitching. Suddenly Anh, naked, her body wet with sweat, glistening in the flaming night, came hurtling out of the hooch and landed next to me. She was crying and screaming at me in urgent Vietnamese. I couldn't understand a word that she was saying, but her meaning was clear enough: Run! Bolt! She began pulling at my arm, pulling me away toward the tree line, where I could see the frantic faces of the villagers silhouetted against the darting flames from the burning bungalows. They were running in and out of the undergrowth, beckoning to me and then shrinking away. And I was almost ready to go with her, to allow myself to be pulled away, when, up ahead, in the general direction of Strider's Bar, there came a lusty and powerful chorus of voices cursing beautifully in English. I disengaged Anh's arm, pointed her off toward the jungle, shouted one word—"Go"—and away she went. I then gathered up my courage and picked up my scattered equipment and plunged off in the direction of the beautiful voices.

I circled around the back way, as there was gunfire coming from the right and from the bar directly in front of me. I threw myself over a low barricade erected to the seaward and crouched down behind one of the palm stumps that heretofore we had been using as a barstool. I was panting and sweating. Coming up as I did from the beach, I could see why the others had chosen this particular spot to make their stand: from this vantage point, positioned as we now were with our backs to the sea and our flanks protected more or less by an estuary on one side and a thick tangle of undergrowth on the other, there was only one effective avenue of mass attack and that was straight on across a sandy clearing, and that was the way that they were coming now.

And coming now: firing, screaming; stalking, silent; coming; the black shadows against the orange flames changing eerily into form and substance; coming; two figures racing along the edge of the clearing, suddenly, as if caught around the neck by a low-slung invisible clothesline, they, in mid-stride, in unison, snap back; coming; voices everywhere; voices all the more horrible because you know not what is being said; voices shrieking in your ear, in your brain, in your very soul; voices; a figure weaving an erratic course directly toward me; no weapon that I can see; simply running, running straight for me; I can see his eyes and teeth—white, mad, laughing, insane; I'm shooting; I can feel the kick; but he's still coming; closer still; finally fifteen, ten, five meters away—his features choked with hatred; his features so clear that I could probably still sketch a passable portrait of him even today; coming; finally someone (I never learned who) nails him; he drops; I take a deep breath and think: All right, all right now; and then he explodes; a severed hand lands on my back with a reassuring pat and then slides off into the wet sand (he was obviously carrying a satchel charge of some type, I cleverly reasoned to myself sometime later); coming; more; one—his head half blown away yet continuing to crawl; coming; and on and on and on, howling, crashing, flashing, thundering; a shadow here, a burst of rifle fire there; "Over there! To the left! To the left!" "Fuck 'em up! Fuck them fuckers up!" "Get some! Who-oo-ee!" "If I only get out of this one, if I only—"; and then suddenly, crazily, no more; it's over and finished, and all that I can hear through the constant buzzing in my ears are the occasional delayed pops from the cartridges going off in the fires and Motown's idiot radio droning on about love, love, love.

"Jesus!" I cried, trying to still my heart and keep my churning stomach out of my throat. "Holy Jesus!"

"Motherfucker!" said Motown, placing a hand on top of his head and pressing down.

"Everybody okay?" asked Strider, looking around. He was breathing heavily. His eyes were wild and bluer than I had ever seen them.

"Seems so," said Doc after a quick visual inventory.

"Good," said Strider. "Real good."

"I know I got two of 'em, for sure," announced Billy excitedly. "Maybe a possible four. Shit, man, did you guys see that one cat coming up the back side there? Gut-shot! Beautiful!"

"Jesus," I moaned.

"How the fuck could you tell what you hit?" asked Doc. "It's so damn dark out here unless—"

"Oh, I got 'em, all right," insisted Billy. "Believe me. Believe me. I got 'em, dead. Two, possibly four."

"Anybody got a cigarette?" asked Doc, changing the subject.

"Here." Strider tossed a pack into his lap.

All eyes were fixed with fascinated horror, looking out at the night; we were back-to-back; our muscles were taut; our ears were pricked; the shooting might have stopped but that didn't necessarily mean that the dying was done.

"Christ, I'm sweating like a nigger," lamented Motown, his huge body shining, dripping with sweat.

"You're what?" asked Doc.

"Fuck you, Doc," said Motown, not bothering to look around.

There was a sudden burst of static light as another one of the bungalows caught fire.

"There goes your hooch, Doc," said Strider, pointing.

"Well, shit," sighed Doc. "It's been a perfect night—morning."

"Gonna get me some ears," announced Billy.

"Jesus," I moaned again.

"Bam! Bam!" shouted Billy suddenly, waving his rifle in the air. "Bam! God, that was sweet! God, how I love it!"

"Take it easy, Billy," cautioned Strider.

"Sure, Strider, sure," said Billy, smiling, his eyes popping, his body shaking. "A possible four. I am sure of it."

The air was bitter with smoke swelling up from the burning bungalows. The bar lay in shambles—bullet holes, splintered bamboo, and broken bottles. Overhead, still noosed by a cord to his perch pole, dangled the little black monkey that we had never gotten around to naming. He shouldn't have been there; the bar boy should've taken him home; but that didn't matter now. He had a small crimson spot in the center of his furry chest. As I looked at him swaying there in the breeze, my mind switched back to church bells and Sunday mornings and the pigeons in the churchyard that I used to shoot with my air rifle when I was a kid. Sunday mornings were the only times when it was safe, when I knew for certain that the preacher would be busy and wouldn't be able to catch me. It was always fascinating to me the way they—the pigeons—looked so peaceful, like they were only sleeping, catching up on a little lost time. You almost half-suspected that if you turned your back and walked away, they'd get up and fly off. But they never did.

"Ah, I spoke too soon," said Doc, pointing up at

the swinging monkey. "Looks like that little fellow didn't make it."

"Well, that's life," said Strider, sweeping a sweat-plastered strand of black hair off his forehead.

What? I thought to myself, what did he say? Life? I wanted to scream, but I only groaned.

Billy reached up with a long evil-looking knife that he always carried and hacked the cord. The little monkey fell with an audible plop. No one said anything for some few moments.

"You know, it's weird," declared Doc finally, "but I'm always surprised when I see these dead animals out here. I mean like somehow you'd think that maybe all this madness should be confined to our own corrupt species. But then, it never is. There's always a spill-over."

"Well, who the fuck gives a fuck?" asked Billy with a little too much hostility.

"Right," sighed Doc. "A dead monkey's just a dead monkey."

"You got it, ace," affirmed Billy, brandishing his long-bladed knife. "And now I'm going out and check out some of them dead gooks."

"And a dead gook's just a dead gook?" asked Doc.

" 'Cept when he's still a live gook," answered Motown. "Best wait till dawn, Billy."

"Don't you worry." Billy smiled maliciously. "This is one white boy that knows how to take care of his own self."

"Yeah?" asked Motown, hitching up one eyebrow.

"Believe it!" snapped Billy.

"Well then, get on wit' your bad self," said Motown.

"Thanks," snarled Billy, "but I don't need no permission from nobody to do nothing."

"Yeah?" asked Motown again, hitching up both eyebrows this time.

"Yeah. I got all the permission I need right here," retorted Billy, slapping his rifle. His hard little eyes fixed themselves on Motown.

"Right, man," said Motown slowly, glaring back at Billy. "Right."

And with that exchange Billy slithered out across the sand and soon disappeared into the undergrowth.

Motown began flipping his safety on and off and muttering to himself. Strider slumped down into the sand and lit a crumpled joint. Doc looked across at me with his sad and thoughtful eyes and shook his head.

"It's all falling apart," he said; his voice registered a note of resignation and disgust. "I don't know why we even bothered. A dream, surely. Doomed and damned from the start, from before the start. It was unrealistic. A hopeless situation. Escape? Impossible! If escape was what it was—was what it was meant to be. I don't know. Hopelessly caught up in a hopeless situation. Only a hopeless situation of our own making this time. Now, that's funny, really funny! Funny like hell and blind babies. Damned if we do, double damned if we don't. Pitched headlong and screaming into the black void of irretrievable disaster. I mean, why try? Why bother? Tell me! You look fairly intelligent. Why try? Tell me! Why?"

"Huh?" I answered, jerking my head around. I didn't know what he was going on about, and I was still more than half-shattered from the firefight. I would've jumped and screamed and fired at the slightest noise or movement. I was keyed up and nervous as a pregnant cat.

"You think I'm whacked out, do you?" demanded Doc.

"Huh? No, it's just that I—"

"Well, I'm not," said Doc. "Or maybe I am. But then, being crazy makes it easier to cope, and speaking of coping, since you're not doing it too especially well—you want some of these?" He held out a handful of red capsules.

"Yeah, thanks," I said, and popped a couple into my mouth. I had trouble swallowing them. My mouth was dry. But I finally managed to get them down.

Doc took four or five pills himself and then returned the rest to his medical pouch.

"These sad charades," he began again. "This desperate dance. It should've been plain to anybody with half a brain that you just can't say: All right, that's it, see you later. Things just don't work that way. And now here we are trapped by our own cleverness. What a mammoth motherfucking joke! Falling apart and tumbling down upon our own stunned little heads. It makes me want to scream with laughter. Jesus Christ, I just don't know. What's the answer? What's the question?"

"Well, don't ask me," I said. "I'm just a tourist here."

"Aren't we all," agreed Doc, looking off sadly. "Aren't we all."

Dawn broke blue over the smoldering village. The trees and remaining structures began to take on depth and definition. The destruction was now plainly and painfully visible. Fully half of the bungalows had been damaged or destroyed. Broken pottery and pieces of crude furniture were scattered about. A small grass fire burned off to one side. In the clearing directly in front of us lay a dozen or so bodies. The flies had already found them and were beginning to feast. Soon the people—first in ones and twos and then in larger groups—began cautiously filtering out of the jungle. And the people, strangely, strangely to me anyway, didn't weep or howl or fall prostrate upon the earth cursing and bemoaning God or the devil or fate or whatever when they sighted the wreckage and ruin that had, only short hours before, been their homes: they simply, quietly, began picking up what was left and still salvageable.

I'll never understand these people, I thought to myself. Never. No way. Not if I live to be a hundred. They're a total mystery and a contradiction.

Suddenly a small girl with long hair flying and oversize sandals flopping darted out from the tree line. I offered up a quick silent prayer: thanks to the pills that Doc had given me, I didn't freak and fire at the child. She charged up to where we were sitting and began screaming, "*Bac si! Bac si!*" (This I later learned meant doctor in Vietnamese.) Doc gathered the little girl up in his arms, brushed the hair out of her eyes, and listened patiently as she cried and whimpered and pointed back toward the tree line.

"She says that her mother and some other folks have been hit," explained Doc wearily. He stood up, staggered a bit, and then steadied himself against the small child's shoulder. "I guess I'd better go see if there's anything that I can do, although I doubt it."

The little girl reached up and took hold of Doc's hand. He looked down at her for a moment and then forced a weak smile. Together they turned and moved away toward the jungle.

"Hold up there, Doc," called out Motown. "I'll go with you."

"Okay," sighed Doc. "You can hold 'em down while I mop their brow and tell 'em everything's gonna be all right."

Then they were gone, the three of them melting away, dissolving into the dense undergrowth to the accompanying squawk of Motown's radio.

"Well, I guess it's just you and me now, huh?" I said, looking around.

Strider lifted his head slightly, opened one eye halfway, and gave me a look like the inescapable truth of that sagacious observation was all too painful.

"Yeah, I guess that's right, all right," I said, and then thought: Christ, I'm answering my own fool questions; I must be flipping. But I needed to talk, to hear words, any words.

"Fuck, they just kept coming," I began; it didn't matter—I needed words. "I couldn't believe it. Just coming and coming and coming. I thought it was all over. I mean really over, the last roundup, gone, good-fuckin'-bye. I must've emptied almost a full clip at that one smiling sucker and yet he just kept on coming, coming, and smiling. Incredible! And then the motherfucker goes and blows up on me! Holy Christ! I was scared. I was so scared I almost shit myself. Right there. It was like nothing I could do could stop him. He just kept coming. I was so damn scared . . . Got any water? Jesus, I need some water.

My throat feels like I've been gargling sand. I almost lost—"

"Hold on there, sport. Just hold on," said Strider, raising himself up onto one elbow. "Now, just settle down. Why don't you check around back there behind what's left of the bar for a few beers. I could use one myself. A few of 'em might've survived. Sure as hell nothing much else did. What a mess! What a fucking waste of good liquor!"

I scavenged around in the debris as I had been instructed and soon came up with a warm six-pack. (I was sincerely glad that someone else was taking charge; it took the pressure off; it gave me a feeling of, if not actual security, then at least of sharing—which to me, at that particular moment, was very important.) Two of the cans had taken direct hits, but the rest were still intact. I took one and passed the others over to Strider.

"Jesus," I began again; I just couldn't stop myself, "how did they ever find us? Do you think they were looking for us or what?"—it's sharing; it's all in the sharing—"Did they know that we were here or did they just stumble on us? Huh? What? I mean, like what the hell's going on? I mean, like . . . okay, what're we . . . what's our . . . is there some kinda . . . I mean, oh Jesus, Jesus, Jesus!"

"Now, dammit, just calm down," said Strider, straightening himself up a bit more. "You ask a mighty damn lot of questions. Who do you think I am, the fucking answer man? You're starting to rattle on like Doc there. Get a hold of yourself. Maintenance, that's the key. One must maintain. Always. Okay? Now, just take yourself a deep breath, a big swig, and a hit off this." He held out another crumpled joint. "Calm.

Nice and slow, okay? Now, just what is it that you're trying to say?"

I took a deep breath, a long pull on the beer, and a couple of hits off the joint.

"Well," I said, "I don't really know exactly. I mean I'm still trying to pin it down. But mostly, I guess it boils down to a search, a search for a reason, any reason, some hopefully logical explanation, an explanation for all this. This! This you and me and Doc and Billy and Motown, this jungle and ocean, this village and these people, this shooting and killing, this way we're living. Why? Why does it happen? Does it have to happen? Why are we here, right here, now, at this particular place at this particular moment? And maybe, since these questions are all probably timelessly absurd and unanswerable—here I am again trying to tie things up in a neat little package with a big bright bow, searching for logic and reason where nothing is logical or reasonable. Shit! Well, all right then, does it matter? That's what I wanta know. Does any of this matter one goddamn bit?"

"Not to me, it doesn't," said Strider calmly.

Too calmly. I didn't like the way that he had said that. I thought that he might be drifting away. I needed those words, that sense of we and us. His eyes held a faraway look now as he stared out at the ocean. What the hell was he looking at with those wounded and wasted eyes? Those eyes so filled with pain. Or, on second thought, was it pain that I saw hovering there so close to the surface? Was it pain or something else?

"Then why are you here, if it doesn't matter?" I asked after a moment of watching. I needed to keep him talking—for my sake, not his.

"Because now I'm a part of it and it's a part of me," he said, turning toward me. (And it wasn't pain, there in those eyes; it was something else entirely.)

"What d'you mean?" I asked; I had to keep him going.

"Well, it's natural, this life, for me, now, anyway," he said. "I could no more return now to the World than I could fly. Jesus! A wife, kids, a car, a job, a house, and crabgrass. It's not possible. It's fucking frightening in fact! But then again, I don't really belong here either. But still I feel more at home, at peace, at peace with myself, here. Now, there's a contradiction for you, feeling at home and at peace here when in actual fact I'm about as far from peace and home as I can get."

"So what'll you do then?" I asked.

"I'll wait," he said. "I'll bide my time and I'll wait. It's coming. I can feel it. It will solve everything. No think, remember? There's no escape. Hell, I'm not even sure I'd try to escape it even if I thought I could."

"It?" I asked. "It?" The beer and the joint and the pills were beginning to kick in, and were making me somewhat more bold in my conversation. "Spell it?" I said.

"It," he explained, "the finish, peace, sleep, surrender."

"No riddles or rhymes!" I cried. "Call it by its real name! Death! Death! That's what you're talking about! That's what you're calmly waiting for like some . . . some . . . like some I-don't-know-what!"

"Yes," he said. "Death."

"And so then you actively seek death?" I persisted.

"I once— "

"Oh, no," he interrupted. "Not really. I simply do not step aside for it. But if it comes—well then, all right, it comes. It doesn't matter. Think of all the great men—no, think closer, think of all the people, the friends, who have seen so little, who have done so little with their lives, who have not even come this far yet, and now never will. At least I've lived. And that's something too. I'd trade nine more months out here in the bush for ninety years back there, back there in so-called civilization, any day. Shit! I've seen it! I've tasted it! I've felt it! Here I have power! Here I'm in control! Me! To go back now to a mundane existence of please-and-thank-you would be unthinkable. It would be a slap in the face to all that I've learned and to all those who have come before. So buy me a drink and I'll lend you a cigarette and we'll discuss the advantages of fatalism."

But talk, discuss, we didn't; we simply sat in the sand and watched in silence together the new day boiling hot out of the sea: the sun rays angling in from across the water (Strider reached up and slipped his shades off his head and down over his eyes; the son of a bitch carried them with him all the damn time; they were probably the first thing that he had reached for when the shooting started); the birds, gulls, arching overhead, diving for fish; a few children, too young, too innocent, to understand or appreciate the near-escape that they had just had, playing near the water's edge; a crab, a kid with a rock; the breeze shifting, blowing in cool now across the water, drying the beads of sweat accumulating on my brow; Anh, dressed now, bringing us two plates of rice and a couple of small dried fish and a terrified smile; the palms swaying restlessly; a distant rumble of thunder (it would later rain); another joint; the rocks jutting out of the water, breaking the waves, sending spray up scattering wildly; a grenade that didn't explode, not five feet away ("Look," he said, and laughed); an old man with one blind eye coming down, talking with Strider quietly, shaking his head; a white cat; a dog with a flea; a coconut rolling in the surf.

"You know, sometimes it's almost enough to make you believe in God," said Strider, smiling slightly, his eyes fixed on the horizon.

"Almost," I agreed.

And it was—almost: the peace, the beauty, the calm, the trees, the ocean, the breeze, the crab, the kid with the rock, the repetition, the sameness, sunrise, sunset, over and over, forever and ever, amen.

"And you, why are you here?" asked Strider after a moment of further contemplation.

"Here?" I asked, pointing to the sand.

"Here," he explained with a sweeping gesture. "Nam. In the first place."

"Well, I once thought that I knew," I said, drawing small intersecting circles in the sand with a splintered piece of bamboo. "I joined. I enlisted. I once thought that it was because I wanted to die, that I needed to die, and that this would be an easy place to do it. But now, now that I've seen so much, so much of death as well as so much of life—well, now I don't know anymore. I'm not sure. I'm not sure of anything anymore. I only know for a fact that the sun's rising and the breeze feels cool and I'm starting to get really looped."

"You know, asshole," laughed Strider with a slap across my back, "there just might be hope for you yet. Maybe."

"But not for you?" I asked.

"No," he said, shaking his head. "I'm past that. And I accept it. And it makes me feel calm."

"Sort of like a sinner who's confessed his sins?" I asked.

"Sort of," he agreed.

He opened up the other two beers and passed one of them over to me.

"To your health," he toasted, raising his beer.

"And yours," I countered. "And may you have those nine more months."

"Yeah," he said. "I'd like that."

Behind us we could hear men and women shouting to one another and hammers banging away. Everyone was on the move. There was no time for sitting in the shade and chewing betel nuts now. They needed to get on with it, get their bungalows back together, get their lives back on line: food, family, shelter—an old man double-timing by with a still smoking plank; a child trailing a rusty saw through the sand; a pretty young girl lugging up two pails of water from the sea.

"Well, shit," said Strider, rising and stretching, "I guess maybe we oughta go see if there's anything that we can do to help 'em. God knows they're helpless enough."

"Okay," I agreed, rising too, "but they don't seem all that helpless to me."

"Oh, they work, all right, and sometimes damn hard too," he conceded, "but there's simply no organization. It's all thrust and scatter, like a flock of sparrows."

"But they still get it done, don't they?" I asked.

"Absolutely," said Strider. "Eventually. In time. They've been getting it done long before we got here and they'll probably still be getting it done long after we're gone. But sometimes they just need a little guidance and sometimes they need a swift kick in the ass. But once you can get them going, get them all moving in more or less the same direction—well hell, then, that's almost half the battle. It makes it easier, easier for everybody—them as well as us."

"Well, okay," I said, "let's get it then."

Strider stopped and looked off into the jungle. He appeared apprehensive.

"What?" I asked.

"I was just wondering where Billy got off to," he answered, glancing down at his watch.

"Well, he said that he was going—"

"I know what he said," said Strider grimly, "and I also know Billy."

"Yeah?" I asked.

"Yeah," he said.

And it was then that we first heard her scream.

15

Two days later the bar and the bungalows had been rebuilt and the bodies had been carted away, and she was still screaming.

The story, as best it could be pieced together from the limited amount of information that Doc and Strider had been able to obtain from Billy and "his girl" between their "sessions," was this: during Billy's arduous search for suitable ears and other detachable body parts, he had sighted off in the dawning distance a young girl wearing a black pajama getup, trying frantically and none too successfully to make an escape through the thick and tangled undergrowth of the jungle. Billy had at first raised his rifle, intending (using Billy's own words here) "to stitch the little bitch from her butthole to her brain." Then, reconsidering, he had thought that maybe he'd like to have a "live one." "Ain't never had me a live one before," he said. So Billy circled around in front of the girl—he knew the surrounding jungle; he knew the trails and shortcuts—and waited. It wasn't long. Soon the girl—her clothes torn, her face smeared with dirt and sweat and tears, panting "like a dog"—came popping out of a snarl of vines and roots, and Billy collared her. "Easy as shitting in the sand," Billy explained. He then ripped off her remaining rags, threw her down on the dew-wet jungle floor, and proceeded to rape her with all the twisted fury and laughing rage that were so readily at his disposal. "You should've heard her scream," he exclaimed. "We did," we assured him.

The girl was about fifteen or so. She claimed to be a VC nurse. She had no medical training or knowledge of medical procedure (Doc quizzed her), but she had no rifle either. She had no idea where she was or what she was supposed to have been doing. Someone had said come and she had followed. She knew nothing. She was hardly what could be called a diehard revolutionary. She hadn't been fighting for freedom; she hadn't been trying to throw off the heavy and uncompromising yoke of foreign imperialism and exploitation (although she did know some of the jargon). She had only wanted food; she had been hungry and alone. Her family had all recently been killed in a bombing raid ("fire rain," she called it) somewhere to the north, and so she had joined up with a roving guerrilla band that was operating in our area. She had slept and she had eaten when and where she could, and had thought no more about it. It had been a job, not a career. She did, nevertheless, express a simmering disgust for the ugly, stinking, round-eyed barbarians who ate little babies for breakfast and slept with the dogs at night—us. She was, Doc had benevolently concluded, not really very dangerous, just a bit out of touch with the realities of the situation. "And who ain't?" Doc had asked.

Billy, however, was another case altogether. Doc suspected that he was not only dangerous but also slipping quite rapidly into a boiling state of fantasy and madness. Billy claimed that the girl belonged to him (he had found her, captured her, "tamed" her— "finders keepers," he had said, and smiled) and now he could do with her as he liked. And what he liked was most severely unpleasant for the scared and hungry young girl who had only wanted something to eat.

"Damn, but she's sure got one powerful set of lungs," observed Doc, reaching for another whiskey and rainwater.

It was midday and hot. Strider and Doc and Motown and I were sitting around the reconstructed and resupplied bar discussing Billy and "his girl." (A small portion of the liquor that we had liberated from the downed helicopter had been wisely held in reserve and buried beneath Strider's bungalow, which fortunately had not gone up in flames during the attack. The cache had now been dug up and the bottles placed on the shelf—we only had one shelf behind the bar.)

"All that fucking screaming's driving me fucking nuts," lamented Motown. "What the hell's he doing to that girl anyway?"

"He says he's interrogating her," answered Doc.

"Interrogating, my ass!" shouted Motown, slamming his huge fist into the bar, sending the glasses and bottles into spastic convulsions. "Hell, he can't speak ten fucking words of Vietnamese. How's he gonna know if she tells him anything?"

"Well, I don't think that really concerns Billy very much," explained Doc. "And besides, she couldn't tell him anything even if she wanted to, even if he could understand. She's a total void as far as information goes. She doesn't even know where she is. Talk about one lost little girl. Jesus!"

"Well, I don't give a shit whether she's lost or not. If she don't stop that fucking screaming I'm gonna stop it for her," said Motown. "It's driving me crazy. All that goddamn screaming, night and day. I can't take it anymore. Oh Christ, there she goes again!"

A scream of glass-breaking, tire-screeching intensity shot out from Billy's bungalow and sped across the village. All activities stopped for a moment, acknowledging the scream, and then continued.

"For fuck's sake," moaned Doc, shaking his head.

"Come on, Strider, do something," pleaded Motown, his face contorted into a grimace of near-physical pain. "I can't take this."

"Doc and I tried yesterday," said Strider, lighting a joint. "We tried to reason with him. But it was useless. He wouldn't listen. He just started laughing."

"I think he's lost it," interjected Doc. "Totally and finally."

"When we tried to take her away," Strider continued, "Billy pulled his rifle and threatened to blow us away if we touched her. And I think he would've done it too, without thinking twice. Maybe he'll just get tired of her or something."

"Okay," sighed Motown, taking a deep breath and shoving himself away from the bar. "Okay. I guess that just leaves me then. I ain't scared of the little psycho motherfucker."

"Now, wait a minute, Mo," said Strider, reaching out and taking hold of Motown's right arm. "You're going off half-cocked."

"Strider, I tell you true," confessed Motown sadly,

"that fucking screaming's getting to me. I've had it. I ain't slept no more'n a couple of hours since she's been here. Now, I can take a lot of shit and you know it, but I can't take that. Fuck, this morning I went down to the far end of the beach, down there, to try to get some relief, to try to get away, and I could still hear her, still hear her screaming her ass off all the way down there. Something's gotta be done. Now! No maybe!"

"All right," agreed Strider, his hand now on Motown's shoulder, forcing him back down. "But wait. Okay? I know your style—or your lack of style. You're about as subtle as a sledgehammer. So just hang tough for a bit and we'll send asshole here in and see if he can do anything with Billy."

"Me?" I shrieked, spilling my drink. "No way! You just said that he pulled on you and Doc! He's lost it, right? He won't listen to me! Hell, he doesn't even like me!"

"Well, none of that really matters," Strider assured me. "You're the man for the job. We can't let this situation get any further out of hand. The villagers are starting to wonder what Mr. Billy's up to, and besides, you can see for yourself that it's giving Motown a headache, so go."

"Oh shit!" I cried. "I can't . . . I don't . . . I mean, I won't!"

"Listen, asshole, quit fucking around and go see what you can do," ordered Strider, pulling me up off my coconut stump. "And take your rifle too. You might need it."

"But what can I do?" I asked, pleading. "I mean like so he's got a girl—a gook—and so she's screaming

220

a little bit. Big deal! It doesn't concern me. I can live with it. Just turn up your damn radio, Motown. I can't reason with a crazy man! He might do anything! He's nuts! He might shoot me! He might—"

"Well," said Strider with a friendly smile and a fatherly pat, "if he don't, I will. Now, move, dammit!"

"Oh shit," I moaned, and walked off toward my bungalow to pick up my rifle.

The walk from the bar to my bungalow and then over to Billy's was one of the longest of my life. Each step called for actual physical effort. It wasn't Billy that I feared so much; it was the madness, the insanity.

I stopped outside his doorway, flicked off the safety, and listened. The screaming had subsided now into a series of low and jerky moans. I knocked on the side of the hooch.

"Door's open," called out Billy. "Come on in."

I entered. The room was dark and musty. There were straw mats covering the window openings. It took some time for my eyes to accustom themselves to the lighting. Finally they did and what I saw confirmed the worst of my fears.

The girl, naked, her body thin, wet with sweat, appeared before me in a frozen attitude of leaping, of taking flight—like some position of strained urgency that might be seen in a modern ballet. She was standing on the tips of her toes with her arms pinned up high behind her back, thrusting out her breasts; her stomach was pressed up against a small wooden table, lending her some limited support; her upper body, heaving, was arched over the table; her head drooped off to one side; her long black hair, falling forward, covered her face. She was held in check in this position by lengths of rope running up to and through the exposed rafter beams in the ceiling. Behind her stood Billy. He had on his sandals and a shirt but no pants. He was laughing, his head thrown back, and pumping away at her from behind while simultaneously yanking on the loose ends of two ropes dangling before him. And with each successive tug on these ropes the girl was jerked up into an even more twisted and rigid position until finally, to me standing there in the dim light just inside the open doorway, she looked no longer as though she were made of flesh and breakable bones but rather like she was a puppet of wood and string—a puppet, to be sure, manipulated by a mad puppeteer.

"My God!" I shouted. "Billy, Billy, what're you doing?"

Billy stopped and turned and gave me a look that one might give to a total and none-too-welcome stranger. For a moment he stood still, silently blinking. Then apparently recognizing me, maybe snapping back briefly into the real world, he laughed and released his grip on the ropes. The girl immediately collapsed into a dangling heap of wild hair, moans, and twitching muscles. He then laughed again and withdrew himself and walked over to the opposite corner of the room where his pants lay. He pulled them on over his sandals.

"Care for a shot?" he asked once his pants were securely buttoned.

"What?" I gasped, my fingers tightening around my weapon.

"A shot," he said, indicating the girl. "She's good. She's tight. She's so good in fact I think I'll keep her. I just can't decide on what to call her. What d'you think about Angie? Huh? Angie? I don't know. I just can't decide."

I was stunned. I couldn't speak. I couldn't move.

Billy recrossed the room, giving the girl a sharp slap across her backside in passing. The girl screamed once and then settled back down into a series of low rhythmic sobs. Billy pulled up in front of a small wooden bench on which sat several half-filled bottles.

"Wanta drink?" he asked politely, picking up one of the bottles.

"Billy, Billy . . ." I began and then stopped. He was smiling; his eyes were jumping in circles.

"You know, when I was a kid my mother never would let me have a dog," said Billy, taking me by the arm and leading me outside into the bright sunlight. "She said that they were dirty and had fleas. All the other kids had one, but not me. Now, that's sad, isn't it? A kid with no dog."

"Yes, I agree. A tragedy, for sure," I said, allowing myself to be pulled along; I didn't want to further aggravate an already volatile situation, and, in truth, I didn't know what else to do. Insane! "A dog's a very important thing when you're a kid," I assured him. "I was lucky. I had one myself. His name was Spot. A car ran over him and I cried for a day and a half. But that's not really the point, is it? The point is—"

"The point is," interrupted Billy, "that now, you see, I still don't have a dog but I've got something that's even better: a gook. Mine! My very own personal, living, breathing, laugh-a-minute gook. And I intend to keep it—her. Sure, she ain't nothing special. Right outta the fucking fields. Still's got mud between

223

her toes. But what the hell? What d'you want for free? So listen, partner, you can just trot on back and tell all my good friends—'cause I know that they sent you; you'd never have come on your own—tell 'em that I found mine, now they can find theirs, just leave me the hell alone!"

"But, Billy," I persisted, "what you're doing—don't you see what you're doing? It's wrong, totally wrong. People just don't own other people. Not anymore. Not in the physical sense that you're talking about. People don't—"

"I do," said Billy, looking at me with his wild and jumping eyes.

"All right. Okay," I agreed. "But, Billy, there's more to it than that. Much more. You simply can't—"

"I can, believe me, I can," asserted Billy. "And now, good-bye and so long."

"But, Billy—"

"And don't come back," he added, gesturing toward my rifle, "unless you wanta use that thing."

With that said, done, Billy turned abruptly and went back inside and slammed the door behind him.

Walking back to the bar, I had not made ten paces before another piercing scream came ringing out from Billy's bungalow.

Insanity, I thought, utter insanity.

"Well?" demanded Motown as I neared the bar. "Well?"

I stopped and looked at him. He made me tired; they all made me tired. I didn't want to speak or think. I walked past him and around to the bar and plopped myself down heavily on my coconut stump. Reaching down the length of the bar, I picked up a loose drink (whose, I neither knew nor cared) and knocked it back. Perhaps after what I had seen, perhaps after having been so close to so much distorted and demented energy, I should have been highly agitated and excited, but I wasn't. I was simply tired, tired of it, them and everything. I wanted only to be left alone.

"Well?" demanded Motown, circling the bar and pushing his blunt-featured face up close to mine. "Well? What did he say?"

I sighed. It was no use; I would get no peace.

"Well," I began, reaching down the bar for another loose drink, "he says that ever since he was a tiny tot he's always felt an enormous void in his otherwise happy and totally fulfilled life, and that now he feels that that void has been finally—"

"Specifically, asshole," requested Strider. "What did he say specifically?"

"Specifically? Oh well, if you want directness," I replied, correcting my course, "he said that he has found his and now we can find ours, just leave him, quote, 'the hell alone,' unquote."

"Crazy," said Doc, shaking his head. "The boy's gone mad, absolutely mad."

"Okay," agreed Strider. "But what do we do about it? Do we tie him up to a tree? Do we try to take him back? Get him some help? What? Come on, Doc, you're the doc."

"I'm no doctor," objected Doc. "I'm only a—"

"Regardless," interrupted Strider. "What do we do?"

Another scream—this one louder yet—jarred everyone at the bar. Especially Motown. It seemed to tear at his very soul. He gripped the bar with both hands and shook it with such force that all the glasses rattled off and fell into the sand.

"Well," observed Doc after the scream had subsided somewhat, "he obviously needs some kind of help."

"He? He?" I cried; I couldn't contain myself. "He? What about her, for God's sake? She's the one dangling from the ceiling like a goddamn piece of meat! She's the one that needs the help!"

All the eyes at the bar turned on me and regarded me heavily in a profound and malignant silence.

"Doc?" asked Strider quietly after a moment.

"Well," said Doc, looking off toward Billy's bungalow, "I've still got plenty of pills left. If we can get him calmed down, maybe we can still talk some sense into him or something. Although I suspect that he may be past talking."

"All right. Fine," said Motown cheerfully. He pushed himself away from the bar and stood up. "I've always liked the boy. If he needs some help, I'll give him some help."

"How?" asked Strider cautiously, evidently uneasy with Motown's smiling offer of aid.

"With this!" roared Motown, ripping my rifle from my hand. "With this! Goddammit! I'll give the son of a bitch all the fucking help he can stand!"

"Wait!" shouted Strider. There was a sense of panic in his voice that I had never heard before. He jumped up and grabbed one of Motown's tree-trunk arms. "Wait! Wait!"

"Wait? Hell!" cried Motown, wrestling his arm free. "Okay! You want him? You can have him. I'll take care of the whore. You guys can take care of Billy.

But that screaming, that goddamn screaming's gotta stop! Now! Right fucking now!"

Motown looked at everyone at the bar and then he turned and started out across the clearing.

"Motown, no!" pleaded Strider, now standing behind him. "You know he's outta control! You know what'll happen if you go in there like that, don't you? Don't you know?"

Motown stopped. He lowered his head and heaved a great sigh. His whole body shook. He turned around. His eyes were moist. He looked helpless, trapped. Huge and imposing figure of a man that he was, he looked now like a lost child on a windy street corner. You could see the agony and confusion written on his face. He was big and powerful and ready for a fall.

"Yes," he said slowly, drawing the word out painfully. "Yes, I know. And I'm sorry, friend. Truly, I am. But what can I do? I can't take it no more. So I'm going. I got to."

Motown started off again across the clearing in silence. Strider returned to the bar and sat down between Doc and me. I lit a cigarette. Doc reached over the bar and down into the sand and came up with three glasses. He blew the sand out of the glasses and poured another round of drinks. And we waited.

"Bad news," said Strider, lifting his drink and looking through it. "Real bad news."

"Yes," agreed Doc. "And it's gonna get a whole lot worse."

From where we were sitting, we had an open and unobstructed view of Billy's bungalow. The door was still shut and the windows were still covered. The girl, however, had stopped screaming by this time. All that

227

could be heard were the birds singing, the wind whipping through the trees, the waves crashing against the shore, and somewhere, far off behind the village, the steady and methodical pounding of a solitary hammer. Motown marched directly across the sandy clearing and stopped in front of Billy's bungalow. He paused there for a moment outside the door, then turned and looked back at us. And even at this distance—perhaps fifty meters—we could still see clearly the conflicting emotions working within him: fury, sadness, pain, regret. He then turned his attention back to the door. He stood there before it for a moment longer, looking at it. I imagined him there (although I don't know; as I have said, his back was turned) taking deep breaths and thinking: Now? Now? Now! The door crashed open with one swift kick which in itself sounded like a gunshot. The girl screamed again. Motown stepped in. Billy shouted something unintelligible. Then there was silence. Then there was a shot (a single shot, not a burst), and then there was silence again. We waited. A minute, a half-minute (I don't know) passed. Finally Motown emerged alone and started back across the clearing; his head hung down; the end of the rifle barrel channeled through the sand, leaving a trail. And he was not halfway back across the clearing before Billy, fastening his trousers and waving his rifle, came running out after him.

"You shot my wife!" screamed Billy, catching up with Motown and spinning him around. "You shot my girlfriend!" He was frantic, waving his rifle and jumping up and down. His face was twisted; his eyes were popping.

Motown stood still, silently looking down at him.

Billy turned toward the bar. Pointing at Motown and still jumping, he cried, "He shot my wife, my whore! Shot her dead! Fucking dead!"

No one moved.

Receiving no support, Billy shifted back to Motown. Shouting up into Motown's face, Billy continued, "You motherfucker! You low-rent nigger-ass motherfucker!"

"Be easy, Billy," warned Motown calmly, coldly, "or it's gonna be me and you."

Billy stopped jumping; his mouth fell open. He stood for a moment gazing up in wonder at Motown. Then suddenly something in his head seemed to click into place. "Me and you?" he screamed; he began backing away. "You're damn right it's gonna be me and you! Me and you to hell! You big nigger motherfucker! Come on! Let's do it!"

They were now standing about fifteen meters apart. Their rifles were at their sides, pointed at the ground. They stood staring silently at each other. I moaned audibly. I started to cry out. Doc grabbed my hand. "Let it be," he cautioned. It didn't matter. There was nothing that I or anyone else could have done at that point to alter the course, to derail the inevitable. Strider in fact was no longer even watching; he was spinning his glass in his hands and looking off into the jungle, into the trees.

"Okay, motherfucker!" shouted Billy. "Go for it! Go for it, damn you! Come on!"

"Is this the way you want it, Billy?" asked Motown; his jaw was set; his feet were spread apart.

Billy was flabbergasted. He seemed to have lost the power of coherent and connected speech. He stood there working his mouth open and shut, his hair whipping about his face, his eyes wide and wild. He was sweating. Neither of them cast a shadow. The sun was directly overhead. It was very hot.

"I want it!" squealed Billy finally. "Yes! I want it! Want you! Now! Go for it! Come on! Come on! Go for it, now! Now, motherfucker!"

Billy ripped up his rifle and got off a couple of quick clean rounds before Motown could respond. Motown was still only a flinch and a jerk behind him, but for Billy it was enough—almost. Motown was already hit, off balance, and beginning to fall before the first shot flashed from his muzzle tip. They were both firing on full automatic at close range. It was all incredibly confusing and all very fast. Yet strangely, at the same time, it also seemed somehow slow and precise. The first round caught Motown squarely in the chest. You could see that distinctly. He began to fire as he fell. He fell straight back as though someone had pulled the ground out from under him. He landed flat in a sitting position with his legs thrust out in front of him. And he remained thus—upright, sitting, firing—until his clip was empty. Billy—well, it's difficult to say exactly when he was first hit because he was in constant motion. The moment that he snapped up his rifle, he lunged off to the right, and from there, caught up in a fusillade from Motown, he continued to lunge and twist and twirl as the bullets tore into his young and handsome body. He hit the ground with a thud, a sigh, and a puff of dust. And he moved no more.

Once the shooting had finally stopped and I could breathe again, I jumped up and raced across to Motown as Doc crossed over to Billy. Motown was spread out on the ground, on his back, with no fewer than three bullet holes that I could see (he was covered with blood) in his upper body. He had a strange smile on his face. His eyes were pinned open. He was staring blindly up at the sky.

I knelt there beside him dumbfounded, speechless. What could I have said? He was dying and he knew it. He just lay there with that crazy, satisfied smile and those bulging, horrible eyes, coughing up bloody globs of phlegm and spit.

"He's dead," reported Doc, coming up behind me.

"Not yet," I said.

"No, Billy," he explained, kneeling.

"Did I get him, Doc? Doc, did I get him?" asked Motown in an eager frenzy.

"Yes," said Doc. "You got him."

Motown reached out and took Doc's hand.

"It was the screaming, Doc. Believe me," began Motown. (I suppose that everyone needs to explain, to justify, to seek forgiveness, understanding—thus, this modest effort.) "It was just that goddamn screaming. Not him. I liked him. Really, I did. We had some laughs together, some good times. He was all right. But it was just that screaming, that goddamn—"

Suddenly his body bounced, his eyes froze, and his smile collapsed. And he was dead.

Doc looked up, looked at me, and sighed. He reached over and closed Motown's eyes. "Well, it won't bother you anymore, Mo," he said gently, softly. "Nothing ever will. Sleep. You've earned it."

The next day we buried Motown and Billy together, side by side, under a huge coconut palm. (The girl's body was cut down and taken away and deposited somewhere by the villagers; where, we never learned nor cared to learn; we had overriding concerns of our own.) Strider and Doc and I, along with several villagers—four old men (probably with nothing better to do) and six young girls (presumably part of the late Motown's herd)—watched quietly and patiently as the two graves were dug—we had a new gravedigger now, the young bar boy—and filled and covered over.

"Well?" asked Strider abruptly as the last shovelful of sand was being patted into place. He had been drinking and smoking steadily since the shoot-out, and now he looked fairly ragged.

"Well?" answered Doc. He seemed somewhat short on tolerance too.

"Aren't you going to say a few kind words for these departed souls, our friends?" asked Strider, taking a sip from a half-empty fifth of gin that he was carrying.

Doc just looked at him. He didn't say a word.

"Come on. Say something," prodded Strider. "This may be your last chance. Asshole would like it too. He goes in for that kinda shit. Don't you, asshole?"

I didn't answer him. I looked back but I didn't answer.

"I don't feel like it," snarled Doc, beginning to turn away.

"Well, neither do I. But come on. Say something. You love to yak," continued Strider. "Besides, they deserve something."

"And something they got," observed Doc curtly.

The villagers, not understanding the words, only the tone, shifted their eyes and feet nervously.

"Right. Okay," agreed Strider. "But say something

232

anyway. Almost anything'll do. They won't care. Nobody will."

"Jesus!" cried Doc, eyeing Strider fiercely. "What's your problem? Huh?"

Strider looked up and smiled and took another hit off the bottle.

"Lemme have some of that shit," said Doc suddenly.

"Sure," said Strider, extending the fifth.

Doc took a long pull on the bottle and then lowered it. His eyes swam over the newly dug graves as he rocked back on his heels, and for a moment I thought that he was either going to throw up or burst out laughing. Instead he handed the bottle back to Strider.

"You want me to say something?" asked Doc, his voice sharp, his eyes hard. "All right, goddammit. I'll say something. Something that you probably don't want to hear. But here it is: these bodies, this blood, belongs to you. It's on your hands as surely as if you'd pulled the trigger yourself. This was your mission, your idea. It always has been. Okay, granted, we didn't have to come with you, to follow you, but we did. I don't know why, but we did. And so now we're here and they're dead and it's because of you. But all right, okay, I understand that everyone ultimately has to take responsibility for his own actions. But still, still, in the final analysis it was always your show. From the very beginning it was your circus. We were only the clowns. You were the ringmaster—or maybe, just maybe, you were the chief clown and we never knew it."

There was silence.

Doc and Strider stood staring at each other. I was glad that there were no weapons about.

"Now gimme that fucking bottle!" demanded Doc, snatching the fifth out of Strider's hand. "I need to get drunk!"

Doc took a small sip and then another and another and another until finally he was gulping it down as though it were water. The gin ran in two streams down his chin, off his shirt, and onto the ground. Wavering on wobbly legs, he burped and reached out for one of the girls, one of the young mourners. He circled an arm around her waist, whispered something into her ear, and then together they headed down the beach. Strider glanced over at me, shrugged his shoulders, and then he turned and walked off in the opposite direction. I stood there alone for a moment longer, thinking of nothing, listening to the wind and watching the sand shift and swirl over the graves, and then I too walked away.

16

It was morning again. It had been raining the night before, and now there was an unpleasant and unfamiliar chill in the air. I felt a cold, a summer cold, coming on. I coughed and cursed and blew my nose. Two days had passed now since we'd buried Motown and Billy. I had been asleep for almost an entire twenty-four-hour period and yet I was still tired. Inside—I was standing outside, leaning against the side of my bungalow, sipping a hot cup of tea—I could hear Anh rustling around, rearranging the dust. She had been rather moody of late. I decided to leave her to herself and go and look up my compadres. I knew where they would be. And they were.

"Good morning," I said as I approached the bar. Neither of them spoke, neither of them even looked up. They both seemed lost deep in thought. There was something in the air, I could tell, something dark and silent and foreboding. I sat down. Immediately—sort of the way a shoeshine boy notices the shoes of his customers before he notices their faces—I noticed that all of the bottles and glasses had been cleared off the shelf behind the bar. It looked sad and desolate. I started to inquire as to the cause for this alteration, but I checked myself. Something was definitely wrong.

On the bar itself, one bottle—bourbon—remained with three glasses; two were filled with liquor; one—mine, presumably—was chipped and empty. The bar boy who was usually there, or at least, hovering within easy shouting distance, was nowhere to be seen. It was then that I discerned the problem, the difference: the village was extremely quiet—no fishing boats putting out to sea; no cooking fires; no children. Just the wind, the slap of the surf, and we three. Hmm, I thought. Then Strider filled my glass. "Well," he said after a moment, "it looks like it's time to move, it looks like it's time to be heading back."

Silence like an ax swing. The wind. The surf.

"Head back, huh?" asked Doc with mild indifference. "I see. We just go back and tell 'em . . . tell 'em what?"

Again: silence; only the surf and the wind.

"Do we tell 'em simply that we got tired of death and dying and murder and rape and so we decided to take a little time off to kick back and try to sort things out, to try to make some kind of sense out of it all?" asked Doc. "Huh? What? What do we say?"

"We'll say, 'simply,' that we got lost," said Strider, not smiling, serious.

"Ah, fantastic!" cried Doc, jumping to his feet. "And I thought that you didn't have a plan. Beautiful! We'll just walk right in and say, 'Gee whiz, fellows, we got a little lost, it was rough, but now we're back and, man, does it ever feel good.' Bullshit! Double fucking bullshit!"

"We'll say," began Strider calmly, purposefully, "that we spotted some VC back at that little ville we hit during that last sweep we were on. They broke for the bush and we pursued. We fell into an ambush, took a couple of casualties, and were forced to pull back. During the fight we somehow got turned around. We lost our bearings and we couldn't link up again. We came up on another little ville and decided to hole up there to give our wounded a chance to heal up. There was no way we could leave 'em, right? Sorry, but they didn't make it. They lingered, but in spite of everything that we could do—well, we couldn't do anything really but wait—they cashed in. We turn in Mo's and Billy's tags and say we buried 'em in the field. We couldn't bring 'em back. There was only the three of us. We didn't know how far out we were, how many klicks. We're lost, right? Lost and wandering. They could hardly expect us to be lugging a couple of bodies around with us through the jungle, you know."

"Yeah?" asked Doc, sitting down again.

"Yeah. Basically," answered Strider. "We can refine it later."

"And how do you propose that we get back to Fable?" asked Doc. "You're not suggesting that we hike it back to the base, I hope."

"No," said Strider. "According to the map, there's another fire base, an ARVN base, down the coast. I hope they're still there. Hell, it might be a whorehouse or a chicken farm by now. Well, anyway, if we stick to the beach, I think we can probably make it in a couple of days. Then from there, well, we're in the hands of God, the ARVNs, and the U.S. Army."

"Oh shit," moaned Doc. "Better get out the Vaseline."

"I know," continued Strider, "that trucking down the beach in broad daylight ain't exactly cool, but hell, it's the best we can do. We'll just have to risk it. Anyway, there ain't nothing else. We can't stay here. We've gotta move."

"That's for sure," agreed Doc. He picked up the bottle and refilled everyone's glass.

"But why?" I asked. "Why do we have to leave? Why can't we stay on here? You said yourself you wanted nine more months, remember?"

"I still do, and maybe I'll still get them," said Strider. "But as for now—well, just listen."

Again the silence, the eerie and unnatural quiet, the sense of calm emptiness. It was like a funeral, a funeral with no one attending.

"So it's a little bit quiet," I said. "I still don't—"

"A little bit?" asked Strider. "Listen again."

And more: not even a dog, not a monkey or a bird; as if nature herself had agreed or conspired with the silence—it was past mere death (the quiet); it was as if life had never existed.

"All right, all right," I agreed. "But can't we go somewhere else?"

"Where?" asked Strider, answering my question with a question. "We can't go wandering around out here for real. We'd probably starve or bump into some VC or some kinda shit. Or say that we did happen to run up on another ville somewhere, what guarantee do we have that they wouldn't feed us good and then stab us in the back while we slept? Remember, there's just three of us now. Here, so far, we've been lucky, real lucky. Let's not push it. Going back ain't gonna be no treat, but it beats the hell out of starving or a knife in the back. Anyway, like I said, I can't see nothing else. I wish I could, but I can't. How about you, Doc?"

238

"Well, as I see it, our options are limited no matter what," said Doc, taking a sip of whiskey. "True, the hike could be a bitch and the story still needs some work. Like they still might want the bodies or a location. They're fucking nuts about bodies. And they're gonna want to know something about those first two guys—maybe we can just deny any knowledge of them altogether, say we never saw 'em. But if they don't press too close for details and we can coordinate our act, then it just might work. I mean like it all depends on the timing, the situation, on who's in command. They might even believe it. Hell, stranger things, a whole hell of a lot stranger things have happened."

"There it is," said Strider. "Coordination and strangeness."

"Yeah, it might work. What's more believable in an unbelievable situation than something that's totally un-believable?" asked Doc. "Totally unbelievable, absolutely incredible, utterly ridiculous. It just might work. A double negative, so to speak."

"I repeat: there it is," said Strider. "Coordination and strangeness."

"Yeah, well, maybe," agreed Doc. "Who's to say?"

The wind, still wet, swept through the village, sending discarded bits of nothing fleeing before it; the trees swayed back and forth in silence; above, gray clouds revolved through restless and threatening skies; and somewhere nearby, a loose shutter banged loudly against the side of a bungalow, transmitting an urgent and unheeded call for attention and assistance.

"But I still don't understand where all the people are," I said, looking around.

The fact that we were returning with a flimsy alibi—

almost transparent—to face possible charges of desertion didn't actually bother me very much at the moment. There was little or nothing that I could do about it; the die was cast. But that silence, that ominous quiet interrupted only by that banging shutter, that bothered me. I needed either answers or no questions. And that shutter and that silence were already questions.

"They're laying out," said Strider. "Waiting."

"And no doubt watching too," added Doc.

"Waiting? Watching? For what?" I asked. "For who?"

"For us. For us to leave," explained Strider. "For us to decide, to recognize the all-too-obvious fact that it's over, that it's time for us to move, to leave. So they're just laying out, giving us time to have an original thought. It's better that way, better for everybody. When we first came here we knew we'd have to leave sometime—or at least we should've known it, recognized it. It was inevitable. And they knew, for sure, better than anyone. People come and go but the rain, the rice, and the land remain. This way nobody feels like he's getting pushed or shoved. Nobody loses face. It's all very sly, all very Oriental. Why rush when you can wait? And these people know how to wait. Forever! So this way, you see, we can even have the luxury of fooling ourselves into thinking that we're leaving of our own accord, voluntarily, because we want to. And you know yourself that when we start having shoot-outs at high noon and killing each other over nothing—well, hell, it's time to move."

"All right. Okay," I said. "So then we're leaving. When?"

240

"Tomorrow," said Strider. "Tomorrow morning. Early."

That night I slept very little. I would close my eyes and then open them again, not knowing how much time had passed. Ten minutes, one hour, no difference. I was no longer concerned about time; it was irrelevant. I had long since thrown my watch into the ocean.

Finally, disgusted and weary, I got out of bed, wrapped a towel around me, and walked outside. It was still pitch-black night. The stars were out and the wind was high. I sat down on the stoop in front of my bungalow and listened to the night sounds: the wild wind, the thrashing palms, the surf. Soon Anh came out and joined me. I had tried earlier to explain to her that I was leaving, that we were leaving, leaving her, leaving the village. She had not said anything in response. Maybe she thought that no response was needed—I don't know. I do know that she understood what I was saying—the words; her English had been showing positive signs of improvement—that she had (as Strider had explained) known before, known that a time would come, but still she had just sat there and listened, and then she had gotten up and moved quickly and quietly away from me. But now she was back with a cigarette and some matches, standing above me, looking down.

"Here," she said, handing the cigarette to me.

"Thanks," I said.

I took the cigarette and curled my arms around her legs and pulled her down next to me. She collapsed for a moment with her head against my shoulder, then she picked up her head, checked the direction of the wind, and lit my cigarette. The match, the flame, lit up her entire face; the wind whipped long through her hair; the stars danced in her eyes. She looked at me and smiled, and then she lowered her head again to my shoulder.

My God, she was beautiful! My God, I felt sick!

"You understand, Anh," I began, "that I'll be back, don't you? Someday, somehow—I don't know how; I don't know when—but I promise you one bright and sunny day you'll look up and I'll be coming down that trail there, and I'll be calling your name: 'Anh! Anh! Where's little Anh?' You wait. You'll see. I'll be back. It's not like I'm running out on you, you know, or turning my back on you. It's just that it's simply time for us to move. It's like Strider said, 'It's better, better for everybody.' You people have been good to us. Real good. You've helped us, fed us. Everything. I couldn't forget you, any of you, even if I wanted to—and I don't. It's burned into my brain—you, this place, everything. And I'll be back. This war can't last forever. You'll see. I'll be back. I will. I swear I will!" My voice was faltering, choked. (Whom was I trying to convince or fool anyway?) "We'll all be back. One day. One day soon. We never forget our friends. Americans are like that, you know. We really are. We're basically good people. So don't you worry, little girl, we'll be back. I'll be back. I promise. I swear."

"No," she said with a serene and easy tone, with something like certainty in her voice. "No. You go. You no come back. I know. You leave. You leave Anh. You no come back. You use. You throw away. I know. I see. You drink beer, whiskey. So many beer.

So many whiskey. You drink. You throw away. You rich. We poor. You use Anh same-same beer. Same-same whiskey. You throw away. Throw away all Vietnam people. You talk: friend. Anh laugh big. You talk lie. All American people same-same: all American people talk bullshit!"

"Now, just hold on there," I warned, tightening my arms around her.

And immediately, like something under too much pressure, like a balloon just waiting to pop, she exploded into a wild rush of arms and legs and elbows and knees. She pulled and scratched and squirmed. Her little muscles strained; her breath was hot. I tried to get a good grip on her but she was too fluid, too full of push and pain. Somehow, looking for a handle, my hand slid in front of her face and she bit for the bone. I relaxed and let her bite. She twisted her head around and her eyes rolled up to mine. I stared back and said nothing. Gradually her teeth eased up and I slipped my hand away from her mouth. Her head came up heavy and went to my shoulder again. She gave a weak, wet little sniffle and ran a finger under her nose and said, "Okay."

"What?" I asked, unsure whether she was asking a question or stating a fact.

"Okay. No problem," she said, straightening herself up again and speaking in the same calm voice as before. "No problem. You rich. Me poor." She raked a loose wisp of hair out of her face. "You go back base. Okay. You go back to America. Okay. You go. You leave Anh. Leave all Vietnam people. Anh know. Anh understand. No problem. Can die anywhere."

"No, dammit! Goddammit!" I shouted. "You don't

understand! You don't understand any goddamn thing! You talk: me rich, you poor. Bullshit! That's got nothing to do with it. I couldn't stay here now even if I wanted to. I've gotta go back with them. I should never have come here in the first place. But I did, and I'm glad! So regardless of whatever happens to me, I'm glad that I came—this, you, everything! It's a reason! It's something! It's a reason for something! Maybe for living! Maybe for dying! I don't know. But now we have to go back—back there. But later—later—later—you'll see! You'll see, believe me! I'll be back! But now—right now, I've gotta—"

"Why? Why?" she cried, turning her big wet and beautiful eyes up at me. "Why? You stay. You stay here. Stay with me. Stay, okay?"

Jesus, I was distraught. I could've strangled on the sound of my own voice and it wouldn't have mattered. I couldn't express myself. Everything came jumping out of my mouth in a jumbled blur of half-breaths and exclamation marks. I'd had it; I was at the end of my rope. The pressure, the fear, the self-doubt, and then the switch: the quiet and the confidence; and now the return. I thought that I was going to lose it. My hands were sweating; my eyes wouldn't focus. I thought that I would go screaming off the edge of the world, off into space, off into the oblivious darkness. But I didn't. I took a deep breath and merely shrieked.

"Why! Why! Jesus, help me! Why! It's them—Strider and Doc! No! Wait! I'm wrong! It's me! Me! It's more me than them! Oh hell, I don't know! I don't understand! I don't know why I came and now I don't know why I've gotta go! I never asked for this! Any of this! Not here! The last of all places on earth that I expected to find this—this! Much less you—something like you! Here! Here! Here in the middle of all this! Jesus! But now—now, I've gotta go back—back with them—back there! But you'll see! I promise you I'll be back! It's not like—"

"No," she cried, shaking her head. "Me no see. Anh no see nothing. Okay. You go. Anh stay. No problem."

"No! No! No! Jesus God, no!" I screamed. "You wait! You'll see! It's not like—"

"No," she broke in again, looking up, smiling, calm. "No talk. Too much talk. Just hold me. Okay? You hold me."

"Sure, little girl, sure," I said. I was shaken, fractured, torn in half. "Sure I'll hold you. And I'll come back too, and I'll hold you again. You'll see. Believe me. I'll hold you forever."

"Yes," she agreed without a trace of joy or sorrow in her voice, as totally devoid of emotion as sand or rock or rain. "Yes," she said, and she was already beginning to put it behind her.

So with the wind whacking through the palms and the surf exploding upon the shore, we, lost and damned, sat holding each other in silence, waiting like the condemned for the dawn.

It came quickly. Too quickly. Bright and treacherous.

Soon, down the trail came Strider and Doc. They had a mixed delegation following behind them: young and old, men and women—talking, staring, smiling. Well-wishers, I thought, I hoped.

I got up, went inside, and began to dress. I put on one of the many pairs of blue jeans that we had liberated from the downed helicopter, a green T-shirt (army-issue), and a pair of tennis shoes, also part of the chopper's booty. My uniform, boots, and other unnecessary necessities, I stashed away in my pack for later use. (As we neared the fire base, our plan was to discard and bury our fine raiment and don our more mundane wear, but for now, that didn't matter; we still had a fair trek ahead of us.) I took one last glance around the room—nothing really: four walls, a bed, a table, two chairs, a roof—and I felt as if I were leaving something much more than what it appeared to be, something much more than it would ever appear to a casual observer. I felt as though I were leaving my home—this: the source of so much pleasure and security. I could almost have cried. The possibilities, the memories all converging, crashing together—the smoky lanterns at night; the pale drift of blue rising from the charcoal fires, mingling with the morning fog; the exotic aroma of the strange and wonderful foods; the peace; the natural harmony; the laughter of the little children outside the windows, looking in; those big innocent all-seeing eyes; the smooth and rhythmical slap of the surf lulling one to sleep at night; the bird calls in the morning; the breeze coursing through the open windows and doors; the endless hum and movement of life and living; the sense of place and possession. Then I heard Strider call my name, so I picked up my rifle and walked back outside.

"Well?" asked Strider, looking up from a mob of children. He was holding one particularly beautiful little girl in his arms.

"Well," I answered.

"Okay," he said, putting the child carefully down. "Then come on. We've gotta go down and see the old man. He wants to make a farewell speech and give us his blessings or some kinda shit. All these cats are the same. Politicians! Shit!"

I took Anh's small hand in mine, and we fell into line. The sun was up now—it must have been about seven o'clock, I guess—the birds were singing and the children were laughing, and as we made our way slowly along the trail to the headman's bungalow, I was overcome by a strange and unfounded feeling, a premonition of some unspeakable lurking horror. I tried to put it out of my mind. Nerves, I kept telling myself, just a case of nerves.

By the time we arrived at the headman's bungalow, the entire village was either following us or was already there waiting. It was quite a crowd and quite a festive atmosphere—handshakes and hugs and kisses. Many of the villagers had brought along little gifts—trinkets, good-luck medallions, Buddha amulets, and the like; several brought small portions of food wrapped in banana leaves, which they pressed upon us with smiling faces and weathered hands.

The headman came out and stood on his porch and looked down at the people assembled there before him. His hair was neatly combed and parted. He was wearing a black dinner jacket (with nothing underneath) that looked as though it might have once belonged to a waiter in one of the old fancy French restaurants in Saigon and a baggy pair of oversize blue jeans turned up at the cuffs and tied at the waist by a length of rope. After a moment he began to speak. I understood not more than half a dozen words of what he was saying (my Vietnamese was still limited to a few basic nouns, verbs, and expletives), so I let my eyes wander about the crowd.

So this is what it's all about, I thought to myself: peasants: farmers and fishermen—old women with black and rotting teeth; beautiful young girls with hair like silk and eyes like fire; young men (yes, a few—goddamn precious few, but still a few), bronzed and smiling; babies running about naked or with only their shirt tops on; old men, calm and wise, sitting in the shade, smoking pipes and laughing. This? This? All the bombs, all the bullets, the charred corpses, and the knock at the door: "Mr. Smith, we regret to inform you that your son . . ." Bullshit! I could scream! Freedom? Democracy? Communism? Lies! Treachery! Words! Old dirty dead words spoken by gray-faced old men in clean clothes with fat stomachs. Old dead useless words spoken to young men with lean bodies and trusting eyes. ("Because, well, because it's right." Right? Right? I'm eighteen years old; what the hell do I know about right?) "You go. You kill. Long live . . ." Long live who? The fat cats? The characters with the clever words and the good connections? They'll never die in a rice paddy screaming for their mothers with their last breath. They'll never squat in the rain eating rice with *nuoc-mam* sauce or cold ham and lima beans out of a can. They'll never sleep in a mudhole stinking of shit and brains and vomit. They'll never turn in the dark, the dark so alive with death, and whisper to a buddy or a comrade: "And when she laughs it's like . . . like music, goddammit, just like music."

(But no—wait. My head's starting to spin; my pen's starting to skip; my thoughts are confused and careless. I must concentrate. I must remember it, remember it all—the details—remember it clearly and put it down the way that it happened because maybe, some-

248

day, someone might want to know: Why? Why? Why? Why?—comes the lost and fading echo, the disjointed chorus of a million silent tongues. But why? All right, I'll leave it. It's too big, too much. It's the then and the there that I must confine myself to. It's the best that I can hope for; it's the most that I'll ever be able to do, accomplish. Not to understand; much less to hope to explain it to others. No! Never! But just simply to report, to describe it as I saw it, saw it through my own bloodshot, bulging, and disbelieving eyes. Jesus! Even now it still makes me crazy. Even now it still makes me want to grab someone around the neck or steal a car and go looking for sturdy telephone poles. But later. There'll be time later.)

Still the old man was talking and still I was holding Anh's hand, and there, standing next to me, was a small girl and she was looking up at us—at Anh and me—and soon the child began pulling at my other hand, the one in which I held my rifle, so I shifted my rifle out of this hand and passed it over to Anh and caught hold of the little girl's hand. She had been looking up at me for quite some time, I later realized— her eyes, enormous and filled with grave concern. Now, with her fragile little birdlike hand finger-locked in mine (satisfied), she turned her attention back to the headman and his speech. Anh squeezed my hand and smiled. And still the old man rambled on.

Strider and Doc, near the front, nodded and smiled and seemed to genuinely understand and appreciate what was being said. Standing there behind them, looking at them, I was suddenly struck by the utterly absurd sight that I now saw before me: Tourists! We looked like a bunch of goddamn tourists—armed, to be sure, but still tourists: Doc with a conical straw hat on his head; Strider with his bush hat—SORRY ABOUT THAT, VIETNAM; all of us wearing sunglasses; our hair long (mine only slightly so, Strider's tied back in a ponytail); our bodies tanned and healthy—muscles toned, stomachs filled; all of us in T-shirts (Doc's was black and had some writing on it which now I cannot recall); Doc in cut-off jeans; Strider in his jungle fatigues, looking, as he always did, as if he had just bought them at a local army surplus store because the baggy side pockets were so convenient for storing one's lids—he never looked entirely real to me, never even vaguely "army"; tennis shoes and sandals; and finally Doc, the artist, adding the perfect finishing touches: his medical pouch slung casually from his shoulder like a traveling bag, a camera (from the chopper) dangling around his neck, with Motown's radio in one hand, and a gaudy and grotesque wood carving of a lion attacking an elephant—a souvenir—in the other. Holy Christ, I thought, and laughed. Holy Christ.

Finally the headman, realizing that he was losing his audience's attention, finished up his speech with three sharp shrieks and then nodded to Strider. Strider bowed and reached up and shook the old man's hand, then stepped up beside him and placed a hand carefully and lightly upon the old boy's shoulder—who was now beaming like he had just won the lottery—and said a few brief words in Vietnamese to the people below. The people bowed and Strider bowed back and then he shook the old man's hand again and stepped off the porch and back down onto the ground. I slipped my hand free from the little girl's, bowed (she bowed too), retrieved my rifle from Anh, and turned, still holding on to Anh's hand. And slowly, like a caterpillar inching along a leaf, stretching out in sections, then contracting and stretching out again, the procession moved away from the old man's bungalow and wound its way along back down the trail and out into the bright and bird-filled morning of our own doom and destruction.

The flowers blooming along the path . . . the small arched wooden bridge . . . the clear cool creek . . . the birds wild in the trees, constant, combative . . . the children dancing . . . the dogs underfoot . . . her hair against my skin . . . the heat . . . the good strong smell of life—sweat, the sea, the jungle . . . the singsong lilt of the voices . . . the swaying column . . . the bobbing heads . . . the flashes of sunlight breaking through the trees . . . an old woman wearing a wide-brim sun hat, waving a peacock feather . . . someone laughing loud, laughing once, then falling silent . . . the sand . . . the footprints . . . the dry rustling of dead palm fronds . . . a water buffalo . . . a duck with a bum wing . . . two kittens under a flowering bush, looking up . . .

And then WHACK! WHACK! WHACK! All movement stopped; faces froze; eyes rolled skyward; ears turned toward the sea. WHACK! WHACK! WHACK! Just over the horizon; just under the new morning sun (the sound deceptively slow when compared to the actual speed). WHACK! WHACK! WHACK! The blades ripping through the air; pure fear; refined terror; even the dogs quiet; only the faint, then the closing, and now the finality of WHACK! WHACK! WHACK! Coming fast.

Strider was standing on the bridge, shouting something and waving his arms. Doc was herding a small cluster of scared children into a stand of elephant grass. People were beginning to shout and shove. A scream. A child off the bridge and into the water. Then the stampede: people pushing; more screaming; chaos; panic surging through the crowd; no real direction, simply confused movement; people scattering, colliding, dropping to the ground, into the water.

A Cobra gunship in the lead with three Hueys bringing up the rear: they came in fast and they came in firing—strafing the bay, the boats, the beach, up the beach, across the beach, to, through, and over us. And I just stood there and watched. I couldn't believe it. It was all so unreal.

The first pass was a joint effort (all four choppers) —precise, almost in formation. It was fast and low and loud; rockets from the gunship whooshing wildly through the screaming air; cannon fire also from the Cobra exploding in an orderly and progressive pattern; machine-gun fire raking the ground at random.

They were on top of us and gone before half of the dead had even had a good chance to start dying. Bodies—people, actual human breathing beings, hacked in half, torn, tossed up into the air. Screams and shrieks and demented howls of terror and pain sprang from the bleeding and bloody earth. The old woman with the peacock feather, now headless, lay on her side, spouting a fountain of blood from her neck, yet still clinging to the feather. Several people with limbs ripped off crawled about, crying or in a daze. A small child literally exploded before my eyes into a nameless mass of nothingness and a shoe. An arm, whole, as if surgically amputated, lay on the trail, in the sand. A young girl cradling a small bleeding body rocked back and forth silently. Several more bodies rolling in the current of the creek floated by and on out to sea. And still I stood, staring in horrified amazement at the carnage and death surrounding me.

I could hear the helicopters circling around to the north. They were still firing. Somewhere, over there, other people are dying too, I thought to myself. The thought neither disturbed nor comforted me—that was happening "over there." Finally I felt something tugging at the waistband of my jeans, and I looked down. It was Anh. She was crouched down, hiding behind my legs, crying. And suddenly, stupidly, I realized that I had been standing exposed, and yet, thus far, unharmed as the world around me had been rapidly going to hell. I pulled her up and motioned her into the bushes. At first she refused to go. She began to howl in her confusing mix of English and Vietnamese. "Hold!" I shouted. I reached out and grabbed a whining child who was stumbling about in a state of shock— blood dripping from the child's ears and nose and mouth—and I pressed the child upon her. And she looked up at me once, once with something akin to hatred in her eyes (or maybe it was something else entirely and I misread it; I'll never know), then she accepted the child and headed into the undergrowth.

Strider was still on the bridge, standing at the peak of the arch. He was about fifty yards away. He had his rifle in one hand; his other hand rested on the bridge railing. He looked unconcerned, composed. Doc was off somewhere in the bush with the villagers. Except for Strider and the dead and the dying and myself, the immediate area was now deserted. I staggered backward a few steps, feeling the full weight and horror of impending doom, and slammed up against a coconut palm. I slid down the trunk and, with my back braced against the tree, I sat and waited. Between where I sat and the sea in front of me, there stood a coconut grove: a hundred or so trees, fairly generously spaced, swaying peacefully in the breeze. Maybe if we just surrendered, I thought; maybe it's all a mistake. ("Americans! Well, fuck me! What the shit are you guys doing here?" "Well, you see . . .") Then I looked over at Strider and the bodies, and I flicked the safety catch to automatic. Jesus, I thought as I watched another body twitch its last, it's been a long road to nowhere.

And again—WHACK! WHACK! WHACK!—angling in across the bay. This time, however, the Cobra was passing farther off to the south, and the Hueys were maneuvering into positions for a landing. They touched down at the far end of the beach, disgorged fifteen or twenty soldiers, and then as quickly and as violently as they had come—the door gunners firing continuously— they dipped their noses, lifted, and whirled away to the north again.

Strider stood yet a moment longer, watching the Cobra's pass with the same relaxed attitude of nonchalance and unconcern, then he opened up. He fired a full clip at the gunship before it finally took notice of him. The Cobra, like something human or, at least, something animated, spun toward him with its body quivering, vibrating. And from here on out it was as though there was something personal between them: first, a few seconds of Strider standing and staring; the Cobra hovering, stationary, leering downward at an angle; then Strider swinging up his rifle and cutting loose again, standing and firing; the Cobra's mini-guns raking the bridge, the water, the surrounding banks; the bullet trails—red and green—zigzagging crazily around Strider; the high-pitched whine of the Cobra's engine; the pulsating wind blast from the blades—the beat, regular, measured, sounding like the beating of an enormous heart; the bridge splintering; the bridge bursting into flames.

Somehow, miraculously, Strider managed to empty three full clips at the chopper without getting shredded. Amazed, stunned, I watched in an adrenalated state of hyper hope and dread, not knowing whether to scream or cheer. It was totally beyond belief: the rage, the roar, the riot, the fire, the smoke, the smell, the trees, the sun, the heat, the fury, the fear, the death, all spinning around and around and around.

Soon the bridge, now fully aflame, began collapsing, collapsing under him, collapsing into the creek. Thick black smoke, forced down to a level of some twenty or so feet by the swirling turbulence from the chopper's rotor blades, fanned out across the bridge, creating a natural smokescreen. The smoke tumbling in upon itself partially obscured my view (and the Cobra's too, I would imagine), but still I could see. And what I saw was Strider glancing quickly away from the chopper, scanning the creek and the creek bank, and then, still with luck or God—I'll discount nothing anymore—or something on his side for a while longer yet, vaulting across one of the last remaining sections of the bridge and into the creek below. And to me, through the smoke, from where I sat, I swear that it looked as if he were smiling.

Jesus, I thought, whispered, shouted, shrieked. "Jesus God!"

The gunship, no longer firing, passed over him, over where he had been, and spun around in front of me, kicking up an angry cloud of dust and sand and sending the coconut palms into a wild and frenzied dance. It hovered, bobbed and weaved about, its tail section swishing back and forth as though it were impatient, yet with its cockpit, like some huge grotesque insect head that is all eyes and antennas, always facing the creek and the creek bank along which, among the dense clumps of bamboo and the collapsing pieces of the bridge, Strider now hid. I don't think that the chopper ever spotted me—I was still braced against the tree, sitting motionless, with the dead in their strange and rigid final postures all scattered about around me like so much loose change—and even if it (the Cobra) had spotted me, I still don't think it would have mattered, because the Cobra already had its target (Strider), and now it was intent on that—him—and nothing else.

Well, I thought to myself (and I did have time to think; after Strider opted for the water, things quieted down somewhat; there was a lull, as they say—Strider was lying low; the Cobra was hovering, looking; the soldiers were advancing toward the far end of the village, away from me), I guess that I've never really done anything by either plan or design that could actually be called "brave." Oh sure, I've jumped out of tall trees as a child on a dare, walked down dark back alleys in strange cities alone, fought people bigger than me (and lost), drag-raced down the wrong side of two-lane country roads at night (and won), but that could hardly be classified as brave—foolish, yes, stupid, yes, but not brave. But then, how many people in this day and age, in what are considered to be the more civilized societies—a term that I won't venture to define—actually have the opportunity presented, or are even forced into a position wherein real bravery or courage is demanded? Modern man's life can be, if he so chooses and can afford it, fairly well-insulated against the need to exhibit courage or bravery. And surely this should be the place and the time—Nam, '69—the place and the time which offers one the opportunities to test and prove oneself. And certainly, in my case, I blew it, the chance, the opportunity. Walking away from the village one month, two months ago—God, how quickly it all goes!—was hardly an act of great fortitude. Perhaps if I had stayed with the company and continued on, courage or the need to exhibit courage would have been called for. But then again, how courageous would staying have been? How much courage does it take to blow away an old man with a walking stick or a baby with a bottle? Or even to stand by and watch without interfering as others do the actual dirty work? Maybe if I had just thrown down my rifle and refused to participate, refused before, before . . . Good God, I can still see that face, those eyes, still feel that limp little body, still hear the breathing and then the silence! Jesus, I don't know. I don't feel like a coward. I don't feel as though I've dishonored or disgraced myself. I just don't know. Perhaps extracting oneself is the best that can be hoped for in some situations, because there are some certain situations that are simply hopeless and nothing more. How does one stop insanity? By becoming insane? Well, fuck it! It's all just a little too academic for me now 'cause if I don't get that fucking bird with this first fucking clip, I'll probably be less than academic: I'll probably be dead. Bravery? This? Shit. I'm back to stupidity and waste and jumping out of trees.

And so thinking, I knelt and took aim.

Suddenly, behind me, there was movement in the grass. I dropped to my stomach and rolled, and out of the bush burst Doc. I shouted at him, shouted: "Doc! Doc!" He ignored me. Maybe he didn't hear me. He was already running, running and screaming and waving his arms. He still wore the straw hat and the T-shirt and the cut-off jeans; his medical bag was still draped across his shoulder—it bounced as he ran. "Doc!" I called out again. But Doc ran on. He ran on toward the soldiers on the beach.

(I never blamed them. What were they to think? The hat, the black T-shirt, shorts, brown skin—we all had great suntans; a hot LZ, they were probably told; a crazy man; a doped-up VC; a suicide charge; the medical pouch—a satchel charge.)

Doc was about halfway through the grove when they spotted him. I doubt they ever heard what he was shouting, that he was shouting in English. He never got that close. His words were long lost and washed away by the metered WHACK! WHACK! of the Cobra's blades. The first burst from the first soldier firing caught him still running, still waving his arms. He spun around once and slapped up against a coconut palm. He grabbed the tree with both hands and half-pivoted back toward me. The hat had slipped off his head. His face held a look of infinite surprise and wonder. He embraced the tree and closed his eyes. His knees crumpled, his arms gave, and Doc toppled over silently into the sand.

I jumped to my feet and let loose with a wild animal howl. Something inside of me had snapped. It was a physical sensation. I was no longer the detached observer with time for contemplation and reflection. My mind was now awhirl with shattered images and twisted thoughts. I was, perhaps, on the verge of hysteria. My full intentions at that precise moment are, even to this day, unclear to me. I only knew that I had to do something, anything. I took two steps forward, out into the bright sunlight, away from the shade of the coconut palm, and lifted my rifle over my head and began vigorously pumping it into the air with both hands while I jumped and shouted and danced about. What this was supposed to mean or signify, I freely confess that I know not. But this was, nevertheless, what I did; these were my actions.

Around me the air, gravid with death, hissed and snarled and spat. The soldiers were still firing, firing in my direction, firing into the high grass behind me. They had altered their course, and were now moving cautiously toward me, toward where Doc's body lay. My God, I thought, if only they knew; it's us, us; there's no need; enough, enough! Behind me, I could hear the shrieks of terror and pain as the bullets tore into the high grass, into the villagers secreted there. And I turned to look, to see if . . . if . . . I don't know. Because at that instant my leg exploded and I crashed sideways into a recent deposit of buffalo dung, screaming.

"I'm hit!" I screamed. "Holy fucking shit! I'm hit! I'm dying! Help me! Oh Jesus! Oh God!"

The pain: white-hot, searing, like nothing I had ever known or even imagined. I cried out again, cursing, begging, choking on the very air itself. I wrenched and turned and reeled upon the ground as if I could escape the pain by means of physical effort. A bloody shaft of splintered bone jutted out through a rip in my jeans. The entire lower half of my leg was shoved over to one side, about two inches out of alignment with the upper half. My head throbbed and pounded. I bit my lip and held my leg and tried to pray.

Then suddenly I became calm. The pain seemed less intense. I was, I believe, sliding into a state of shock. I was losing a lot of blood; that was for certain. My jeans and the sand beneath my leg had already turned dark and sticky. A pool of blood and sand and leaves and twigs and small insects began to form. With each beat of my heart, the pool became wider, spreading out. It was strange to watch. My blood! I began to feel light-headed. My stomach churned. I wanted to throw up. I pulled myself up into a sitting position and snaked over into the shade again. It was cool there. A butterfly lit on the end of my tennis shoe.

And slowly, like a man emerging from the depths of a dream, I became aware that it was quieter now. The shooting had stopped. The Cobra on its own private mission of vengeance, undisturbed by anything not directly related to Strider, had worked its way off farther downstream. Across from me the soldiers were standing around Doc's body. There seemed to be some kind of argument going on. Two of the men—one in a baseball cap; the other bareheaded, blond—stood over Doc's body, shouting and pointing at each other. The rest of the men were clustered about in groups of threes and fours, looking at their feet or into the trees, looking anywhere except at Doc. In the high grass, the villagers had also quieted down—reduced now to a mere whimper. Things began to seem a bit unreal: I was wounded, it was quiet, and there was a butterfly on the toe of my tennis shoe. I took out a cigarette and lit it.

So now I bleed to death, I thought to myself. Simple. Easy. Free. Like a Roman in a bathtub. Absurd and yet, somehow, logical too. Perhaps it was to be expected. Nothing from nothing leaves nothing.

The soldiers across the way were within easy earshot now. I could have called out to them for help, but I didn't and they made no attempt to approach. They seemed to be waiting for someone to tell them what to do. The two soldiers standing over Doc's body were still arguing—shouting and pointing. The argument had become more heated. Their voices reached me in an obscene cascade of threats and counterthreats. The soldier wearing the baseball cap reached up suddenly and snatched the cap off his head and flung it to the ground. The man's head was bald on top and fringed with white hair. And I felt a swift, sharp, almost electrical shock course through my body. I was speechless, breathless. I knew that head! That head, red and sweaty. That head, with the skin pulled tight. That head, with its ratty little eyes and its broken smile. That head, small yet evil—evil like the devil himself. That head belonged to the colonel, the man whom we had so rudely expelled, the man who had sworn so certain a vengeance upon us ("You'll die! You'll all die!"). And now I could see it; it began to make sense—sense in a mad, diabolical, crippled sort of way. I looked around for my rifle. It had flown out of my hands when I had been hit. Now I could see it nowhere about. I felt naked and alone and angry and afraid.

Soon a breeze kicked up from out of the sea and the butterfly floated away. I was feeling little pain now. I was still bleeding like a stuck pig, but the pain just simply wasn't there anymore. My blood had totally soaked the ground around me. I was sitting in it now—a couple of inches deep; it was dammed up against the base of the coconut palm behind me. I was amazed (in spite of the fact that it was my own blood that was amazing me) just how much blood the human body could hold—or, more accurately, in my case, just how much it could lose. I was feeling positively stoned. I could hardly keep my eyes open. I wanted to lie down and go to sleep—there, in the shade, with the sea breeze blowing gently in my face. Simple. Easy. Free. Just drift away into the cool, cool nothingness of forever. But I didn't; I couldn't. I forced open my eyes and propped myself up once again with my back braced against the coconut palm. I wanted, I needed, I had to see what was to happen. I had seen so much that I now felt that I had to see the end too. Not that I imagined that I could change or alter events in the slightest, but I—for myself, for my own peace of mind, for the long cool nothingness ahead—I had to see the finale. I thought that I had earned that much at least.

Finally the soldiers reached an agreement of some sort. The agreement, however, didn't appear to be the end result of high fellowship, good faith, or mutual purpose. It appeared rather to be the result of numbers, as it was only after several of the men rallied to the young blond soldier's side and stood next to him, exhibiting their weapons and a weary air of patience and disbelief, while the colonel stomped and kicked and howled and cursed and then eventually exhausted himself, that the discussions were at last concluded.

The soldiers split up into two groups. One—the main body—veered off into the village, continuing their sweep. The other, consisting of the colonel, the blond soldier, and three others, advanced toward me. The colonel led. The others followed at staggered intervals, apprehensive—their eyes constantly checking the jungle and the foliage. The colonel looked at nothing. He walked with a measured and determined stride. He had hate written all over his face.

To have had my M-16 and a full clip at that moment, I would have gladly given my leg, both of my legs—which, in truth, is not nearly so great a sacrifice as it might now sound: I thought that I had precious little time left to live. I was even on a nod. I would nod out for a second or two and then jerk back to life again—nod and jerk, nod and jerk. And each time, between each nod and jerk, between each brief interlude of peace and nothingness, the colonel and his red reptilian face would appear closer, more menacing. Everything was happening now in a jumbled series of starts and flashes like a film crudely clipped and spliced.

Nod and jerk: the colonel's marching on ahead, actually marching, actually picking his feet high up into the air; I wonder to myself if he's counting; he looks ridiculous; all that extra effort—Motown in my head: "This is the tropics, man, stay cool, take it easy, it's hard 'nough just natural, ain't no need to add to it"; the colonel's face is beet red; his face and his boots both shine; he pauses occasionally; he kicks an empty coconut shell; he turns and curses the men behind him; the others are lagging far back; they seem to want no part of it—whatever it is; the colonel marches on; his hands are swinging; his body is coming toward me at a slight forward slant; I want to laugh but my eyes are losing their focus and I'm very, very tired . . .

Now, in the distance, out at sea, there is a low slow roll of thunder; dark heavy clouds are gathering on the horizon; a fire crackles somewhere behind me; there's smoke in the air; the soldiers in the village are firing off short bursts; I'm hearing this now as if I were underwater—garbled, distorted; and yet quite clearly, through the water, above the thunder and the shooting, from behind me, I can hear a rising hysterical wail of a single child and voices, soft yet tense, trying to quiet it and then the tail end of a muffled scream and then silence; and even the silence sounds strange; the trees above are swaying back and forth; birds are flirting about; another butterfly, amazingly beautiful, red and orange and blue, floats by; and now even my thoughts are becoming confused; I can't recall exactly why I'm here; here, sitting in a pool of warm blood, watching a man with a red face marching toward me; I know that I'm waiting for something, but for what, I'm not sure; and still the man—he has a pistol in his hand now (I hadn't noticed that before) —marches on . . .

It's the colonel, I remember suddenly; I'm simultaneously relieved and made anxious; and there was Billy and Motown and Doc and Strider and the two on the trail whose names I never knew— Strider!; where's

Strider? I ask myself; he was here and then gone, gone like a dream, like smoke, and now I'm alone, all alone; and the wind whips through the trees; and the birds cry out more shrilly; I'm starting to lose the feeling in my fingers; my legs—both of them strangely— have long since gone numb; I have written them off; but my fingers!; I try to make a fist; it's no use; and the colonel marches on; the others have caught up with him now; he had to stop and wait for them; they advance as a group; my breathing is becoming irregular, labored; I'm almost panting; I want to call out but I can't; my mouth won't form the words; there is a definite short circuit between my brain and the rest of my body; I can only sit and watch and wait; I might as well be dead, I think to myself . . .

I feel as empty as a shell propped up and positioned on a shelf; I control nothing anymore, not even my own death, perhaps least of all my own death; I sit and I wait; and the trees and the birds and the tall grass rippling in the breeze and the people and the bodies and the blood; and still the colonel marches on; he's very close now; his face is twisted and pinched together at the temples; he never picked up his baseball cap after he threw it to the ground, now the sun beats down upon the top of his head, giving no quarter; rivulets of sweat course down his face and drip onto his shirt front; he signals back to the men to spread out; they exchange brief comments among themselves and then spread out in an advancing horizontal line; the chopper has worked its way down to the mouth of the creek, now it turns and heads back this way again; and it seems as though everything is rushing forward in a silent violent blur—suddenly there's something happening on my right; I can't quite see it; the colonel turns and shouts and points; the soldier closest to the creek bank jerks up his rifle, then freezes; he glances around quickly, looking back at the others (none of the others have raised their weapons), and in this position—looking one way, his rifle pointed in another—he stands like some crazy statue, a monument to indecision, and then slowly he lowers his weapon; the colonel's screaming; I can't make this out either; I'm underwater again; and then I see Strider; he's alive, up and running; he's running parallel to the creek, back toward the bush, back toward the jungle; he's passing in front of the smoldering remains of the bridge now; the wind whips the smoke around and he runs through it, smiling; running and smiling . . .

Strider's still running; my eyes are straining against the blur, trying to pick out a little more detail; like a runner or a swimmer pushing for the last lap, so now am I; I have to see, I have to know; my hearing is still jerky, but through sheer effort or will or something, at least my vision is becoming somewhat clearer; he's running; he's no longer carrying his rifle; he is, however, carrying something else; I concentrate; it's the hat, the bush hat—SORRY ABOUT THAT, VIETNAM; he's running and smiling; he looks like some marvelous animal of muscle and grace, sure of his own speed and his own place in the scheme of things; then shots ring out; I can hear the dull pops like distant firecrackers; I turn and there's the colonel with both hands wrapped around the butt end of his revolver, firing; and Strider's still running; foolish man, I think to myself of the colonel, foolish ugly little man; pop, pop; I laugh to myself; on he runs; the colonel's barking orders and trying to reload; the others ignore him and move on toward me . . .

I can see it seconds before I hear it, just out of the corner of my eye; now I hear it too—the flat methodical whacking—and I know with absolute certainty the true meaning of fear and dread; the Cobra races up the creek, spins a quarter-turn, and lets loose with its mini-guns blazing; Strider dodges to the right, to the left, then abruptly he turns, turning away from the creek, turning toward me; I can see his face; he looks calm; he's breathing hard from all the running, and he's no longer smiling, that's for sure, but he still looks calm; on he runs, leaping, zigzagging between the coconut trees; the Cobra passes over him, firing; the ground erupts just in front of me, between the soldiers and me; the soldiers dive for cover, clutching heads and helmets and screaming; on he runs; the Cobra swings up and around and lets loose with another burst; Strider's only about twenty meters away from me now, still ducking and dodging, still zigzagging through the trees; suddenly an arc of machine-gun fire peels across his path; it stands him up straight, stops him cold; he does a strange little dance like a fighter trying to shake off the effects of a blow; he lurches forward a few more feet, stumbling over roots and rocks and coconuts and things, and then he drops . . .

He's looking at me; he's lying on his stomach, with his face up, looking at me; there's blood trickling out of one corner of his mouth—it's steady, a continuous flow; he looks calm, calm like a cat, almost satisfied; he's working his fingers in the sand and looking at me, working his fingers and looking; I'm sitting more or less upright, looking down; from this angle I can see his back; it's totally blown out; it's red and raw like so much ground beef; there's blood everywhere—blood and mangled flesh and bits of bone and torn pieces of organs; I want to look away but his eyes have locked onto mine; they hold me fast; they say it all; it's all right there, all written in his eyes; there's something fine and sad and heroic there, something tragic and triumphant in those eyes; the chopper whirls in for one more pass—one last nail in the coffin: rockets and mini-guns—and I look away; only it's not Strider this time; this time it's the villagers in the high grass behind me who get the call; there's more screaming and shrieking; the grass bursts into flames; there's panic, frightening in itself—people running, crying out, holding on to each other; and soon there's the sick sweet smell of burning flesh in the air . . .

The soldiers—the main body—are still working their way through the village; I can mark their progress by the burning huts; the fires send up thick greasy individually spaced columns of black smoke, like a row of smudge pots; the gunship returns from its last pass and hovers overhead watchfully; it hovers just over the tops of the coconut palms, its skids almost touching the tops of the trees; the green heads of the palms lash about wildly in wide, loose-necked circles; the soldiers in front of me are still lying on the ground; they look up at the chopper as though they are none too certain of its intent; the colonel's still working on his pistol—it appears to be jammed or something; he's down on one knee, sweating and turning a deeper shade of red; from time to time he lifts his head up and shouts an order into the pulsating air; no one obeys, no one hears; the chopper's making too much noise—the wind blast, the wild trees, and the swirling sand . . .

I lock back onto Strider's eyes; he's still looking at me, still working his fingers in the sand, working and looking; the bush hat that he had been carrying is lying a couple of meters away, on its side, next to a large green coconut; it's stained with blood; the air is heavy, oppressive; the sun's working itself up higher into the sky; the day's getting hotter; it'll be a scorcher if it doesn't rain, I think to myself; the heat and the loss of blood have set my head to spinning; I can't hang on much longer; if it wasn't for Strider –Strider and his snake-stare eyes—I would probably have keeled over by now; I know this; I'm beat; but Jesus, I think to myself, if he can hold on, hold on with no back left, then hell, so can I; I hold on; the soldiers in front of me are up and moving toward us again; the Cobra's still hovering overhead—the wind, the sand, the noise; the colonel's down on both knees now, taking his pistol apart; the grass fire is spreading deeper into the jungle; ash floats through the superheated air; a huge tree has caught fire now; it stands straight with flames leaping up out of its top, orange against the blue sky . . .

Strider's still looking; he's no longer working his fingers in the sand, but he's still looking; his eyes are calm and intense; his breath comes to him in a jagged series of painful gasps; the pain doesn't show on his face—nothing shows on his face; he looks and breathes and nothing more; it's all winding down now; patience, I tell myself, it'll all be over soon; there's still an occasional shriek or two coming from the high grass, but that's about it; except for the chopper and the thrashing trees, it's mostly quiet; the colonel's up and marching again; he's behind the soldiers now; he no longer has his pistol with him; a soldier on my far left fires off a quick clip into the high grass as he walks; the blond soldier shouts something at him; the soldier ejects the empty clip and slaps in a new one without looking or breaking his stride . . .

The shadows have shifted now and I'm sitting in the sunlight; I'm sweating and spinning; I look over at Strider; he's not looking at me anymore; he's staring off into the distance; his eyes are fixed and vacant; from where he's lying, from the angle and tilt of his head, I wonder to myself if he can see the ocean; I hope so; the sea and the soil—all things ever returning; I want to say something, but again, I can't; I can't even swallow now; maybe he feels me looking at him—I don't know—but he turns his head; he blinks and focuses and then across his bloody mouth slides a small but, I believe, genuine smile (I have to believe that); and for a moment, for a brief—too brief—second, there's something indefinable, something strong and hard and right that passes between us unspoken; and maybe that's all that one has a license to expect—a moment obscure and passing, a moment strange and fugitive, special and familiar; and maybe that's enough—I don't know; but in any case, this time, this is all that's offered; suddenly Strider jerks; his neck contracts into his shoulders; his eyes jump wild; one arm shoots out and grabs at nothing; then slowly, very slowly, his chin sinks into the sand with his eyes still open . . .

He hasn't moved; his eyes are still staring into the sand, only inches away; his arm is still thrust out in front of him—limp, palm up; the soldiers are upon me now; one is cutting away my pant leg, using a bayonet; another is preparing an injection—a medic; he has a medical pouch but also an M-16; the rifle lies across his lap as he works; the blond soldier is here too; he's kneeling on one knee, checking the high grass, scanning the trees; his rifle is on automatic; his eyes are youthful and hard; another soldier is coming up behind him, coming from where Strider is lying; "dead," he says; he calls the blond soldier lieutenant; there's more talking; occasionally it's directed at me; but I don't hear much of it and what I do hear doesn't make a lot of sense: "soon" "all right" "outta here" "crazy" . . .

This is it; between the injection and the bleeding, I'm finished; I'm finished and they're gone—Strider, Doc, Motown, Billy, and all the rest; the thousands upon thousands, the wave upon wave smashing against the rocks—sand; and all that's left are the names and the numbers and the old fading photographs; and the people, the people without names or numbers or faces, the brown swirling nameless faceless mass surging along forever to the unbroken rhythm of living and dying, again and again; and they just keep coming; and the few faces that you ever remember—there was a boy with a broken kite, a young girl cleaning fish (she had fish scales on her hands and face), an old man with a twisted stick leaning against an orange tree, a big round smiling woman with only a half-dozen teeth in her head singing to a water buffalo, a baby sleeping on a straw mat, and Anh; Anh! Anh! my God, my little girl, Anh—where are you now?; eyes like diamonds, hair like silk; and the fire in the high grass burns on;

then I look up; the Cobra has shifted itself forward a bit more; it's directly over me now; the trees are beating themselves senseless; and there's the colonel, red-faced and sweating, his body curled, his shoulders hunched; he's smiling; he's standing over Strider's body and smiling; suddenly he sees the hat, the bush hat, his hat; the wind whips it about; it rolls and tumbles at his feet; he tries to step on it; he misses; it shoots away; it lifts, swirls, and falls; finally he traps it with his foot up against a coconut palm; he reaches down and he picks it up; he slaps it once against his leg; he sees the blood and frowns and then he raises the hat to his head; and my eyes following the hat drift up, up higher into the trees, the wild beating trees, and there, just before I go out, just before I go over, I see it—falling, green and fast.

17

I opened my eyes and began slowly pulling myself up from the submerged wreckage of drugs and delirium. I was alive. I was alive and yet I seemed to be in some sort of large tomb. It was cool—cold, in fact—and silent. I was laid out on my back, looking up. The roof above curved down in a uniform arc to the floor. The room was lit brightly with fluorescent lights and stank of a sterile cleanliness. It was that—the smell—that first helped me to begin to put it together. I was in a hospital, a recovery ward, a long half-cylinder of galvanized steel over a concrete base. I took a deep breath of the chilled antiseptic air and pulled the top sheet up close around my neck. From behind my head I heard a slight jingling sound. I turned and there I saw an elongated plastic bag filled with a clear dripping liquid and a coil of rubber tubing running down to my arm. An IV, I thought to myself brilliantly. I was steadily coming around.

Along each length of this half-cylinder ran a row of ten beds. Each bed had a body in it. Some were rigged up with IVs like myself; others had tubes and plastic pipes running to and from noses and throats and, in some cases, under the sheets too. Except for the occupants of the beds, no one else was in sight. Next to each bed was a small wooden table on which the patient's personal effects and various types of medication were set. Next to my bed, on the table, was nothing. There was no natural lighting in the room—no windows. There was a thick metal fire door at one end of the building, and it was closed. Above this door and at the opposite end, high up on the walls, were fitted two large window-unit air conditioners. The air conditioners hummed and the IV bags dripped.

Suddenly I flashed onto the thought of my leg. A wave of ice-pick shudders prickled down my spine. For some few moments I couldn't bring myself to look—the crutches, the cane, the flip-out leg. Finally I braved it, and it seemed to be there. At least there was no abrupt dropping off of physical form under the sheet halfway down my leg. In fact, quite to the contrary, there was bulk, an enlargement of a kind—a plaster cast, I later came to realize, running from a few inches above my knee down to my foot. I wiggled my toes and they wiggled back. I was alive and more or less physically whole.

I spent a considerable amount of time at this very splendid amusement of wiggling my toes and fingers and flopping about. There was no one to talk to. All the other patients seemed to be asleep. From this I surmised that it must be night on the outside. Here, inside, it was impossible to tell one way or the other. After a while I lost interest in the wiggling and fell still. Silent and cold, I lay there in my bed staring up at the curved metal roof and thinking about nothing. I was still fairly well-drugged. Not thinking was easy. Strider would have been proud of me; "no think," he used to preach. I simply imagined that I was dead.

How long I lay there like this in the cool and the quiet, I have no idea, but I rather think that it was a long time. When I next checked in mentally, I found that several of my fellow patients were already awake and several more were in the process of waking. It was always the same, always sad and depressing to watch—the eyes would first pop open, the muscles would tighten (sometimes only the facial muscles) and then relax, the eyes would close again for a moment, and then there would be the inevitable sigh of resignation and defeat. And once they were finally awake, they said nothing; they simply lay still and stared with morose unblinking eyes into the long blank space of another dull day ahead in which the minor became major and any diversion was pure godsend.

At some slow point during all of this waking and watching, the metal fire door suddenly swung open and in marched a tall man with extremely white skin, wearing a sneer and a set of captain's bars. I knew immediately that I had a visitor. The man marched—his heels clinking on the concrete like crickets in a jar—straight up to the foot of my bed, chopped a quarter-turn, and slapped my injured leg with a thick roll of papers that he was carrying in his right hand.

"How do you feel, shit bird?" he asked with a threatening smile. "How's the leg?" He slapped it again. "They taking good care of you? How's the food?"

"Well, I—" I began.

"Good," he declared enthusiastically. He looked around the room once and then back down at me. "You're one low piece of shit, private," he laughed. "Just about as low as they come." He shook his head and smiled at me as one might smile at an old dog or a drunk who was noted to be thoroughly incorrigible yet harmless. He unrolled the papers in his hand and stood for a silent second admiring them, and then he coughed and swallowed a throatful of phlegm.

"I have here a report from Lieutenant Collins," stated the captain, his voice now crisp with familiar authority, "on the action that took place at that little shithole ville at which you and your partners were found yesterday. What was the name of that little-piece-of-shit place anyway?" He looked at the top page and found what he was looking for. "Ah, yes. Okay. From everything in this report as well as what records we have been able to obtain on you from battalion thus far, such as the date and place and events at the time of your disappearance, I would say that just at first glance it would seem to me as though a very solid case can be made for your arrest and court-martial on charges of—"

"My what?" I asked, feigning astonishment. I had suspected that something like this might be the cause behind this visit, but still I wanted time—time to be alone and collect my thoughts before it would become necessary to deal with this and with them. I was still trying to remember how Strider's story was supposed to come out. I could remember parts of it but the logic seemed somehow skewed now.

"Arrest, court-martial, jail, prison," explained the captain cheerfully. "Long Binh. Hell, Leavenworth! Just imagine it: miles and miles of nothing but you and all those butt-fucking queers. You'll love it."

"But—" I tried to interject. I needed it slow. I was in no way a hundred percent. I needed it a little bit at a time, not miles and miles of cells and sodomy thrust upon me.

"Butt's right," laughed the captain. " 'Cause that's just where you're gonna get it. Ah, the criminal class—truly disgusting!"

"Yes, but—" I tried again.

"Save it, soldier," ordered the captain, reverting back to his earlier tone of command and business. "You bugged out on us, you and your friends. You guys had a pretty nice little time up there, didn't you? Lieutenant Collins reports that you even built yourselves a bar. Cute. But now, you see, the cuteness and fun are all over, and we want our pound of flesh. The other lucky bastards are all dead—by the way, we found the other two bodies as well." He checked his papers again. "Julius Carvel and William Able." He rolled the pages back up and looked down at me with a maniacal glint in his bulging eyes. "So, I guess"—he began tapping my foot with the roll of pages in time to his words, lightly at first, then harder— "that . . . just . . . leaves . . . you."

Whack!

"Understand?" asked the captain sharply, his hands white-knuckling the roll of pages.

I made no reply. I was thinking about Julius Carvel and William Able—Motown and Billy, no doubt. How long was I out there with those guys? Why didn't I know their real names? Their whole names? And what about Strider and Doc? Who? What? Where? Was it all nicknames, aliases, make-believe, fog, and dream? Wasn't it real? Wasn't there pain and sorrow and joy and laughter? Wasn't there? Wasn't it real? I remember . . . I think I remember . . . I remember . . .

"Good," said the captain, smiling.

He relaxed his stance and swung loose his arms. He walked around from in front of the bed and plopped himself down upon the foot of my injured leg, wrenching it—cast and all—over sharply to one side.

"Jesus!" I cried, shooting up into a sitting position.

He sat up quickly, shoved my leg out from under him, and sat back down.

"Sorry," he said, and smiled again.

I looked at him; he looked at me. His hair was brittle and grew forward like the bristle of a boar; his uniform was clean and pressed; his teeth and fingertips were stained yellow with nicotine. He took a bent loose cigarette out of his top pocket, straightened it, and then lit it. He drew heavily on it and continued to look at me. After a moment he began to speak again. This time it was the voice of the jolly assassin, the joking executioner—filled with cat-purr menace and easy butchery.

"But sadly," said the captain, blowing a long cloud of bitter blue smoke into my face, "as much as the thought of you sweating out the next twenty or so years in some shithouse cell somewhere personally pleases me, it seems as if it's not to be. Because, you see, we now have before us a small problem—a p.r. problem, you might say, a problem of image and the goddamn shit-eating press. But then, you don't know anything about that, do you? How could you? You've been off in the fucking jungle fucking little gook girls, haven't you? Shit. But now, you see, we have this little thing called My Lai on our hands which the goddamn press got hold of about a month ago and have been going crazy over ever since looking for someone's ass to fry. Namely the U.S. Army. They seem to think that we're all a bunch of baby killers over here. The fucking faggots." He pulled deeply on his cigarette again and lifted his eyes up to watch my IV bag drip a couple of drops. He sighed and shook his head. "So you see," he began again in a tone slightly more subdued, "if we bring you up on charges now, what do we get? One chickenshit asshole in the slammer and more trouble. A lot of damn bad publicity, which we don't need and can't use. And you're not worth it. They'd have a fucking field day with this. Five assholes off living it up in the jungle, a goddamn shoot-out between two of them, two more wasted by our own people, and then this goddamn colonel and his fucking chopper loaded with crap—hell, it would all come out. And it would only double the deep shit we're already in. You know, asshole, you would've saved everybody a whole helluva lot of trouble if you'd just gotten your ass wasted too. But you didn't, did you? A lame piece of dog shit if I've ever seen one." He looked at me and shook his head again, no doubt considering my general worthlessness and the total lack of justice in the world. "So what we're gonna do," he continued after a moment, "is we're gonna let it wash. It never happened. None of it. Zero." He paused and smiled. "Almost. 'Cause as soon as that leg of yours heals up good"—he slapped it again— "we're gonna find a nice little spot for you right up close where it's nice and warm and send your no-count ass back into the motherfucking field. And who knows"—he was yellow teeth from ear to ear now— "anything might happen. It's sad—the accidents, you know. Like say it's night and somebody gets a little

279

jumpy, thinks he hears something, and bang, the wrong person gets it. Tragic. So cheer up, motherfucker, all's not as black as it seems."

I could feel blood oozing around inside my cast. Small dark splotches were beginning to appear on the top sheet now. My leg, after having been sat on, throbbed and twitched with an eager and precise rhythm of its own. In my mouth was an unpleasant taste of something like peanut shells. Sweat was popping out on my brow, popping out and then drying quickly in the cold air.

"You know, shithead, you don't look so good," observed the captain. "It's lucky you're in the hospital."

Other people were moving about the ward now—doctors and nurses and orderlies. The place was slowly coming to life. I was wondering to myself what a "me-lie" was—for that's how it sounded to my ear—and why it was keeping me from prison. The captain's smiling underthreat of a bullet ("good morning") in the back didn't particularly bother me for some reason. Perhaps I was finally becoming somewhat immune to it all. Or perhaps it simply no longer mattered. Directly across from me, a soldier was propped up with a pillow behind his back, reading a well-thumbed comic book. A few beds down from him, two others were quietly playing cards.

"But what about the people?" I asked.

"People? What fucking people?" asked the captain, looking around.

"The villagers," I explained. "The people in the village. There was this girl—"

"Gooks," snorted the captain impatiently.

"No, people," I protested. "People just like—"

"Dead," said the captain. "That's what we do to gooks. That's our job. Your job too, asshole. We waste 'em. Oh sure, I guess a few of 'em got away and there were a few more who surrendered—that's how we found out about that shoot-out and found the bodies and the chopper—but mostly they're dead. Lieutenant Collins reports that the place was thick with VC. He called in an air strike—"

"VC?" I stammered. "But they were just—"

"Vietcong. Victor Charlie. The opposition. Them," droned on the captain, not listening, speaking to me out of some dreamlike state of fond sweet memories. "Sometimes you gotta admire the little bastards. They can really take it. You'd almost think they liked it or something. But then that's just gooks for you. They aren't really but about half-human anyway. I can remember this one time I was out with . . ."

Dead, I thought to myself. An air strike, no less. As if mini-guns and rockets and bullets tumbling through space at two-thousand miles per hour—"dead before you hear the shot"—weren't enough. Well, that should've done the trick. Napalm and the works. The world goes up in a bright orange cloud of boiling gas. Talk about a case of overkill. Why don't they just go on and nuke the whole damn place and be done with it? They don't seem to be all that selective in their—our?—slaughter as it is. They—we?—could wait about forty or fifty years and let the place air out and then reintroduce democracy. I'm sure it would take. And Jesus, these idiots really seem to think they've bagged themselves some hard-core VC too. That'll win 'em some hearts and minds. All those little scorched ant bodies. Some more nice publicity for them—us? "Show us the burnt and mutilated, the crippled and blind. You did this?" "But it's a war." "That's no excuse; you're Americans."

I was getting turned around, confused. Distinctions were difficult; the lines were blurred. I tuned back in on the captain's story to cut down on the thought time.

". . . so when we finally dragged 'em all out, there were ten of 'em, ten of the motherfuckers all living and sleeping and eating and shitting and everything down in this little gook rat hole about half as big as a goddamn toilet. What a fucking mess!"

He laughed, his eyes glistening in the fluorescent glare from above. Recalling his past adventures seemed to make him genuinely happy—almost excited. He took a deep breath and slapped my leg again. His face eased into a smile. "Well, I guess that's about it, huh, shit bird?" He stood up and looked down at me, still smiling that ready false smile of his that bespoke of nothing so much as disdain and contempt. "And remember, if you ever need any help, don't call me." He turned and began walking away. "Worst of luck to you," bade the captain, flashing his handy smile one last time over his shoulder.

My bed was situated in the middle of this room. The captain was walking fast; he was almost to the fire door. I was weak, stretched to the limit. One side of my bed was now liberally soaked with blood. I worked myself up on to my elbows and, with my voice rising strained and broken, like some demented beggar howling at passersby, I called out after him, calling:

"But what about the colonel, Mr. Captain Sir? What happened to the colonel?"

A bottle broke. A heavy quiet thumped through the ward. All eyes whirled on me and waited.

The captain's hand was already on the horizontal latch-bar of the door, preparing to push it open. He stopped and turned and marched back to the foot of my bed. His smile had vanished.

"Colonel Winfield P. Comfort died early this morning of wounds that he received yesterday while leading an assault against a heavily fortified enemy position," stated the captain in a manner that suggested recital rather than reaction, "and will be awarded—"

"You mean he got conked on the head by a goddamn coconut!" I shouted gleefully. I started laughing. It hurt to laugh. It jerked my leg around and grated the loose bones together (I could feel them now), but still I couldn't help it. It all seemed absolutely hilarious to me. "A goddamn coconut!"

The captain stood stiff and silent, watching me laugh. His face went rapidly from white to pink to scarlet. His mouth began to twitch. He was trying to control his anger. The roll of pages in his right hand slapped against his own leg with an unconscious and random violence. You could see the process—the control—working inside of him. He obviously knew about control. Finally his anger peaked and he subsided into a state of mere hatred.

"Fuck you," said the captain, his voice calm and purposeful. "Wait till we get you back in the field, motherfucker, then you can laugh all you like."

And with that dark promise, he turned again and headed back toward the door. A doctor standing nearby stepped out between two beds and grabbed the captain by the arm. The captain spun on the doctor as if he might hit him with his roll of pages. The doctor, however, seemed not to notice this. Instead he bent— the doctor being taller than the already tall captain— and whispered something into the captain's ear.

"Don't worry about him, Doc," said the captain loudly. He twisted his arm free and looked back at me. "He's already taken care of."

The doctor, straightening up, looked briefly at the captain's face, and then he bent down again as if to say something further to the captain, but the captain, freed now from the doctor's grip, brushed roughly past him and stalked out of the ward.

"A goddamn coconut!" I shouted out again as the door clicked shut. "Right on the fucking head!"

I was still laughing. It was marvelous. The colonel. The coconut. Conk! Adios, motherfucker! Jesus, what a joke!

The doctor who had been speaking with the captain came around to the side of my bed. He wore black-rimmed glasses with thick lenses which magnified his red and sleepless eyes. He threw back the bloody top sheet and immediately called for a nurse.

"Prep this man," commanded the doctor, moving my leg gently from side to side. "I want him in the OR in ten minutes. We've got to get that cast off and have a look at that leg. We'll probably have to reset it."

"Yes, sir," said the nurse, now standing next to him. She was pretty. She had blond hair. It was pulled back and wadded up in a bun. Her eyes, like those of the doctor, had a washed-out, world-weary look.

The doctor stepped across the narrow passageway, pointed me out to one of the other doctors, and then headed quickly from the room. The nurse set a metal tray down on my bedside table. She picked up a small vial and a hypodermic needle, tilted the vial up and filled the needle, and then none too gently jabbed it into my arm.

"You should've seen it," I told the nurse. I was no longer laughing but I was still in a rather excited state. "It was unreal. The whole thing. From day one."

"Yes?" she asked, pausing with the empty needle arrested in midair.

"It was like . . . like . . ."

"A movie?" she suggested, her mouth broadening into a smile.

"Yes!" I exclaimed. "That's it! It was just like—"

"Or like something out of a book, maybe?" she offered with a sympathetic kind of seriousness.

"Yes," I agreed a little more cautiously. She seemed to know the routine. "Like something out of a—"

"Then for God's sake," she demanded, "why don't you write it down and send it in to *Reader's Digest* or something and quit making such a damn nuisance of yourself?"

"Well," I said, considering, "no one would believe it."

"Then why the hell should I?" she asked, snatching up the tray and turning, and leaving me alone, forever and hopelessly stuck in the shadows of a distant yesterday, with the joke and the pain and a story to tell.